"You don't understand.

"My sister Ariel and I haven't spoken in six months," Melanie went on. "I never wanted to see her again after what she did. When Stephanie called and begged me to come to dinner to celebrate the birth of Ariel's little girl, I...I hung up on her! Oh, God, she was my best friend. That was the last time we talked...."

Kent had to resist the urge to take Melanie into his arms when she buried her face in her hands and painful sobs shook her. Instead, he racked his rattled brain for something soothing to say while he was processing what she'd told him. Melanie wasn't making any sense, but she was obviously distraught.

"I'm sure she realizes why you were upset," he said. "That's what best friends are for. Whatever happened between the two of you, it's never too late to make amends."

"You don't understand," Melanie repeated. "I've known Stephanie for years. She was my best friend, yet I lost my temper with her because she befriended my sister. I can't ever make amends for that, because she's lying on the floor of that bedroom dead. My best friend is dead."

Dear Reader,

Who among us has not longed for the opportunity to turn back the clock for a second chance at something? Whether it has to do with a relationship, career choice or some other life-altering decision, there have certainly been times I have longed to go back and *get it right this time*.

That's the dilemma facing Melanie Harris and Kent Mattson, the characters you are about to meet. Like the rest of us, they learn that while it is impossible to redo the past, it is very possible to meet the present head-on when life offers unexpected opportunities. It's been my experience that getting that second shot at happiness is only the first step. In the end, as Melanie and Kent find out, it's what we do with that second chance that can make all the difference.

Enjoy the ride these two people are about to take you on. You're going to find they keep you guessing until the very end.

Happy reading!

Julia Penney

HER SISTER'S KEEPER
Julia Penney

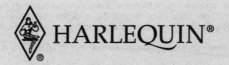

TORONTO • NEW YORK • LONDON
AMSTERDAM • PARIS • SYDNEY • HAMBURG
STOCKHOLM • ATHENS • TOKYO • MILAN • MADRID
PRAGUE • WARSAW • BUDAPEST • AUCKLAND

ISBN 0-373-71330-4

HER SISTER'S KEEPER

www.eHarlequin.com

Printed in U.S.A.

To all who go above and beyond the call of duty.
We owe you our thanks.

CHAPTER ONE

WHEN MELANIE HARRIS had envisioned celebrating her six-month wedding anniversary, she never imagined she would spend it sitting in an impersonal office, waiting for an appointment with the renowned Dr. Kent Mattson. Then again, she hadn't anticipated how quickly things could have turned bad. She glanced at the unmoving hands of the wall clock, then tried to read the magazine in her lap, but the words on the page were a meaningless blur.

She sighed, bit her lip and, for the hundredth time, wondered what was keeping her in the chair. All she had to do was get up, walk out into the bright California sunshine and put the whole sorry chapter behind her.

There was the door.

She stared at it for a moment, then set the magazine down and stood with sudden resolve. She'd just taken her first step toward freedom when the receptionist entered the waiting room.

"Dr. Mattson will see you now, Ms. Harris," she said with a pleasant smile. The receptionist was a middle-aged woman with a calm, patient expression, obviously accustomed to dealing with the steady stream of emotional wreckage that flowed through Dr. Mattson's office. "I apologize for the wait."

Melanie, a mere two feet away from the door, froze with indecision. She could hear her heart beating in the stillness of the room. Her mouth was dry, her palms damp. She didn't belong here, but, after all, she'd promised Stephanie that she'd endure at least one visit. She owed her best friend that much. It was Stephanie's enviable strength that had propped Melanie up for the past six months. Six months of wishing she were dead rather than face another sunrise.

"Promise me you'll see Dr. Mattson. He's the best there is and he can help you," Stephanie had pleaded. "You *have* to put this behind you. None of what happened was your fault."

Wasn't it, though? Wasn't she standing here in this office, hand reaching for the doorknob, because she'd blindly and willingly believed everything Mitch had told her, in spite of the warnings from those who'd known him so much better than she had?

"Ms. Harris?" the receptionist said, a concerned frown furrowing her brow. "Are you all right?"

Melanie felt herself beginning to crumble. In spite of her resolve not to show any weakness, her eyes stung and her voice trembled when she spoke. "If I were all right, would I be here?"

The receptionist never missed a beat. "Ms. Harris, there isn't one among us who doesn't need someone like Dr. Mattson at some point in our lives," she soothed, stepping forward to touch Melanie's arm. "Please, come with me." She guided Melanie across the waiting room to another door and gave her a reassuring nod before opening it. Melanie drew a deep breath, shored up the last of her resolve, and entered Dr. Mattson's inner sanctum.

Expecting an older, overweight man with gray hair, horn-rimmed glasses and a placid, patronizing expression, Melanie was surprised by the sight of an athletically built man dressed in blue jeans and a chambray shirt, sleeves rolled back to reveal powerful forearms. A man whose dark, tousled hair showed not a hint of gray, whose keen blue eyes were offset by the weathered tan of his face and whose strong masculine jaw looked as if it hadn't felt a razor since erasing the five o'clock shadow of the night before. In fact, he looked much more like a cowboy who had just come in from a hard morning's work in the saddle than a clinical psychologist. She wondered for a moment if she were in the right place, but before she could retreat, the receptionist closed the door behind her with a firm click.

She was trapped.

KENT MATTSON KNEW he was running behind, but he was distracted. He couldn't stop thinking about the murder scene he'd been called to that morning. But, unfortunately, his work with the LAPD paid peanuts compared to his private practice. Two days a week he listened to clients who were victims of Hollywood; it was a shallow world by most counts, juicy by others, yet immensely profitable to those in a position to help them. Without that extra income he'd have lost Chimeya long ago.

Too, he derived an ironic satisfaction from an increasingly healthy bank account bolstered by these movie industry casualties. It was these very same stars and starlets moving into the valley who had sent property taxes soaring and jeopardized the long-term survival of the historic ranch that had been in his family for three generations.

He glanced down at the latest file his receptionist had placed on his desk. Melanie Harris. The name was vaguely familiar, though he couldn't place it. He scanned through the file but his mind kept returning to the morning's murder.

A soft rustle of movement interrupted his thoughts and he glanced up to see a woman standing in the doorway. She seemed uneasy, which wasn't unusual for a client's first visit. He rose to greet her.

"Ms. Harris. Please, come in. I'm Kent Mattson," he said, crossing the room.

Melanie Harris was a tall, attractive young woman in her late twenties or early thirties. Her clothing was predictably fashionable, her hair a deep, lustrous shade of mahogany and swept back. She wore no makeup, which was highly unusual in this part of town, but the best makeup artist couldn't have hidden the dark smudges beneath those tragic green eyes, nor mask the fact that she was at least ten pounds underweight.

Kent gestured to the chair across from his desk. "I was just reviewing your file," he said, waiting for her to sit, but she remained standing just inside the door. "I see you were referred by your regular physician, Patricia Phillips. Won't you have a seat?"

She hesitated, and he sensed that she was very near to bolting. Her eyes held his for a moment, like a startled doe caught in the headlights of a car, and he was struck by her expression. He turned away and moved toward the side table, and poured himself a cup of coffee. "I have several bad habits," he said, glancing over his shoulder. "One of which is drinking too much coffee. Could I fix you a cup, or would you prefer tea? I have black, green or herbal." He noted that some of the initial anxiety had left her eyes, but the wariness remained, and he doubted very much that the sadness would ever leave.

"I'm fine, thank you," she said in a quiet voice.

Good. At least she could talk. Be a tough job for him if she couldn't. He carried his mug to the window and stared out at a skyline smudged with brown haze. "I see from your file that Dr. Phillips was concerned about your weight loss and chronic insomnia." He took a sip of coffee, wondering why her physician hadn't just prescribed Prozac or Valium. The movie industry was hooked on those pills. Still no response from Ms. Harris, who remained standing just inside the door, poised to flee. "So," he said, turning to face her, "we know why Dr. Phillips thinks you should be here. I guess what I need to know is why *you* think you should be here."

He felt another jolt as his eyes locked with hers. If she wasn't a big-name movie star yet, she would be. Those eyes alone would guarantee that, even if she couldn't act worth a damn.

"I'm here because I've been told I need your help," she replied.

He ran his fingers through his hair and sighed. "That's something you're not going to get from me until you're ready for it. When you're here because you *want* to be here, you'll be ready. Until then, you're just wasting your time and mine."

Her face betrayed no emotion whatsoever, but he noticed a quick flash of pain in her eyes. "In that case, Dr. Mattson, I'll be going," she said, and turned toward the door.

Kent might have let her walk out except for that flicker of anguish. She was in trouble, real or imagined, and needed help. That was, after all, why he was there, despite his current preoccupation, which he did his best to shake off. "Once you start running from your past, Ms. Harris, it becomes very hard to stop," he said. "How much longer do you want to live like this?"

His words made her pause, her hand closed around the doorknob. He saw the determined set of her shoulders as she stood motionless, and then she leaned forward until her forehead touched the door, her body rigid. After several long moments she straightened, turned and looked at him.

"I'm tired of running."

"Good," Kent said, relieved that he hadn't driven her away. "You've just taken the first step. If you choose to stay, we can begin."

FOR MELANIE, remaining in Dr. Mattson's office meant returning to a place in time that she never wanted to revisit again, yet she knew instinctively that to silence the demons, she had to confront them. She also realized that alone, she was incapable of fighting that battle. As much as she wanted to walk out, she knew it would be a mistake. For six months she'd suffered.

Ever since her wedding day.

She remembered every detail as if it were yesterday. The original DiSanto gown, a slim, strapless shiver of satin and pearls. Stephanie helping her with the tiny buttons up the back. The sweet-spicy scent of the old-fashioned pink roses that made up her bridal bouquet. The deep, rhythmic rumble of the Pacific Ocean and the golden afternoon sunshine spilling through the tall Palladian windows while Ariel wove pearls into her hair….

It was perfect, until the tap came on the door and Janet, the wedding director, peered into the room. "It's almost time. Two minutes until they start the wedding march.

Victor's waiting to walk you to the rose arbor. You look just beautiful, Melanie."

Would she ever forget that moment? Stephanie had finished fastening the last button and had gone to gather up the bridesmaids, leaving her alone with Ariel, who had been uncharacteristically quiet throughout the endless preparations. Ariel, her hands full of pearl hairpins, her face as pale as Melanie's gown, her fingers trembling so badly that Melanie, noticing all of this for the first time, reached her own hand to close on her sister's.

"Ari, for heaven's sake, what is it? What's wrong?"

Ariel pulled away from her, shaking her head, denying that anything was amiss, but something very definitely was. Melanie rose to her feet, concerned. "Are you ill? Please, Ari, tell me. What is it?"

Her sister's blue eyes had filled with tears. "It's nothing," she said with such dramatic pathos that Melanie knew her sister thought her world was coming to an end.

"Ari, this isn't the time for theatrics." Melanie put her hands on her sister's shoulders. "Tell me what's wrong."

The tears spilled over. "Oh, Mel, I'm pregnant," Ariel blurted out around a choked sob. "I wasn't going to tell you. I didn't want to tell you!"

This was hardly the moment for Ariel to be breaking this news. In five minutes Melanie was supposed to be walking down the petal-strewn path to her wedding ceremony.

"I'm happy for you, Ari," Melanie managed, hugging her sister. "Now stop crying. This isn't the end of the world. You're not the first unmarried woman on the planet to get pregnant." Ariel began to weep in earnest and Melanie's patience grew thin. The minutes were ticking down, and Mitch was waiting. "Ari, who's the father? Does he know about this?"

Ariel buried her face in her hands and cried out in despair. "Oh, God, Mel, it's so awful. I didn't want to tell you."

"I would have guessed sooner or later. It's pretty hard to hide a pregnancy after a while, kiddo. Look, we'll talk more about it at the reception, okay? It's going to be all right, Ari," Melanie said, stroking her sister's hair back from her flushed face with genuine affection, because as much as Ariel could drive her crazy, Melanie wanted the best for her. "I'll help you through this. Trust me. You'll be a great mom."

Ariel was not reassured. "I wasn't going say anything, except for being pregnant. You're my sister and I love you. I would never hurt you, Mel. Never."

Melanie felt a twinge of unease. "Of course you wouldn't. You're not making any sense at all."

Another tap at the door, and Janet looked in. "We're waiting on you, Melanie." She frowned. "Is everything all right?"

"Just give us a few more minutes," Melanie said, and when the door closed she gripped Ariel's shoulders and leveled her gaze. "Talk to me, Ari."

Ariel shook her head again. "I'm three months pregnant. I was going to get an abortion. I went to the clinic and I…" Fresh tears brimmed over and Melanie released her to grab a nearby box of tissues. "I just couldn't go through with it," Ariel said, sniffling and dabbing at her eyes.

"That's all right. Does the father know?" Melanie repeated.

Ariel gulped and nodded. "He said I was trying to trap him, that the baby wasn't his, and then he dumped me."

"Sounds to me like you didn't lose much when you lost him," Melanie said, hugging her sister again. "Paternity tests would prove he's the father if you really want to go that route, but you certainly don't need financial help raising a child, and you're a whole lot better off without that kind of man in your life. Blow your nose and try to forget the jerk for a while. We have a wedding to attend, and you're my maid of honor."

"God forgive me, Melanie, I don't deserve any honor at all, least of all that one." Ariel fell to her knees, taking two handfuls of Melanie's gown and pressing them to her tear-streaked face for a moment before looking up at her sister. Her words tumbled out in a rush. "I can't forget the baby's father because…because it's Mitch. I wanted to tell you, but you seemed so happy, happier than I've ever seen you.

"I didn't want to hurt you, I wasn't going to say anything, but then…last night at the rehearsal dinner, I overheard him talking to one of his friends. He was saying…he was saying that he thought you were worth marrying because you'd be the one who could break him out of being a stunt man, and get him the acting roles he wanted. You were so close to Victor, he was sure you could make it happen. Before I got pregnant he was always after me to talk to Victor about getting him an acting role, but I never did because Mitch couldn't act. He was awful. Oh, Mel, don't you see? He used both of us the same way. You can't marry him. He's a no-good bastard!"

As her sister spoke, a chill swept through Melanie. Three months ago she and Mitch had fallen in love. Three months ago Mitch had been sleeping with Ariel…until he found out she was pregnant. "No," she whispered.

"Oh, Mel. I'm so sorry." Ariel rose to her feet and reached for her, but Melanie jerked away.

"No," she repeated. "That can't be true. Mitch loves me...."

Ariel shook her head, tears still streaming. "Mitch doesn't love anyone but himself. I know you've heard the rumors. Believe them, Mel. He's a womanizer, a user. He's handsome and he's daring, but he's no good. Don't marry him. Don't let him hurt you the way he hurt me!"

Melanie turned away from her sister and found herself staring at her reflection, at her beautiful Ines DiSanto wedding dress.

She reached her hands to smooth the satin gown and lifted her chin, defiantly eyeing the woman in the mirror. She would not cry. She would never, ever cry. Let them stare and let them talk. Melanie Harris would hold on to her pride, if nothing else. "Let's go," she said to Ariel.

"Mel, please, let me tell Janet the wedding's off," Ariel begged, holding back. "She can talk to the wedding party, she can tell Mitch..."

"This wedding's not off, baby sister," Melanie said, reaching for Ariel's hand. "We can't disappoint all those guests, can we? Come on."

With a cry of protest, Ariel was tugged along as Melanie exited the bedroom. Holding her gown up in one hand, she strode determinedly past an openmouthed Janet, wide-eyed bridesmaids and a shocked Stephanie and Victor, and down the wide granite steps of Blackstone toward the rose arbor in the formal garden overlooking the Pacific.

The guests were standing as the quartet played the wedding march, waiting for her entrance. Their faces mirrored the pleasant anticipation of such moments—expressions that faltered when Melanie came into view, dragging a wildly sobbing Ariel behind her. The quartet stopped playing and lowered their instruments, as startled as the wedding guests, but Melanie only had eyes for the man waiting for her at the arbor.

Mitch Carson.

He watched their approach with amazing calm for a man who had to have sensed impending disaster. Ariel was wrong about him. He was a damn good actor.

"Here's the woman you should be marrying, Mitch," Melanie said with icy calm, thrusting her weeping sister forward. "For the life of me, I can't quite imagine you as a doting father, but I understand you have six more months to prepare. I wish the two of you a very interesting relationship."

She barely remembered leaving Victor's estate and climbing into her car wearing the gown that had cost her nearly half a year's salary as a location scout. She drove along the coastal highway, clutched in the depths of a nightmare she couldn't escape. A nightmare that hadn't passed in six long months. Six months of her sister's hysterical phone messages imploring her forgiveness. Six months of Stephanie begging her to reconcile with Ariel. Begging her to get professional help. Six months of deteriorating job performance, sleepless nights and deepening depression.

And then the latest message from her sister on her answering machine, just one week ago. Ariel's voice had been shrill, barely intelligible. Mitch was dead, killed on location during the filming of the latest Kellerman thriller. A routine stunt had somehow gone wrong and there was an explosion, a terrible fire. The police would be investigating, the whole thing was so suspicious.

Ariel was devastated, because she and Mitch had been trying to work things out. Apparently she had discovered something below the man's shallow layer of womanizing self-indulgence. Something that had made Ariel believe he was ready to settle down with her and the baby.

The shock of Mitch's death had no doubt triggered the birth. Melanie learned of the frantic rush to the hospital from Stephanie, who had driven Ariel and stayed with her for the birth. Stephanie, who only two days ago had begged her to attend the special dinner Vic and Tanyia were hosting to celebrate Ariel's newborn baby girl.

"Please come, Mel," Stephanie had pleaded. "It would mean so much to Ariel. She needs you right now. And the baby…your niece…is so beautiful. You have to see her." Melanie hadn't gone to the dinner, of course. No way in hell could she bring herself to do that…yet.

Suddenly, Melanie dropped her head into her hands. She was so terribly tired. This wasn't like a movie set, where the director could call out, "Cut! Let's try that again." This was real life, and there were no second takes. Her life was a mess. She would never be able to forgive Ariel for her betrayal. She no longer liked her job, because as long as she worked for Victor, she was constantly reminded of her wedding day. She didn't want to be in this place, this office. She disliked Dr. Mattson for making her relive this nightmare, disliked the muted beige tones of his office, designed, no doubt, to comfort, and she even resented Stephanie for getting her into this situation in the first place.

Melanie drew a shuddering breath, straightened in her chair and gazed about her with dismay. She glanced at her watch. Exactly ten minutes had passed since she'd taken a seat in Dr. Mattson's office, and she hadn't uttered a single word. He was sitting there patiently, waiting for her to spill her guts and cure herself, but she just couldn't bring herself to tell the story to a stranger. No way she could ever confess to a three-month whirlwind romance with a renowned womanizer that her friends had all quietly warned her against. No way could she ever talk about her sister's treachery, the same sister she'd worked so hard to protect and support after their parents had died.

She'd fulfilled her promise to Stephanie by coming here today, but she was done with it. She would pull herself together and keep her secrets buried in the past. If the past haunted her for the rest of her life, running from it was a price she deserved to pay. Fools deserved to suffer.

Dr. Mattson said nothing when Melanie rose and started for the door. She paused for a moment, as out of breath as if she'd just run a mile in soft beach sand.

"I'm sorry," she apologized before leaving his office, fighting for control. "I guess I'm not ready for this, after all."

Kent knew he should say something to stop his client from going out that door. Instead, he sat rooted in his chair, unable to move or speak as she swept out of his office, closing the door firmly behind her. He'd been glad that Melanie Harris had remained silent, allowing him to think about this morning's murder…but by doing so he had failed his client miserably.

Kent leaned forward on his elbows and ran a hand through his hair with a weary sigh. This conflict of jobs was impossible. He'd just let a client leave without receiving any help from him whatsoever. He had to decide between his job with the police department and his growing affinity for a healthy bank account. A knock roused him, and his receptionist stood in the doorway. "I'm sorry to disturb you, Doctor, but Ms. Harris insists on paying before she leaves."

"Tell her that's not our policy. Get the insurance information from her and…"

Melanie herself appeared, edging around the receptionist. She had her checkbook in hand and a determined look in her eye. "I prefer to pay as I go, Dr. Mattson. What do I owe you for that session?"

"I'm afraid your money's no good here, Ms. Harris. If you couldn't share this office for thirty minutes with me, then I obviously don't deserve payment. Should you at any time change your mind, give me a call." Kent pulled a business card out of the brass holder on his desk, rose to his feet and extended it toward her.

"You should probably know that I've never believed in…therapists. Half the people I work with see one regularly," she said with a flash of rebellion, but she took the card.

"And you think they're being weak for seeing a…*shrink?*"

"Yes, as a matter of fact, as well as extremely self-centered," she replied with a faint flush of embarrassment. "If I stayed for the allotted time, would you accept my payment?"

"Not for your first visit. The rules are the rules. However, you're more than welcome to stay. I'll even fix you a cup of coffee or tea, and you don't have to say a word. At least that way, if you do come back, you'll be officially into your second visit and I can charge you an arm and a leg."

"I won't come a second time, Dr. Mattson. I can guarantee you that."

Kent walked over to the side table. "Coffee, or tea?"

She hesitated, and he knew he'd won when her chin dropped fractionally. "I'll take green tea, please," she said, and resumed her seat. While Kent fixed her tea and replenished his coffee, she sat gazing at the office walls. "Thank you," she murmured as he handed her the mug. She rose from her seat and walked to the bookshelf, perusing the leather-bound volumes. She studied the framed photographs on the wall. His diplomas from grad school and the criminal justice academy. She stepped closer to read the assorted plaques, lifting her cup to sip her tea. Her eyebrows raised and she glanced at him.

"You won a national police pistol-shooting contest?"

"Three years in a row," he said. "The fourth year my boss sent me to a symposium on forensic psychology in New York City, so I couldn't enter."

"And did he win, with you out of the picture?"

Kent grinned and nodded. "*She* won. My boss at the police department happens to be a woman, and a damned fine shot."

"Then, you're a police officer?"

"Only part-time, for now," Kent said. "I divide my time between my office here and the LAPD."

" Interesting," Melanie said. "This is quite a trophy wall you have here, Doctor. I wouldn't expect such hobbies from a…psychologist. But then again, this is Beverly Hills."

"You betcha. We shrinks gotta get our thrills in while we can." Kent took a swallow of coffee, kicked back in his chair and glanced at his watch. Five more minutes until she bolted. Five more minutes to make her realize she needed him so he could pad his bank account a little more.

"Your parents?"

She'd returned to the photographs. "Yes. That picture was taken ten years ago. They've both passed away since."

"I'm sorry. I know how hard it is to lose your parents. I lost both of mine when I was eighteen. Car accident." She glanced back at the photograph. "That looks like an old Mexican ranch in the background."

"Chimeya. One of the oldest in California. Authentic, right down to the two-foot-thick adobe walls. I was raised there."

"That must have been nice," she said, studying the photograph closely. "Horses, dogs, cattle and lots of wide open space. A good place for children to grow up... I suppose it's been sold off and developed, like everything else worth preserving in this day and age."

Kent was surprised by the bitterness in her voice. "Actually, the ranch is still very much in the Mattson family. I live there."

Her eyebrows raised again. "Then the ranch must not be around here, that's for sure. There's no smog in that picture."

"Nope. Chimeya's far enough away to escape the smog, in the foothills of the Sierra Nevadas."

"And you commute?"

"The ranch has a decent landing strip."

She gave him an appraising stare, then turned her attention back to the pictures. "Your horse?"

"His name's Seven. He likes Budweiser beer, doggin' steers and long rides into the hills."

"Ah, so you're a cowboy at heart." The faintest of smiles warmed her pale features as she spoke.

"I guess you could say that. I started out giving psychotherapy to the horses, but it didn't pay, and on several occasions my efforts got me kicked. So I went to school to learn how to psych out human beings."

She laughed, a beautiful sound. He caught a faint whiff

of her subtle perfume and wondered if something had
happened to the air-conditioning in his suddenly very
warm office. Just as he was pushing out of his chair to
check the thermostat, Melanie set her teacup down and
faced him.

"Thank you, Dr. Mattson. I'm sorry if I was short with
you earlier. It wasn't easy for me to come here."

"You survived the experience with flying colors," Kent
said.

The faint smile warmed her face once again. "I fulfilled
a promise to a friend and a recommendation from my
doctor," she amended. "My allotted time is up. Thank you
again. Please, let me pay you."

Kent shook his head. "Against policy. If you want to
come back, by all means, do so, but you don't pay a cent
until your second visit."

"Then I'm afraid this is goodbye," Melanie said, extending her hand.

Kent took it in his own, surprised at the firmness of her
grip. The tremble he'd detected earlier was completely
gone. "Goodbye, Ms. Harris," he said. "You have my card
if you should have a change of heart."

She pulled her hand out of his and left him standing
there, still marveling at the idea of a woman sitting in
silence for ten whole minutes. He wouldn't have thought
such self-restraint was possible. Too bad to have lost that
potential gold mine, but there'd be others. Not nearly as
pretty, though. Not by half. The woman's legs would stop
the most jaded drivers on Santa Monica Boulevard. Kent's
phone rang as he was tucking his very brief notes into the
Melanie Harris folder.

"Murphy here. We have a situation."

"Damn, Murph, gimme a break. This is my day of raking in the big bucks so I can afford to keep working for you," Kent said, pushing the file aside and rocking forward in his chair. "What's up?"

"We're at the Beverly Hills Regency. A young woman was found dead in her room an hour ago by maid service." There was a brief, ominous pause. "There are no signs of foul play, but I'd like you to have a look at the scene if you can. T. Ray's still with the body. This looks very similar to that young woman who was found earlier this morning."

"Say no more. I'm on my way."

"Kent?" There was a hiss of static as Captain Carolyn Murphy paced with her cell phone the way Kent had seen her do on many occasions. He could picture the rigid set of her shoulders and that dark gaze gathering like a storm. "The thing is, according to the desk clerk, this victim checked into the hotel last night with a newborn infant. There are baby things scattered around the room, but the baby's missing."

His heart rate accelerated and his adrenaline level soared. "Don't let them disturb anything at the scene, Murph. I'll be there in fifteen minutes." Kent hung up the phone, buzzed his receptionist and informed her he was leaving early.

"You have three more appointments, Dr. Mattson," she reminded him with disapproval. "Mrs. Forsythe, Sienna Bernstein and…Wanda Wendell." The latter name was spoken with understandable trepidation. Wanda Wendell's sole reason for living was to make other people's lives miserable.

"Call them and reschedule. I have a police emergency."

Kent reached for his jacket and grabbed his car keys and

briefcase on the way out the door. His mind was racing even as he descended the stairs two at a time, the five flights faster by far on foot than by elevator. He burst out the ground floor stairwell and took the basement shortcut to the parking garage, running to his reserved parking area. He was out of breath by the time he reached the place where his new Audi should have been, and stared at the dark, vacant slot in disbelief. What the hell? Grand theft auto wasn't supposed to happen in this garage, which was precisely why he'd paid an outlandish fee for a reserved space in a place that had an armed security guard controlling access. Kent began a fresh sprint toward the gate, heart hammering.

The security guard was young and ignorant, professing no knowledge of Kent's Audi leaving the garage without him. Kent didn't have time to argue. "Call me a cab, and make it quick," he snapped. He heard a car approaching the gate from behind and stepped out of the way, glancing at the driver as the window lowered and a slender, graceful hand extended with the ticket. Melanie Harris. Her timing was a minor miracle, considering the infamously slow office elevator. Kent threw his arms up to stop her. "Ms. Harris! Could you give me a ride to the Beverly Hills Regency? My car's been stolen and there's a police emergency."

Those turbulent green eyes met his, and she didn't hesitate. "Get in," she said, and as Kent climbed into the passenger seat of her silver Mercedes sports coupe, breathing the mingled scents of leather upholstery and perfume, hearing the muted strains of Handel's Water Music from the stereo, she waved off his thank-you. "Think nothing of it," she said, pulling out into the midday traffic and accelerating smoothly ahead. "Consider my thirty-minute debt to you repaid."

CHAPTER TWO

MELANIE HARRIS drove with the practiced skill of someone accustomed to navigating busy city streets. They had spoken barely five words since he had hopped in the car and given his destination. As she deftly shifted the Mercedes into gear and pulled into the light prelunch traffic, Kent flipped open the file he had been reading when Melanie first stepped into his office. He wanted to glean as much from the notes as possible before he had to process the second scene.

Try as he might, he found it difficult to concentrate. He found himself distracted by the woman sitting just inches away. There was the perfume, for one thing. Subtle and pleasant, it kept wafting over from the driver's side of the car. It was one with which he was unfamiliar, but he had a suspicion it would be forever linked with Melanie. He gritted his teeth and began reading the notes, but his eyes kept skipping from the words in front of him to Melanie's legs. Tanned, shapely and in perfect range of his peripheral vision. After several minutes he gave up and stared out the window, trying to put his thoughts in order. He might have succeeded but for the fact that Melanie seemed to feel it was her duty, as driver, to initiate polite conversation.

"I hope you don't mind classical music, Dr. Mattson,"

she said, in reference to the CD playing in the car's state-of-the-art sound system.

He turned from watching the passing scenery to look at her. "Water Music's definitely one of Handel's all-time classics, but I guess I'm more of a rock and roll kind of guy."

He went back to glancing at his notes, silently damning himself for sounding so Neanderthal. Still, his response had obviously discouraged Melanie, because she gave up on the small talk and concentrated on her driving instead. Too bad Kent couldn't do the same with his notes. It was those legs of hers. What red-blooded man could possibly concentrate on the details of an unsolved murder when such a pair of legs was sitting a mere thirty inches away?

MELANIE WAS no stranger to the Beverly Hills Regency, and this was by no means her first visit to the city landmark, a place she had often seen at its busiest times. The luxury hotel was a longtime meeting place of the famous. It was where the rich came to play, to see and to be seen. As such, it was a popular spot for tourists and paparazzi ever on the prowl for celebrity sightings. Melanie had often dined at the formal Green Palms Restaurant or lunched at the trendy Brick Oven Cafe. Part hotel, part spa, part culinary destination, the "Beverly," as the locals called it, was always crowded, so a packed driveway was to be expected. But as she turned off Wilshire Boulevard, Melanie wasn't prepared for the sight of dozens of police cars, emergency vehicles, satellite trucks and television vans parked haphazardly on the driveway and even on the hotel's prized gardens. When she slowed to a stop at the entrance, a squad car was blocking the way. She turned to her passenger, who was already holding out an official ID card for the uniformed officer, who waved them through. Melanie drove slowly between the police cars while Dr. Mattson scanned the scene.

"Park there," he said, pointing to a slot between two police cruisers scarcely wider than her own car.

She barely managed to squeeze into the space and wondered how she'd ever get her car out of this chaotic maze. A tall black woman with close-cropped hair was coming out of the Beverly's front doors and scanning the crowds. She spotted Dr. Mattson climbing out of the car and strode over.

"Hey, Murph," Dr. Mattson said. He reached back into the car to collect his battered leather briefcase.

The handsome, well-dressed woman was obviously in no mood to exchange pleasantries. "Follow me, Kent," she said, turning and striding briskly back toward the main doors.

Dr. Mattson left without so much as a goodbye, a thank-you or a backward glance. Melanie watched until they both disappeared into the building. In her rearview mirror she spied another cruiser, lights flashing, parking directly behind her and blocking her exit. She sat for a few moments as the engine idled, then switched off the ignition and blew out a breath.

"*Now* what?" she said.

KENT HAD WORKED with Carolyn Murphy for five years, and the two had become almost instant friends. Together, they had worked on numerous cases, and while Murphy at times had displayed disgust, frustration, anger and sadness at the varied degrees of human degradation they had come across, she always took it in stride, keeping her "eyes on the prize—catching the bad guys."

A good team, they'd caught a lot of bad guys. Murphy had the hard, no-nonsense approach of a career cop. She gave no quarter and asked for none. A crack shot, she held a black belt in karate, was fluent in several languages and was the product of the meanest streets of South Central L.A. When necessary she could schmooze with the lackeys at Police Central, but she much preferred working in the trenches with her squad of detectives. For a grandmother of two, Kent had discovered early on, she was one hot-shit woman.

As they crossed the lobby toward the bank of elevators, Murphy glanced at him. "Your car. Did I hear over the radio that it had been stolen?"

Kent had been hoping to keep the information from her, but the garage attendant must have called it in. Too bad he hadn't been that on the ball *before* the Audi had been stolen. "Yeah, they took it right out of the parking garage. Imagine that."

He waited for her to chide him, but her grim expression never altered as she hit the elevator button, an indication to Kent that she was preoccupied. Otherwise she would most definitely have rubbed his nose in I-told-you-so's. Murphy was the one who had cheerfully read him chapter and verse of the California crime stats on the Audi as soon as she learned he'd purchased one.

"The Audi TT convertible?" she'd said, arching her eyebrows with wicked intent. "Nice car. Do you know how many stolen cars were reported to the LAPD last year? One thousand, one hundred and fifty-two. Know how many were sports cars? Eight hundred twelve. I predict your fancy little set of wheels will last two weeks, max."

Kent had managed to keep it for three whole months.

Small consolation, he thought as he stepped into the elevator. If Murphy's behavior was any indication, Kent had a pretty good hunch his missing car would be the least of his worries by the day's end.

"So, do we have a name?" Kent asked as the elevator climbed.

"As a matter of fact we have two," Murphy said. "Does the name Ariel Moore mean anything to you?"

"Should it?"

"Just what rock were you hiding under this week, cowboy?" Murphy asked.

Kent just looked at her, waiting.

"If you paid attention at the supermarket checkout line, you'd know Ariel Moore is the hottest rising star in town."

"And you know this *how?*"

"I know this because my grandson has her poster pinned up above his desk. That, and the hotel manager filled me in. Apparently she stays here frequently in this same two-bedroom suite. The reservation was made under Ariel Harris, which is her real name. But," she added, "here's the interesting twist. The dead woman is Stephanie Hawke, and no one has seen Ariel Harris, aka Moore, or knows what happened to the baby that checked in with Ms. Hawke. We assume the baby was Ariel's, since she gave birth only a week ago. Which you'd also know if you paid attention to the supermarket tabloids."

Their arrival at the eleventh floor halted any further conversation and they exited the elevator. The hallway was silent. As Murphy strode briskly down the carpeted corridor, she told him that all the guests on that floor had been escorted into a large conference room soon after the police had arrived. When Murphy stopped to speak to a group of uniformed officers, Kent continued to the suite.

He was glad to see a minimal number of people in the room itself. His captain had done a good job of keeping the scene clear of extraneous badges, not always an easy task. This suspicious death had all the indications of becoming a high-profile case and Kent knew high-profile cases brought the promotion and publicity seekers out of the woodwork. He hesitated at the door of the suite and paused for a moment to clear his mind and center his focus.

Kent had once had a university professor tell him that crimes and crime scenes were all about patterns. Find the pattern, and the answer would naturally follow. From his own experience, Kent knew that could take skill and patience. By their very nature, crime scenes were chaotic. Trying to take one in all at once would be overwhelming, so Kent liked to break it up into manageable chunks. First, he eyeballed the entire scene, committing everything to memory. These first impressions would later be compared alongside the official crime-scene photos, police logs, investigating officer notes, forensic notes, medical examiner reports and his own written log.

Much of the official information and reports would arrive via fax or computer to his office at Chimeya. It was there, notes and photos spread around his desk, a fire blazing, Loki curled up on his favorite rug next to the hearth, that he would start the detailed and painstaking review and let the patterns emerge. When he hit an impasse, and it happened from time to time, then he talked to Susan. He was too much the scientist to believe in ghosts, spirits or the hereafter, but that never stopped him from posing questions to the one woman he had loved and who had been taken from him seven years ago. Now, as then, she could still guide him to the answers, but before there could be any answers, he had to collect the information necessary to pose the questions.

Kent drew a deep breath and stepped into the suite, crossing to the bedroom. There was the bed, still neatly made. The curtains were drawn, a sliver of sunshine coming in through the crack between the two drapes. The television was on, but muted. In the soft glow of the bedside lamp he could just make out the figure on the floor. He moved in closer to examine the body of a young woman with dark, shoulder-length hair, fully dressed in gray slacks and a white linen shirt. She lay curled on her side as if she'd lain down there to sleep, but her eyes were half open, gazing into infinity the way the eyes of the dead sometimes did. One hand was reaching out as if to gather up the small beaded purse that had fallen to the floor beside her. Kent squatted on his heels, looking for jewelry on her person and remembering with a stab of pain how they'd tried to take Susan's wedding band and engagement ring. How they'd nearly torn her finger off, trying to remove them…

The memory caused his stomach to twist. After five years he still wasn't used to this routine. He hoped to God he never got used to it. This young woman was still sporting three rings and a necklace, and he mentally ruled out robbery as a motive. He shook his head, rose to his feet and resumed scanning the room. No sign of a struggle. Nothing appeared to be out of place. He looked closer at the victim, seeing no evidence she had been restrained or physically abused. Kent jumped as a hulking figure lurched up from the other side of the bed. "Shit, T. Ray, are you trying to give me a heart attack?"

T. Ray Boone laughed as he rose, and as Kent willed his heart to slow its beating, he found himself wondering how he had not seen T. Ray on the other side of the bed. The medical examiner's bulk was not easy to miss.

"Sorry 'bout that," T. Ray said, his Southern accent as deep and mellow as the tupelo honey produced by his native Mississippi.

By this time, Murphy had rejoined Kent. "What do you have, T.? Anything new?" she asked.

T. Ray consulted the clipboard in his latex-gloved hands. "Tell you what, y'all just change the name and location and it's the same as that lady you dragged into my carving room this morning."

"Not quite," Murphy said. "According to the desk clerk, when this one checked into the hotel last evening, she was carrying an infant. The night auditor had a guest call down to complain about a baby crying shortly after midnight. Obviously, the baby is now missing."

T. Ray shook his head. "Well, I can't speak for that, but what we have here is a female, Caucasian, age twenty-three to twenty-six, dark hair and eyes. Dead at least twelve hours, which puts time of death right around midnight. I'm going with dehydration and possible acute organ failure as a cause of death, which screams poison to me, same as that other one, but that could change with the autopsy. Maybe I'll get lucky and find something in the blood chemistry, but I gotta warn you guys…" T. Ray's brown eyes took on a somber look. "If this *does* turn out to be some kind of viral thing, you might not want to be gettin' too close without a haz-mat suit."

"Thanks for the belated warning," Kent commented. "Did you find any evidence of viral or bacterial infection in the other woman?"

T. Ray shook his head. "Nope, I didn't, except for the secondary pneumonia. No reason why that young thing should've gotten so critically sick and died all alone at night. No reason at all for her vital organs to just shut down, that I could find. That's why I'm thinkin' poison."

"But no evidence of foul play?"

"None. Blood was clean, body was clean. If it was poison, I don't know what the hell it was, but give me five minutes with this one in the morgue and I can tell y'all whether it's the same as the other," T. Ray said.

Kent glanced around. A pacifier lay on the floor near the body. A baby blanket was draped over the desk chair. And a baby bottle half-full of milk was on the side table. "What the hell happened to the baby?" he muttered to himself.

"That," Murphy responded, "is something we're trying to find out as soon as possible. We're hoping the infant is with its mother, but we can't locate Ariel Moore to confirm that." Murphy's cell phone rang, and she turned away to answer it.

Kent didn't bother to listen in. He was far more interested in gathering as much information, tangible and intangible, from the scene as possible. The two deaths bore too many similarities not to be connected. If T. Ray suspected poisoning, that meant someone had killed them. He knew the sooner he could start building a behavioral profile of the killer, the faster they could capture whoever was doing this and, hopefully, prevent more killings.

Members of the crime lab were entering the room in a steady stream, dusting for prints, shooting photos and hunting for any trace evidence the killer may have left behind. Soon, Kent knew, he would be perceived as in the way. Even in a state where people routinely took their pets to animal psychics, Kent's particular contributions to the efforts of law enforcement were not always appreciated. Not everyone in the LAPD had reacted with enthusiasm to the addition of a forensic psychologist. Kent had been surprised and flattered when Murphy had stepped forward and requested he be assigned full-time to her department and, after a grueling six-month stint at the FBI facility at Quantico, given the official designation of a homicide detective to quell the growing departmental dissent. It was a move neither had ever had reason to regret.

He saw Murphy was off her cell phone and walked over to her. Knowing that her take on things was oftentimes dramatically different from his own, he wanted her initial reactions to the scene. Kent's back was to the door and before he could ask the captain his first question, he saw Murphy glance over his shoulder and a look of irritation flash across her face.

"What's she doing in here? This is a crime scene, not a sideshow."

Kent turned and saw Melanie Harris standing just inside the suite's bedroom door. It looked like he had caught her in midwave; her hand was raised but something had diverted her attention, leaving the elegant fingers floating in midair. Even as he turned toward her, he could see her eyes widening in shock. She took a sudden step backward, stumbled on the threshold and would have fallen if Kent hadn't moved as quickly as he did.

It had been seven years since Kent had held a woman in his arms the way he was holding Melanie now. He carried the protesting woman from the room, vaguely aware of the wall of badges parting to allow him passage and Murphy's angry voice demanding to know how a civilian had gotten access to the crime scene.

"Please, put me down, Dr. Mattson. I'll be all right," Melanie protested as he carried her into the adjacent bedroom. Kent set her down near the bed, aware that Murphy was right behind him.

"Are you sure you're okay?" he said.

"Go scope out that room, Kent," Murphy interrupted before Melanie could respond. "T. Ray wants to bag the body and get started on the autopsy. I'll get the paramedics to check her out."

Kent took advantage of Murphy's orders and fled the room, Melanie's distress affecting him more than he liked.

"The pretty lady okay, Doc?" T. Ray's crooning drawl greeted Kent as he reentered the crime scene. T. Ray was standing beside the bed, alternately staring down at the body and then scribbling in his notebook.

"She'll be fine," Kent responded, pulling on the latex gloves Murphy had handed him in the elevator, and wondering if the same could be said of him.

"'Course she will, my man. You caught her before she could hit the floor. Smooth moves for a Beverly Hills shrink." T. Ray lowered his pen and projected a solemn, patronizing air. "Look, I'm real glad you took my advice about getting back into the social scene, but if this is your first date, y'all could be in big trouble with that one. Pizza parlor would've been a better bet." A mock frown concluded this brief lecture, then T. Ray said, "You let me know when you're done snoopin' around, Doc, 'cause I'm itchin' to get to work on this one."

There was a room-service cart draped with a white linen parked near the door. A single long-stemmed rose, apricot-colored, in a slender glass vase with a spray of baby's breath and a sprig of leather leaf, was on the cart, along with a covered plate, a napkin, still folded and unused, several pieces of silverware and a teapot with accompanying cup and saucer.

"What did she order for room service, T. Ray?"

"Looks like a bowl of clear beef broth, some soup crackers and a pot of ginger tea. Didn't touch any of it, though. I'm not surprised. She must've been pretty sick for a while, judging from how dehydrated she is."

Kent checked out the bathroom, noting the neat array of feminine toiletries beside the sink, and the thick terry-cloth towel, damp and crumpled in a careless heap on the floor after the victim had apparently taken a shower.

"Has the bathroom been checked out?" he called to T. Ray.

"Head to tail with a fine-tooth comb. You know how Murphy is. They've vacuumed for hair samples and sprayed for blood, videotaped, photographed, measured and sketched. Paw around all you want, Doc, just don't touch the body. That's *my* domain."

Kent pulled his own notebook out, annoyed by the tremble in his hand as he wrote. Melanie reminded him of Susan. There was no use denying the way she made him feel, and it wasn't just the beauty and grace of her. There was something else, some intangible quality he couldn't quite put his finger on…. He moved through the guest room methodically, jotting notes and making sketches, his years of police work inuring him to the buzz and bustle of activity around him until he heard Murphy speak his name. He glanced up as she strode into the room.

"How's it going, Kent?" she said, her words terse and her dark eyes flashing with a restlessness he'd grown used to over the years.

"I'm about done here."

"Good. Your young woman's asking to speak with you,"

she said. "The paramedics have checked her over. She's in a state of moderate shock, not surprising considering that's probably the first body she's ever seen. The next time you ask a woman out, I suggest taking her to the movie theater instead."

"She's *not* my young woman," Kent said with a flash of irritation. "She's just a client who gave me a ride to the scene and for some reason followed me up here."

Murphy's eyes narrowed skeptically. "Whatever you say. I'll have one of the officers drive her home when she's ready. She's in no condition to sit behind the wheel of a car. She's pretty shaken up, though she won't admit it."

"Thanks. And I'm sorry about her barging in like that. I don't know how she ever got through the barricades."

"The officer thought she was with you. You're forgiven, just barely. What do you make of the victim?"

Kent crouched on his heels again to examine the body. "Looks pretty much like the victim we found this morning. I'm thinking we're going to see the same cause of death."

"If that's the case it will be the first real clue that these two women have a common denominator." She straightened with a frustrated shake of her head, then touched Kent's arm. "Better go see your young woman. She could use some professional soothing, but make it quick. I'm going to ride along with T. Ray to the preliminary postmortem."

Kent rose to his feet, too distracted to correct Murphy for a second time about his lack of involvement with Melanie. At the present moment he didn't feel the least bit professional, or even remotely capable of soothing another human being. The two crime scenes today, plus Melanie's involvement, had brought back too many memories of Susan. Nonetheless, he forced himself to return to the

adjacent room, where Melanie was sitting up on the edge of
the bed, refusing to take the hot drink that one of Murphy's
officers was offering. As soon as Melanie spotted Kent, she
rose to her feet. Her face was still very pale. Murphy was
right. She was badly shaken and appeared on the verge of
tears.

"It's all right," Kent said to Melanie, giving the officer
a nod of dismissal after retrieving the mug of hot cocoa
from her. "I'm sorry you had to see that, but you
shouldn't have followed me up here. This is a crime scene,
and civilians aren't allowed."

"I…I didn't know if you wanted me to wait for you or
not…." She sat back down again. "You left so suddenly, I
didn't know what to do. I was parked in and couldn't leave,
so I thought I should find you and ask…."

Kent felt a pang of guilt. He *had* left her abruptly, with
no explanation. "You should drink some of this," he said,
extending the mug. "It might make you feel better."

Melanie shook her head. "Thank you, but nothing will
make me feel better right now."

Kent sighed. He set the cup on the bedside table and
drew up a chair. "Look, if you think it'll help, I'll write
out a prescription, something that you can take when you
get home…."

She shook her head, then drew in a sharp, gasping
breath and covered her face. She remained rigid for a few
moments, then dropped her hands. Her eyes burned into
his, filled with the same nameless torment he'd glimpsed
in his office…only this time it was far more intense.

"You don't understand," she said in a voice that
trembled with emotion. "My sister Ariel and I haven't
spoken in six months. I never wanted to see her again after

what she did. When Stephanie called and begged me to come to the special dinner to celebrate the birth of Ari's little girl, I…I hung up on her! Oh, God, she was my best friend. That was the last time we talked…."

Kent had to resist the urge to take Melanie into his arms when she buried her face in her hands and painful sobs shook her slender, vulnerable form. Instead, he racked his rattled brain for something soothing to say while at the same time he was processing everything she'd just said. Melanie wasn't making any sense, but she was obviously distraught. Hadn't Murphy said the victim's name was Stephanie Hawke? And the movie star with the young baby was Ariel something-or-other? Was it possible that Melanie was connected in some way with this crime scene? Kent's thoughts were jumbled.

"I'm sure she realizes why you were upset," he said, confused. "That's what best friends are for. Maybe you should consider calling her back and accepting that invitation to dinner. Whatever happened between your sister and yourself, it's never too late to make amends."

Under the circumstances, this was the best Kent could manage, but if Murphy had thought his professional training would be of some comfort to Melanie, she'd been dead wrong. Never in his entire career had Kent's words generated such a negative response. Melanie dropped her trembling hands, raised her streaming face and stared at him for a few moments in silent shock.

"You don't understand," she repeated. "I've known Stephanie for years. She was my closest friend, yet I lost my temper with her because she befriended my sister. I can't ever make amends for that, because she's lying on the floor of that bedroom, dead. My best friend is dead."

CHAPTER THREE

TWO HOURS AFTER officially identifying Stephanie's body at the Beverly Hills Regency, Melanie was waiting in numb silence at the police station, fingers curled around a cup of lukewarm vending machine coffee, staring blankly at the constant parade of officers, detectives and civilians that shuffled past the row of seats outside of Captain Carolyn Murphy's office. She'd never been so cold in all her life, though she knew the chill she felt had nothing to do with the ambient temperature of the station house.

Stephanie was dead. She'd died at the Beverly, in the same top-floor two-bedroom suite Ariel had booked every time one of her movies was released. According to the investigators, Ariel had allegedly made the reservation over the phone, using her Harris surname instead of her stage name to maintain privacy, but according to the hotel clerk, *Stephanie* had checked into the room with a young infant. Baby things had been strewn throughout the suite, the baby was missing and nobody had seen any sign of Ariel…but she *had* been there.

Nobody had seen her enter or leave the hotel, but the little beaded bag lying on the floor near Stephanie belonged to Ariel. Melanie had spent most of the past two hours telling investigators almost everything she knew about her best friend and the missing Ariel. But Melanie was exhausted and so emotionally drained that some of her memories felt almost dreamlike now. It was hard to recall that last distraught message from her sister, word for word, so she hadn't volunteered any information about Mitch. When Captain Murphy had questioned her about who the father of Ariel's baby was, Melanie had told her the father was dead—and repeated the fact that she and her sister hadn't been on speaking terms for the past six months.

Could Ariel have had something to do with Stephanie's death? Was her sister somehow involved? Why had Stephanie been at the suite with Ariel's baby? Where had Ariel been with her fancy beaded purse? She only carried that when she was going out someplace jazzy for the evening. It was one of her favorite little costume extras. The forgotten purse and baby things bespoke an ominous degree of haste and panic in Ariel's departure from the room.

"Melanie?"

She heard Dr. Mattson's rough, masculine voice and glanced up, feeling a welcome jolt at the sight of him.

"Sorry this is taking so long," he said. "I know how hard this must be for you, but we needed to compile your notes as soon as possible. The first twenty-four hours of an investigation like this is critical."

"I understand," she said, clinging to his every word. "Have you located my sister?"

"Not yet. She's not at her apartment and hasn't been seen there for some time. We've put out an all-points bulletin to locate her and the baby. I'm sure she'll turn up soon. Look, you've had a bad shock, and you really shouldn't be alone. Is there someone I can call for you who could come pick you up? A relative or friend?"

"I'm fine, Dr. Mattson. Really." To prove her point, Melanie tried to stand, but she sat back down abruptly as her knees betrayed her and a wave of dizziness darkened the edges of her vision. "I'll be fine in a moment," she amended, taking several deep, slow breaths.

In point of fact, the last place Melanie wanted to go on this ghastly day was home. She wanted desperately to talk to someone about Stephanie, but Rachel, her coworker and a friend of Stephanie's, wasn't answering her cell phone, and neither was Victor. He might be able to shed some light on Ariel's activities. According to Stephanie, he had very generously offered Ariel the caretaker's cottage at Blackstone to use until she and Mitch sorted out their lives, but to Melanie's knowledge Ariel had declined. Ariel, addicted to the nightlife, was too fond of her apartment in the city, which was conveniently close to all the clubs and bars she loved to frequent.

Nonetheless, it had surprised Melanie that Victor had offered the cottage to Ariel. It had surprised her even more that Victor hadn't mentioned this to her at all, that she'd had to learn about it from Stephanie. No doubt Victor had only been trying to help the struggling Ariel who, despite the high fees she'd commanded as a successful actress prior to her pregnancy, let money flow through her hands like water, saving little against just such a contingency as an unexpected maternal hiatus. And, of course, Mitch—damn the man, she still couldn't think about him without feeling that sharp stab of pain—only made the big money when he was taking the big risks as a stuntman.

It was probable that the couple had faced grim financial restrictions as Ariel's pregnancy had progressed. For the life of her, Melanie couldn't imagine the two of them trying to make a go of it. Ariel was so ethereal, her head lost in the clouds, drifting and dreaming her way through life. Mitch was so animal, so basic and so dangerously sexual. Maybe that was what drew the women to him.

Melanie shivered and tightened her arms around herself, focusing on Dr. Mattson's rugged face, the stubble darkening his jaw and making him look more masculine than ever. He was as weary as she, yet his eyes were clear and keen, and honest in a way that Mitch's had never been. In spite of the horrors of the day, she felt drawn to him, safe in his presence, and she most definitely didn't want to go home. Not yet, anyway.

"You really shouldn't drive," Dr. Mattson was saying. "Look, I'd be happy to drop you off at a friend's house…."

Melanie was taken aback by his unexpected offer. "Thank you, Dr. Mattson. I'd appreciate that. And, if it's not too much trouble…my car is still at the Beverly."

"Not to worry," Kent said. "I'll arrange for an officer to deliver it to your house, just give the desk sergeant over there the address and your car keys." He held up his hand as she began thanking him again. "It's the least I can do, after all you've been through today. I'll go round up an unmarked car, and you just point me in the right direction."

BLACKSTONE WAS NEARLY an hour's drive from the station house, not because it was all that far as the crow flies, but because the Santa Monica Freeway was choked with bumper-to-bumper traffic. Melanie was content to leave the driving to Dr. Mattson. Twenty minutes into the trip, as she gazed out the passenger window in a blank haze of exhaustion, he said, grinning, "Are we there yet?"

She cast him an apologetic look. "It's not much farther.

I'm sorry, Dr. Mattson. I should have taken a cab. You've had a long day, too."

"I don't mind." He shrugged. "This is actually a pretty drive. Living so near the ocean you'd think I'd see it more often. Fact is, I hardly ever lay eyes on the Pacific, except when I'm flying to the ranch."

"You're lucky to have a place where you can get away from it all."

"I couldn't survive without it," he said. "Especially with this job. There are days when it's hard to find the good side of anything, kind of like today. But then I think about Chimeya at sunrise, when the sun rounds out of the east, the sky lights up from inside itself and the mountains glow like fire…. There's nothing else like it, and no place better for centering the soul."

Melanie felt the tension in the pit of her stomach ease as she listened to Kent. "It sounds lovely," she said. "Are you really going back there tonight, with all that's gone on today?"

"I do my best thinking there, and there's no commuter traffic. Just a fast taxi and a straight one-hour shot to heaven."

Melanie studied his profile as he spoke. She wanted to ask him if he was married, but didn't know how to phrase the question without sounding nosy. How could he *not* have a partner in his life? He was damn near perfect. In fact, she was still searching for some annoying fault, some irritating quality that would reaffirm her belief that she was far better off without a man in her life. He had to have at least one or two bad habits, aside from drinking too much coffee.

"You told us that your sister had a lot of male friends," he said, glancing at her, "and that you hadn't spoken to her in six months, but maybe you could tell me a bit more about who the father of her baby was? Who knows? It might give us some clues to help us find her."

His tone was casual, but Melanie felt the anxious knot form in her stomach again, even as a voice within whispered, Tell him. Tell him everything.

She wanted to. She sensed that Dr. Mattson knew she was withholding information. His long silences had been filled with the loudest unspoken questions that Melanie had ever endured. She bit her lower lip and stared out at the thinning blur of traffic as they sped away from the city. The irony of this situation was not lost on her. What she couldn't, *wouldn't,* talk about in Dr. Mattson's office was no longer her secret to keep. Not as long as Ariel and the baby were missing. She drew a painful breath and released it slowly.

"The father was Mitch Carson, and he was my fiancé."

As Kent drove down Blackstone's private drive, access to which had been ensured by Melanie's obvious acquaintance with the security guard stationed at the gatehouse, he was struck by how isolated and unique this property was. He liked the way the natural beauty of the place had been allowed to flourish, an unusual sight amidst this obsessive modern culture of manicuring every blade of grass.

He also liked the way Melanie had begun to open up to him, talking about her fiancé, her sister and her wedding day. It hadn't been easy for her to broach the subject, but once she started, the words came faster and faster, tumbling out in a rush to release all the pent-up emotions of the past six months. When she had finished, she slumped back in her seat with a dazed look, as if she couldn't quite believe she'd finally confronted the demons of her past. For the last five minutes she'd been silent, gazing out the window. Kent was glad for the break in conversation. It gave him a few moments to process her revelations and how they may or may not be connected to the day's events.

"That's the guest cottage," Melanie said, rousing as he rounded a curve and a simple gabled dwelling tucked in a grove of eucalyptus trees came into view. "The mansion's on top of the ledges, another quarter of a mile beyond here." She sat up straighter. "Look, the door's open. Maybe Victor's inside. If you'll stop here, Dr. Mattson, I'll go check."

Kent parked the unmarked police car and followed her to the cottage. The spicy sweet scent of the rose bushes lining the brick path mingled with the salty Pacific air. Grapevines adorned both sides of the arbored entry and a purple wisteria twined against the shingled outer walls. Six o'clock in the afternoon, and the sun's rays were strong and golden, spilling into this small Tudor-style cottage as Melanie pushed the door completely open.

"Victor?" she called out as she entered. "Vic?"

Kent stepped over the threshold and into the dim coolness that smelled faintly of cedar paneling, leather and wood smoke. He stood for a moment, letting his eyes adjust to the lower light level, then followed Melanie into the living room, which was dominated by a beautiful field-stone fireplace, the old andirons still cradling several half-burned logs. Built-in bookshelves lined both sides of the fireplace, and comfortable leather furnishings and a braided rug complemented the restful feel of the cozy space.

"We used to live here, Ariel and I," Melanie murmured, looking around.

"For how long?"

"Three years." Melanie walked to the bookshelves and

scanned the titles. "Victor offered it to me a few months after I began working for him. He knew I was struggling to raise my sister and having a hard time making ends meet on a gofer's pay. We lived here until Ariel landed her first big movie role and Victor's wife had a few too many glasses of sherry and came here to tell us she thought it was high time we moved on." Melanie glanced at him with a wry smile. "I never told Victor that the reason we left was because his wife was jealous of Ariel. At the time I thought that was ludicrous. Ariel was only nineteen. She was still just a baby…or so I thought."

Kent followed Melanie up the narrow stairs, where four doors opened onto the landing. The first room Melanie looked in was big, with a queen-size antique sleigh bed and two dormer windows framing an ocean view over the treetops. "This used to be my room," she said. "At night, with the windows open, I could hear the waves pounding against the Blackstone ledges."

The bedroom was simply furnished and uncluttered. There was one framed picture atop the bureau, which Melanie studied for a few silent moments before turning away abruptly. Kent glanced at the photograph, a high quality black and white of a lean, athletic man on a Harley wearing an arrogant grin, leather pants and a dark T-shirt. Arms like Sylvester Stallone's and features reminiscent of a young and virile Marlon Brando.

Melanie drifted out of the room and into the corridor. Kent followed as she passed a second door that opened onto a tiny bath. He glanced inside. Old-fashioned porcelain sink with brass bistro fixtures, small claw-foot tub, vintage pull-chain toilet. Everything clean and neat as a pin. A third door opened onto a smaller bedroom. "This was Ariel's room," Melanie said, stepping inside and looking around. "The wisteria vine growing against the cottage was so thick and strong that she'd climb down it like a monkey and spend the night raising hell with her friends. Ariel hated school, and couldn't have cared less about her grades. It's a wonder they graduated her."

Melanie paused outside the fourth door off the landing. "This used to be what we called the study, but Ariel never used it for studying." She was still smiling as she swung the door inward. She gasped and froze, hand still on the doorknob. Kent glanced over her shoulder and saw a charming nursery, painted in pale pastels, complete with a crib, baby toys and a changing table. A tiny writing desk set beneath the window and a day bed completed the furnishings. "Stephanie must have been wrong. Ariel *did* come back," she said, gazing around the small space. "I knew she'd been trying to work things out with Mitch before he was killed. She must have hoped he'd move in with her here and help raise the baby."

"What?" Kent burst out. "Correct me if I'm wrong, but didn't you tell Captain Murphy that your sister lived in Beverly Hills?"

"Yes. That's true. She has an apartment there which she loves, but according to Stephanie, Victor offered the guest cottage to Ariel a few months before the baby was born. Stephanie told me she didn't take him up on his offer, but she was obviously wrong."

Kent stared, first at Melanie, then back at the baby things. He had to restrain himself from cursing aloud. "So you're telling me your missing sister might have been living here?"

Melanie shook her head, puzzled. "It doesn't really

look like they were living here. I mean, there are no personal belongings, just that damn picture of Mitch and a nursery that looks as if it's never been used. I'm sure Victor would have told me if Ariel had moved in."

Kent stood beside her, analyzing every detail of the small room. The entire cottage had an empty feel to it, and this room was no exception. Even the desktop was bare, although… Kent spotted the small, cream-colored envelope propped against the base of the table lamp at the same time as Melanie did and they crossed the room together. On the face of the envelope, in a childlike scrawl, a name had been written and underlined twice.

Mel

Kent heard Melanie's sharp intake of breath. "Oh, Ari," she said as she reached to retrieve the message.

"Wait," he said, staying her hand with his own. "You shouldn't touch it. It's evidence…." Her hand was ice-cold in his, and as she lifted her pleading eyes, he felt his resolve begin to crumble. After a few moments he sighed and reached into his jeans pocket for the fresh pair of latex gloves he'd grabbed earlier at the Beverly Hills Regency. "All right," he said. "I'll open the letter and lay it on the desk for you to read, but you can't touch it. Understand?"

She nodded.

The envelope wasn't sealed, which made things easier for Kent. He withdrew the folded sheet of matching stationery, acutely aware that Melanie was clinging to the edge of the desk and her face was even paler than it had been before. He hesitated, caught between knowing what was right and what his heart was telling him to do. Not only did he stand to lose his badge twice over for doing this, but Melanie was probably going to faint on him again.

And yet, she deserved to read the note. Hell, if it was his sister that was missing under suspicious circumstances and his best friend that T. Ray was examining probably at this very moment in the hospital morgue, wouldn't he want to study the note before the investigators arrived and took it to the crime lab? Damn straight he would, no matter what it said, good or bad. And so Kent carefully unfolded the piece of stationery and laid it flat on the desktop.

Dear Mel, I've messed up everything so bad…

The words seemed to float up from the pages to her eyes. As she read, the unmistakable delicate scent of CK One, Ariel's favorite perfume, wafted up from the paper. Melanie swallowed hard, blinked a tear from her eye and prayed that the letter would hint at Ariel's whereabouts, and reassure her in some way that her sister was all right.

I've ruined my life and, worst of all, I've destroyed the lives of the people I love most. I don't blame you for not wanting to talk to me. I don't even blame you for hating me. After what happened with Mitch, I guess it's what I deserve. But, I have to tell you— beg you to understand—I never, ever meant to hurt you. What I did was selfish and stupid, I know, but when I first met Mitch it was love at first sight, or at least that's what I thought. You must be able to understand that.

Melanie certainly could. It was the same effect Mitch had had on her when Victor had introduced them on the location of *Hammerhead Row*. The movie was full of explosions, fights, high-speed car chases and numerous other risky stunts, and Mitch had been the body double for the lead actor.

Melanie remembered the almost electrical charge she had felt when she and Mitch met. *Hammerhead Row* had been shot almost entirely on location in San Francisco, and that required Melanie's constant presence. The initial mutual attraction between them had led to lunches, which soon evolved into dinner dates at various city hot spots. By the time the movie was into its third week of production they were sleeping together. In fact, Melanie could still blush recalling those first passionate encounters in Mitch's trailer. By the time the film wrapped they were living together and by the premiere, they were engaged. And all that time, Mitch was playing both Melanie and Ariel.

Melanie forced the memories out of her mind and turned her attention back to the letter.

I don't expect your forgiveness, but maybe one day you will want to meet your new niece. She's so beautiful, and I hope she takes after you. Strong, smart, brave and dependable. All the things I'm not. All the things I admired so much about you. All the things I lost. And please try to forgive Mitch. I think, no, I believe, he realized how much he had hurt both of us. He wasn't a bad man. He was just caught up in the Hollywood scene and he let it go to his head. He really wanted it to work between us and to support this baby. I regret she will never know her father.

Mel, I love you. If nothing else, please believe that. I would like to tell you that in person, and maybe someday in the future I can. We're going away for a few weeks but maybe when I get back we can come visit you. Motherhood is going to be the toughest part I've ever played. It's going to be hard and it's going to be lonely, but I can do it. I have you for a role model, after all. You're so strong, and I've been so weak, but that's going to change, I promise you that. And I ask you to promise me one thing. No matter how you feel about me, if anything ever happens to me, please, I beg you, take care of my little girl.

So, for now this is goodbye. When we get back, I'll call you. I can only hope it is a call you will take.

All my love,

Ari.

These were the most honest, self-aware and heartfelt words she had heard from her sister in years. And, thanks to Melanie's obstinate refusal to talk to her sister, this last communiqué was one-sided. "What a fool I've been," she whispered.

"Are you all right?" Kent asked.

He was standing very close. *Probably ready to catch me again.*

"Just give me a minute," she said, not turning. Instead, she looked up from the letter and out the window. The sun was over the Pacific and the waters gleamed with a thousand jewels on the waves. It had been their favorite time of day. In happier times, it was the kind of late after-noon when she would have come home from a long day on set with a huge bag of Chinese takeout and a wealth of Hollywood gossip to share with her little sister. The two would take the food and a blanket down to the private beach below the estate and have a feast, staying until the last golden rays fell below the waves.

"We never did see it," she said out loud.

"Excuse me?" Kent said.

"The green flash, we never saw it in all the time we were here."

Kent was looking at her oddly. Perhaps he was thinking the letter was the final straw needed that day to break the back of her sanity.

Without turning from the window, she said, "You mean to say that you live and work on the California coast and you've never heard of the green flash?"

"Hey, I just work on the coast. I'm a mountain man, born and bred."

She finally turned toward him. "Few people have seen it and lots of folks don't even believe it ever happens. But the story goes, on evenings when the conditions are right, as the sun sets behind the ocean its last rays, just for an instant, shine through the waves far out to sea. In that instant the sunlight flashes green across the sky. Ari and I spent a lot of nights down on the beach waiting to see it."

In the ensuing silence, Melanie was able to collect herself and, for the first time in those awful months since the aborted wedding, think clearly. It was as if a fog was lifting and she could look inside with brutal objectivity. She had spent the last six months foolishly blaming everyone but herself for her misery. She had blamed Mitch for his philandering, she had blamed Victor for introducing her to Mitch and most of all she had blamed Ari for ruining her life. Now she realized the only blame belonged on her shoulders. She had been faced with a choice: deal with what had happened and move on, or wallow in self-pity and melancholy, thereby punishing everyone around her.

Her choice had cost her dearly. One by one her friends, all but Stephanie, had given up on her, leaving her to her own state of misery. Her work had suffered to the point that even Victor had warned her that her career was in real jeopardy. And the heaviest toll of all had been the erosion of her relationship with Ariel. Well, no more. The dreadful, endless day that had started with the desperate move of seeking help from an outside professional had somehow brought her to this point of realization: The only one who could help her was her. On the spot she made a series of promises to herself. No more excuses. No more self-pity. No more wallowing in the past.

She straightened, squared her shoulders and turned to Kent. "Dr. Mattson, we have to find my sister as soon as possible."

SOMETHING IN Melanie's voice made Kent look closely at her. Gone was the vulnerable patient who had bolted from his office. Gone, too, was the bewildered woman who had just suffered through the discovery of her best friend's corpse, the official identification of the body and nearly two hours of police questioning.

Instead, he had the distinct impression he was seeing the real Melanie Harris for the first time, and he marveled at the change. Kent would have predicted months, if not years of intensive therapy to put back together the broken woman he had met that morning. He raised an eyebrow.

"Do you know where she was planning to go?"

"No, I don't, but at least we know she's all right. This letter was dated two days ago. She knew she was going away and must have been planning to have Victor give me that letter," Melanie said. "Victor might know where she's gone."

"Who's this Victor you keep mentioning?"

"Victor Korchin. He owns this estate. He's my boss, and a good friend."

"Why is that name so familiar?"

"Victor's a film director."

"Ah, yes. Korchin Studios." Murphy had mentioned that name to him earlier. This time, Kent did curse aloud. "No doubt Victor has close ties to your sister, who happens to be a successful actress," he prodded.

Melanie hesitated. "Yes. Victor's been like a father to her."

"But somehow you just forgot to mention to us this little connection between the two of them?"

Melanie dropped her eyes from his accusing stare. "I'm sorry."

"I hope he knows something about your sister's whereabouts, since she didn't leave many clues in that letter and the only other person we might have questioned is dead. I'll have a couple of detectives dispatched here immediately to question him and search this place properly, now that we've messed up any potential evidence." He reached for the cell phone clipped to a holder on his hip, but before he could make his call, it rang.

"Mattson here," he said.

Melanie could tell that Kent was on the receiving end of a call from his boss.

"Hold on a sec," Kent was saying as he fished a notepad

out of his pocket and leaned over the desk, pen in hand. "Okay, what do you have?" He listened, scribbling furiously. "Got it. Thanks. And Murph? You might want to send a team out to Victor Korchin's estate. Ariel Moore and her baby might have been living at the guest cottage here. We found a letter that she wrote two days ago to her sister, and she could still be somewhere on the premises. We haven't approached the main house yet." He gave her the address before ending the call and turning back to Melanie.

"Do they have any leads?" she asked.

"No, but they've made a positive ID of the other victim found earlier this morning."

"There was *another* victim? Who?"

Kent paused. "What the hell. You'll probably hear it on the evening news." He flipped through the pages of his notepad. "Her name was Rachel Fisher, age thirty-seven, and she lived at…"

"Sixty-five East Corinth, right on the beach," Melanie said, her mouth going dry as her heart skipped several beats.

Kent appeared stunned. "Don't tell me you're psychic."

Melanie shook her head, trying unsuccessfully to rid herself of an all-too-familiar feeling triggered by one of her earliest childhood memories. When she was a little girl and Ariel just a newborn, their parents had taken them to a family gathering at an aunt and uncle's farm in the country. It had been a day of picnics, games, cousins and, to a young Melanie, seemingly endless fussing over "baby Ari." By midafternoon she had grown resentful of the fawning over her new sister. Determined to recapture some of the attention, Melanie was drawn to the huge and ancient apple tree behind the barn. She knew Uncle Tukey loved red apples and set out to prove her worth by scaling the tree and fetching the biggest, reddest apple she could find. As it happened, the biggest, reddest apple was hanging from the tree's uppermost branches. With scarcely a thought to her mother's standing admonishment to remain in sight of the grown-ups at all times, she skipped around the back of the barn and clambered up the tree.

Melanie had climbed higher and higher, until she was a full fifteen feet off the ground. She looked down only once, and that was enough. She was an accomplished tree climber, but this was certainly higher than she had ever gone before. Smiling in anticipation of the look of happy surprise on Uncle Tukey's face when she presented him the trophy apple, she shinnied out onto the branch, which was swaying a bit under her weight. Clinging to the rough bark with one hand, she extended the other and, just as her fingers brushed the red fruit, the branch gave one last mighty sway and snapped.

She remembered feeling not as if she were falling, rather as if she were suspended in midair and the ground was rushing up to meet her. Everything was pretty hazy after that. She must have screamed because there was a knot of adults and cousins around when she came to, all with the same concerned look on their faces. Melanie's plan to divert their attention from Ariel had worked, but the price had been a costly one—a broken arm and a month-long grounding. All of that was a dim recollection, however. What had stayed with Melanie was that feeling of inertia while inevitable events rushed toward her. It was one that had followed her all her life and, as she looked at Kent, she felt it again for the second time that day.

"Dr. Mattson, I know Rachel. I know her address because *mine* use to be Sixty-seven East Corinth. We were next-door neighbors until I moved closer to the studio. She's one of Victor's best screenwriters, and I've known her for years."

A DOZEN THOUGHTS were competing for Kent's attention, but rising fast among them were these: two young women had died mysteriously, mere miles and hours apart. Both were affiliated with the movie industry, and both knew the missing Ariel Moore and her sister, Melanie. It was obvious from the expression on her face that Melanie had made the same sinister connection.

"What's going on?" Her eyes reflected her confusion and fear. "Dear God, do you think Ariel and the baby might be in some kind of danger?"

"I honestly don't know," Kent said, putting his hands on her shoulders as he looked at her. "But I can promise you this. We'll find your sister and her baby as quickly as we can. In the meantime, I'm not about to let you out of my sight."

CHAPTER FOUR

MELANIE TURNED AWAY from Kent and gathered her wits. "Was Rachel killed at home?" she asked. "Do you think the same person killed them both?"

"Rachel's body was discovered on the beach below her apartment by a jogger early this morning," Kent said. "This early in the investigation we can't be sure, of course, but there's a strong possibility the two deaths are connected."

"But who would want to kill either of them?" Melanie bit her lower lip, damning the quiver in her voice.

Before Kent could respond, they heard the throb of an approaching engine and the crunch of tires on the gravel drive. A green-and-yellow John Deere garden tractor puttered into view, a spry-looking elderly man perched on the seat, dressed in drab workingman's clothing and wearing a straw hat. "The gardener?" Kent asked.

Melanie shook her head. "Victor Korchin," she said. "I'm hoping he can tell us where Ariel is." She turned from the window and hurried for the door, but Kent reached for her arm to hold her back.

"Wait," he cautioned. "Until Captain Murphy gets here, the less said about anything that's happened, the better. You'd better let me talk to him."

"That's ridiculous. I just want to ask him about Ariel."

Melanie pulled out of his grasp and backed up a step. "Victor has a right to know about Rachel and Stephanie. You can't possibly think he's involved in any way."

"This is a murder investigation. I'm talking about police procedure here and we've already violated a number of important protocols. I'd like to keep my job, if you don't mind."

"I won't mention them," she promised, inwardly seething at the way he was treating her. She wheeled around and exited the little nursery, dashing down the stairs in angry haste. As she rushed forward to meet Victor, she heard the faint sound of sirens approaching from the main road. Victor stopped the tractor and cut the ignition.

"Melanie," he said, climbing off the seat. He seemed surprised and pleased to see her. "Have you come to see Ari? This is good, so good, but I don't think she is here." Victor's eyes focused over her shoulder. "Come up to the house, bring your gentleman friend, we'll share a glass of wine and talk…." His expression changed as he heard the approaching sirens. "What's wrong, Melly? What is it?"

"Oh, Victor," Melanie said, crumbling at his use of her pet name. "We were hoping you'd know where Ariel was. It's very important that we find her." Melanie turned as Kent stepped up beside her. "This is Dr. Kent Mattson, and he's…"

"Is Ariel sick? Is the baby all right?" Victor interrupted, his face becoming pale. "Something terrible has happened. What is it? Dear God, tell me."

"I'm sorry, sir," Kent said. "I'm afraid you'll have to wait for the police to arrive. Maybe you'd better sit down." He guided Victor toward the passenger side of the unmarked car before walking away to meet the police cars, and Melanie's heart broke at how old Victor looked as he half collapsed onto the seat with a dazed, apprehensive expression.

"Melanie?"

"I'm here, Vic." She knelt beside him. "I'm right here."

"What has happened? Why can't you tell me? Is Ariel all right? And her baby?"

Melanie closed her hands around his, feeling their cold tremble. "I don't know, Victor. I honestly don't know. Do you have any idea where she might be?"

"At her apartment, maybe? She spends most of her time there, now that Mitch is dead."

"She isn't there. We've checked."

"I just cast her as the lead in our next production, *Celtic Runes*. Did she tell you? We were going to begin filming shortly…. Is she sick? Is she in some kind of danger?"

Victor was so distraught that Melanie was on the verge of telling him everything she knew when she felt Kent's hand on her arm, drawing her to her feet as the police cars, a seeming platoon of them, careened around the corner and skidded to a stop, blue lights flashing, sirens cutting out one after another. Kent propelled Melanie along with him as he approached Captain Murphy's car. She fixed Kent with a steely expression as she exited her vehicle. "Well?"

"The man over there is Victor Korchin," Kent said. "According to Melanie, he was like a father to Ariel. All he knows is that she's missing, and he learned that from us not five minutes ago. We told him nothing about the two murders, and we didn't touch anything inside the cottage except for the letter in the nursery, and I wore gloves when I took it out of the envelope." Kent glanced at Melanie, then ran his fingers through his hair. "If you don't mind, I'd like to get Melanie out of here. It's been a helluva long day for her."

Murphy gave Kent a curt nod of dismissal as she moved toward the unmarked car, signaling two other officers to accompany her. The three of them assisted the visibly shaken Victor to the captain's vehicle. Halfway there he paused.

"Where are you taking me?" he asked, removing his straw hat. "I will need to leave a note for my wife that I am going." He reached into his trouser pocket and drew forth a large handkerchief to dab the sweat from his forehead.

Melanie took a step forward, but before she could voice a single word, Kent pulled her back. He escorted her firmly to the car and planted her in the passenger seat. "But, Dr. Mattson, I can't just leave Victor like this…."

"Not another. word," he said, his eyes steely. He shut the door and returned to where Murphy stood, bending close for a brief conversation before returning and climbing behind the wheel.

Kent backed up carefully, threading through the maze of police vehicles. "Murphy's aware of the details. She'll handle the questioning from here on out. She's an expert at that."

He was heading back down the winding driveway as he spoke, driving cautiously and yielding the right of way as other police vehicles approached. Melanie stared at his calm, impassive profile, experiencing another wave of heated indignation at his words. "You talk as if Victor's a suspect."

"It's standard police procedure," he repeated. "Murphy might not take him to the station house, but we have to question everyone who has any connection to these women." He paused, then glanced sidelong at her. "I don't suppose there's anyone else Ariel was close to that you haven't told us about, or any other places she might have been living?"

Melanie faced front and laced her hands tightly in her lap. "No."

"Okay." He turned left when he exited Blackstone's impressive gate. "Then I think it's time we found you a safe haven for the night."

"Just drive me home, please," Melanie said, battling an overwhelming weariness. "I want to be there if Ariel calls. She could be in terrible trouble."

"It's not a good idea for you to be alone."

"You can't possibly believe that I'm in danger, too," Melanie said.

"Until we know for certain that you aren't, I'm not taking any chances. I'd like you to give us permission to stake out your apartment for a few days, just in case, and if you insist on staying there, I'd like you to consider having an undercover officer on the premises. A woman, of course," he added, as if she might have thought he was volunteering himself.

"Absolutely not," Melanie said with a firm head shake. "My apartment is in a very safe part of town and I'll be fine there by myself. I'm not going to argue about this, Dr. Mattson. I appreciate your concern, but please, just take me home."

As HE ENTERED Melanie's apartment for the first time, Kent fully expected that he'd be overwhelmed with Hollywood pretentiousness and was pleasantly surprised by the homey simplicity of the place. It was a small apartment—the kitchen, dining room and living room all blending into one open space—furnished in an inexpensive yet tasteful style.

"It's small," Melanie had said as she unlocked the door, "but I don't need much." She flung her purse on the sofa, ran her fingers through her hair and heaved an exhausted sigh that turned into a moan as her eyes fixed on a broken bowl on the kitchen floor. Her shoulders slumped. "Oh, no. That crazy cat of mine thinks he has the right to sample anything I accidentally leave out on the counter." She knelt to gather up the broken pieces, her hair tumbling around her face in a soft glossy fan. "Trust Shakespeare to help himself. He knows the counter's off limits, but apparently Anatanyia's Mexicali shrimp dip was too much of a temptation. Never cared for it myself—too spicy. I'm sorry about the mess."

"I'd like to check out your apartment before I leave, just to make sure everything is okay," Kent said.

She glanced up at him, hands full of broken shards, and nodded. "All right. Thank you."

It didn't take him long to figure out that nobody lurked in the closets or hid in the bathroom, and no murderer lingered in the bedroom, but something caught his eye beneath the bed. The tail of a cat protruded from beneath the dust ruffle. "I found your dip thief," he called to Melanie, "hiding out under the bed."

"Typical," he heard Melanie say, and he stood for a moment, wondering why the tail didn't move. Cats were cautious creatures by nature. Kent knelt and lifted the bed-spread. The cat was lying on its side—big, orange and unmoving. He reached his hand to touch the animal. There was no response, and he was not surprised. The cat was quite dead and he noticed a bit of white froth around the animal's mouth.

With a surge of adrenaline Kent was on his feet, running to the kitchen. "Don't touch that!" he snapped. Melanie had a wad of paper towels in her hand to wipe up the remnants of the dip that soiled her kitchen floor. She froze, then rose slowly to her feet.

"What's wrong?" She stared at him, her eyes widening. "Where's Shakespeare?" Kent closed the distance between them, as if by being near her he could protect her from the next bad shock of her horrible day.

"He's dead," Kent said. "I'm sorry. Wash your hands immediately and don't touch the dip. We'll need to get a sample of it to the lab and get it analyzed…."

"Dead?" she echoed faintly. "Shakespeare? Dead?"

"Did you eat any of that dip yourself? Even to be polite?"

She shook her head. "No. Like I said, I never cared for it. It was supposed to go in the trash this morning but I forgot to take it out with me when I left."

"Where did it come from?" Kent asked.

"Stephanie dropped it off here the morning after the dinner party…." Her eyes filled with tears that spilled over onto her cheeks.

"Who is this Anatanyia? What dinner party? When?"

"Victor Korchin's wife," she said. "The party was at Blackstone the day before yesterday. It was held to celebrate the birth of Ariel's baby. I was invited but I didn't go, I didn't want to go. I wasn't ready to see her yet, I wasn't ready to forgive her, and so Stephanie brought me the dip to tell me about the party and how beautiful Ariel's daughter was and…" Melanie's voice choked off for the second time and she leaned into him, pressing her hands to her face and drawing a deep, shuddering breath. She was trembling like a leaf in high winds. Kent supported her with one arm, while his other hand reached for his cell phone.

Murphy answered on the fourth ring. "This had better be important, Kent, because I'm in the middle of an interrogation that you should most definitely be witnessing."

"I may have just discovered what killed those two women," Kent said. "Send a crime team to Melanie Harris's apartment, would you? Tell them there's a dead cat in the bedroom and some dip on the kitchen floor that may contain a poisonous substance. And Murph? I think we'd better assign twenty-four-hour surveillance of her apartment, as well as an officer to stay with Melanie. I don't think she's safe here by herself, but she insists this is where she wants to be, in case her sister tries to contact her."

Kent felt Melanie stiffen in his arms as he stuffed the cell phone into the holder on his belt.

"Dr. Mattson," she said, drawing away from him and drying her cheeks. "I really don't want to stay here now. Not after what's happened to Shakespeare. If you could drop me at a hotel…." There was a flicker of dread on her face as she remembered that Stephanie had died in a hotel room surrounded by people. She shook her head, a small, helpless gesture. "I don't know what to do. I don't know where else to go."

Kent hesitated. He could take her to a safe house. That could certainly be arranged. But he sensed that she needed more than just a safe place. She needed a sympathetic ear and companionship. "I know where," he said. "You'll come home with me tonight. Chimeya may be too remote and rustic for your Hollywood tastes, but you'll be safe there."

She shook her head. "I can't do that," she said. "Thank you for the offer, but it's too much of an imposition."

"Then I'll assign Sergeant Bertha Dewburgh as your bodyguard. No one'll bother you with Big Bertha nearby, and she'll stick with you like glue. Takes her job real seriously. Guaranteed, Big Bertha and two plainclothes detectives'll keep you safe in any hotel room. I'll make the call, if you're sure that's the route you want to take."

Kent reached for his cell phone again, and Melanie stayed him with a touch of her slender hand. "All right," she relented. "I'll go with you to Chimeya."

Kent tucked the phone away for the second time with an abrupt laugh. "Good choice. Come on. If we hustle, we can be at Chimeya before dark."

"All right, just give me a few minutes to pack some things," Melanie said.

"I'm sorry, but that's a negative. Nothing can be removed until the crew from the crime lab gets a look at it."

"Crime lab?"

"Yes, unfortunately, your apartment has been classified a crime scene. But don't worry, by tomorrow you should be able to send for a few things." Kent offered a cryptic little grin. "In the meantime, I have a strong hunch you will be well taken care of and outfitted once my housekeeper gets a hold of you."

KENT'S LOVE AFFAIR with flying had begun at an early age, and he attributed that love to strong genetic encoding on both sides of his family. His father had flown in the Navy and survived two tours and eighty-six missions in Vietnam. He called those his years spent "downtown." His grandmother on his mother's side had been one of the women pilots who served the United States military in World War II. In 1942 she'd been the youngest pilot in the Air Transport Auxiliary, ferrying planes and supplies to frontline airfields in Britain and France. She'd flown Spitfires for the most part, though she'd been rated for multi-engine aircraft as well, and had piloted nearly a thousand planes with only one forced landing.

Kent had toyed with the idea of joining the military after graduating from college and following in his father's footsteps, but as strong a temptation as flying the most sophisticated fighter jets was, his love of freedom was even stronger. Having grown up in faded Levi's and worn cowboy boots, he couldn't picture himself in a crisp white uniform, smartly saluting his way up the ladder. So he opted for the next best thing: first, his private pilot's license, and then commercial training at the best facility in the nation. He could have landed a job flying for one of the big airlines, but again, his love of freedom won out. He'd bought his own plane and piloted his own dreams.

Kent was aware of Melanie's trepidation as he pulled the unmarked police car into a parking space near the terminal at the small airfield.

She sat up, smoothed her hair and glanced out the window. "Oh, God," she said, eyeing the fleet of private aircraft parked beyond the buildings. "You weren't pulling my leg. You really do commute by airplane."

"You betcha," Kent said. "In an hour we'll be at Chimeya. C'mon."

He was out of the car and opening her door, waiting as she got out slowly and clutched her purse to her chest, a frown puckering her smooth brow. "Dr. Mattson, there's something you should know…."

Suddenly enlightened, Kent reached for her hand. "Fear of flying is very common. Don't worry, you'll be safe with me."

Melanie's green eyes widened with surprise. "How did you know?"

"I specialize in psychic psychology." She followed him as he entered the terminal. "Hey, Paulette," he said to the woman sitting behind the counter, who was reading a paperback. "I'm heading home for the night."

Paulette reached for the flight-plan log and tossed a set of keys on the counter. "Gotcha, Doc," she said, staring at Melanie with interest. "She's all fueled up and ready to roll. Have a nice evening. See you tomorrow?"

"Bright and early," Kent said, scooping up the keys and signing the log book.

"Doc?" Paulette said just as Kent was exiting the office. "Better watch your climb out. An FAA dude was here when you blasted off last Friday and we got written up for not busting your chops."

"Right," Kent said with a somber nod. Damn the FAA and their overly restrictive rules at these little airstrips. He paused, one eyebrow raised. "Are they anywhere near here today?"

Paulette heaved a frustrated sigh and attempted to look stern. "Nope."

"Good." Kent walked toward the line of planes parked on the edge of the tarmac, admiring the sleek silver lines of the TBM 400 turboprop he'd owned for two years now. He heard Melanie's light, quick footsteps keeping apace, following him as he did a routine preflight check, then gave the smooth, shiny fuselage an affectionate slap and turned to catch a glimpse of those beautiful, if slightly anxious, eyes. "She's good to go, if you are," he said.

He admired her shapely legs as she climbed aboard the plane, marveling at how even a glimpse of her femininity could send his heart rate off the scale. He was obviously more sexually deprived than he'd thought. Strapping his passenger into the copilot's seat, he analyzed the way her delicate perfume flavored the atmosphere of the cockpit, and gave the fragrance his final stamp of approval.

After securing himself into his own seat he handed her a headset. "Once we get airborne we'll need these to communicate. Steering on the ground is accomplished through the brake pedals, since the yoke only works once we're in flight. Sounds good, doesn't she?" he said as the engine roared to life. He advanced the throttle and took his feet off the brakes. The TBM 400 moved smoothly forward out of the lineup, and he swung her to the right as soon as she was clear of the other planes. "She's a sweet plane to fly, tops out at three hundred knots. Speed is addictive, no doubt about it, and this little lady really kicks ass."

So far he'd gotten no response from Melanie, who was looking increasingly pale and tense. He was beginning to wonder if this flight wouldn't tip her over the edge. Maybe she'd finally see that green flash once they were airborne. "Put your hands on the yoke," he said to her. "Follow through with me and get the feel of her."

Her slender hands reached out reluctantly and closed on the controls. Kent advanced the throttle a little more, taxiing toward the compass rose. "Okay, let's run through our preflight checklist…mixture rich, check fuel selector, wiggle the elevators and rudder and make a visual check. They look good to me. Trim in neutral, see that white line? That's neutral, right where it should be for takeoff.

Magneto check…our RPMs shouldn't exceed 125, so we're good. Check the suction gauge, suction is up. Engine instruments and ammeter…amps are okay, not fluctuating. Check heading indicator…we're about ten degrees off of true so we'll reset to three-five-zero."

He glanced at Melanie, who was frowning with concentration as she watched and listened. "Fun, huh?" He returned his attention to the control panel. "Vertical velocity is zero and the field elevation here is three hundred feet, which tells us that the pressure is about three thousand and nine. High pressure, should stay that way. We'll have smooth sailing to Chimeya." He keyed his mike. "Tuttle's, this is November 221 taking the active."

"Roger that, Doc," came Paulette's immediate response. "And please remember to stay in the pattern."

"You know I will." He checked the final approach and saw that it was clear. He pivoted the turboprop on the compass rose, paused several seconds, then advanced the throttle smoothly and took his feet off the brakes. At eighty-five knots the plane left the ground and he pitched her up into a steep power climb to five hundred feet, before heading northwest toward the rugged wall of mountains known as the High Sierras.

After Paulette was done venting her half-hearted frustration at his steep climb out, he explained to Melanie through the headset, "If there were any air traffic in the area you couldn't break out of the pattern like I just did, but I like to keep my power up until we reach altitude. Here. You take her now. Maintain a heading of 340 and climb to three thousand."

"No way," Melanie said, giving him a shocked look but keeping both hands tightly clenched on the yoke.

"A light touch is all she needs," Kent said. "Loosen up a little."

"Dr. Mattson, I really don't think…"

"The plane is stable, she wants to stay in the air. If you took your hands off the controls, she'd neutralize herself, in most instances."

"That's all true, I'm sure, but…"

"Watch your altitude. You want to keep her about five hundred feet below those clouds."

This time her eyes packed an electrical charge that would have rivaled a lightning bolt as she flashed him an incredulous look. "Oh sure, no problem. Where's your tape measure?"

Kent grinned. "Once you've flown for a while, you kind of get a feel for these things. You'll see." He spoke without thinking, and felt a kick of surprise in his gut at the easy way the words had slipped out, but she hadn't even noticed. She was frowning at the altimeter, then squinting at the clouds. She shook her head, a quick, frustrated movement.

"She wants to climb right into those clouds, and I'm not asking her to."

"Trim her up a hair and take the pressure off. Like this." He adjusted the trim and immediately noticed her expression brighten.

"That's much better," she said, smiling. "How did you learn to fly?"

"My dad taught me."

"Did he also teach you about classical music?"

"Not especially. Why?"

"In my car this morning you recognized the music I was listening to. You even named the composer."

"It was one of my mother's favorites, not mine." He found himself wishing he had some light classical music to plug into the plane's sound system. Might be just the thing to soothe her nerves.

He glanced at his watch. Forty minutes 'til wheels down. "You're doing just fine," he said. "Steady as she goes...."

CHAPTER FIVE

MELANIE WAS SO EXHAUSTED that she hardly felt any fear at all after half an hour of flight time. She watched the sprawl of houses diminish into nothing but brown rolling hills, then the rolling hills got bigger and the mountains got closer and the dense fog of pollution disappeared, and suddenly she was aware that the city was far, far behind them, and ahead loomed a rugged wilderness of exquisite beauty. She gazed out at the mountain peaks, drenched in the last of that day's sunlight. Strange to think that the sun would set, just as it always had, and that it would rise again in the morning. That the world would go on, seemingly unchanged, yet changing with every moment. Changing brutally with Stephanie's death, with Rachel's death, with Ariel's mysterious disappearance. Changing in ways Melanie couldn't begin to comprehend.

Kent began descending about twenty miles out, aiming for a gap between the shoulders of two impressive peaks. "This can be a tricky landing when the weather's dirty," he said. "The wind howls through this pass, and you only have so much leeway."

She could believe that. The steeply timbered slopes on either side of the wing tips looked much too close for

comfort. She felt her stomach drop out as he cleared the
pass and the plane slid sideways and down through the air.

"Sorry," he said. "Have to side-slip aggressively here to
lose altitude fast."

"My goodness," Melanie breathed, her hands clenching
on the arms of the copilot's seat as the ground rushed up
at a dizzying speed. She closed her eyes at the last moment,
certain they were going to crash, and then felt the solid
bump of the plane's tires against the grass runway and the
press of her body against the restraining harness as the
plane swiftly decelerated and rolled to a stop.

"You okay?" Kent said as he pivoted the plane around
and began taxiing back.

"Fine," she replied, wondering where the ranch buildings
were. All she could see in this high mountain meadow was
the narrow grass landing strip, a weather-bleached little hut
at the far end, and a light-colored pickup parked beside it.
Minutes later the plane pulled up to the hut, Kent helped her
down the steep stairs and assisted her into the truck.

"Chimeya isn't far from here, less than a mile," he said,
as he drove up a dirt road that threaded through a grove of
piñon pine and topped another rise before descending into
a second, much larger valley surrounded by mountains
and cradling a vast stretch of open grassland. They could
see a thread of water winding through the valley. "That's
Chimeya Creek," Kent said. "The ranch is just this side of
it, almost hidden in that grove of cottonwoods."

Melanie sat up straighter as she spied a herd of cows
and some horses grazing in the open spaces between small
groves of trees. "Is Chimeya a working ranch?"

"Technically, though if it were up to the horses and beef
cattle to support the place, it would've folded long ago."

"It's so beautiful," she said, admiring the soft blue haze of twilight in the valley juxtaposed against the bright alpenglow on the snow-clad mountain peaks. "How lucky you were to grow up in a place like this." When she spotted the ranch buildings, her professional eye was instantly intrigued. "Wow. Did Clint Eastwood film any westerns here?"

Kent laughed. "The very best of the good, the bad and the ugly, that's Chimeya, all right. But no, the only things ever shot here were family photos."

He parked the pickup in front of a massive wooden gate that spanned a fortresslike adobe wall enclosing both wings of the historic building. A large longhorn steer skull hung on the huge crossbeam overhead. Kent swung one half of the gate open and gestured for her to enter. As Melanie stepped in, she was struck by the symmetrical, timeless beauty of the old adobe fortress, whose brown walls ended in a series of connected flat-roofed houses with blue doors opening onto the courtyard. The dark ends of the roof logs sticking out from the tan adobe walls resembled rows of cannons. She wondered what tales this historic outpost could tell.

As they crossed the inner courtyard, bright with flowers, she heard the sound of running water. A fountain graced the center of the spacious plaza, spanned by a trellised arbor of ancient grapevines whose twining trunks were as thick as a man's leg. Red tile pavers surrounded the fountain and there were several rustic wooden benches for sitting in the shade. Soft yellow light glowed from the deep-silled windows that overlooked the courtyard. She paused for a moment, taking a deep draft of the cool mountain air.

"Jasmine is what you're smelling," Kent said, taking her

arm and escorting her toward the entry, which was fronted by a long series of log pillars supporting a sturdy ramada of wooden poles. "Stannie loves the stuff. Grows it against the old walls. She says the scent centers the soul. Say *that* one five times fast." He opened a hand-hewn wooden door hung on ornate wrought-iron hinges and led Melanie into another world. While she stood in mute wonder, he kicked the door shut behind them with a loud bang. "Stannie?" he bellowed, tugging her into the hacienda's great room, where she looked around amazed, for if a room could reach out and give a comforting hug, this one was doing it now. "Stannie!"

Melanie took in the flickering yellow flames of a fire in the corner fireplace, the richly colored tapestry of the Navajo rug that adorned the floor, the comfortable, mission-style furnishings, shelves stuffed with books. Then she heard a quick clicking on the tiles.

"Loki, you useless scoundrel." Kent greeted a most peculiar-looking dog who trotted into the room, eyes bright and ears cocked. The dog was multicolored, brindled, with a black circle around one eye. One ear stood straight up, the other flopped over. His fur was long in some places, short in others, tufting out here and there and giving him a completely disheveled appearance. As Loki looked up at Kent he gave what Melanie could only describe as the strangest smile she'd ever seen. All teeth and twisted lips, it would have been frightening if its meaning were misinterpreted. "You should've been barking at our arrival. You signed on as a watchdog, remember?" He glanced apologetically at Melanie. "Loki's getting old. His hearing isn't what it used to be."

Melanie crouched to wrap her arms around forty pounds

of dog for desperately needed love and affection. "Hello, you beautiful old thing," she murmured as Loki kissed her face with unabashed enthusiasm.

"Beautiful is one thing Loki's not," Kent said. "But I guess he can't help how he looks, and sometimes I think his ugliness gets him more attention; mostly in the form of pity. He was always more my wife's dog than mine." Kent started for the arched doorway that led to the inner part of the house. "Stannie!"

Melanie was startled to hear him mention a wife, though she realized she shouldn't be. Of course he would have a wife. Men like Kent Mattson didn't stay single for long, and just because he wasn't wearing a wedding band didn't mean a thing.

"Ah, there you are," she heard him say, and as she rose to her feet a gaunt, thin-lipped older woman swept into the room with an indignant scowl.

"Of course I be here, you'll be the one that's late again, aren't tha', now?" she said, wiping her gnarly hands in her apron. Her steel-gray hair was knotted into a severe bun at the nape of her neck and was skewered through with what looked like a meat thermometer.

"Stannie, this is Melanie Harris," Kent said, touching the elderly woman's shoulder to direct her fierce gaze at Melanie, "and she's had a very bad day. Her sister's missing, and her best friend and a coworker both turned up dead. We're starving and need something to eat. I hope you've kept supper warm."

"Aye, that I have." Stannie nodded, her intense dark eyes softening on Melanie and her strong Gaelic accent gentling. "I'm that sorry about your hardships, miss. I knows what it's like to lose a loved one. Oh, believe me, I knows."

"Thank you," Melanie said, grateful for Loki's warm body pressing against her leg. She dropped her hand to the top of the old dog's head. Loki's fur felt as rough and wiry as it looked.

Kent's eyes dropped to Loki, who was pressed against Melanie's side. "Stannie, where are the boys, and have I gotten any faxes?"

"Oh, aye, the machine's been goin' nonstop for the past hour or so. I refilled the paper tray when they started comin'. The boys have eaten already, like a pack of starvin' wolves, and I sent 'em to the bunkhouse half an hour ago. I was figurin' you'd be needin' peace and quiet, with all that paperwork to look through."

"Good. See that Ms. Harris gets something to eat, would you, Stannie?" he said as he turned. "Then show her the guest room. She's exhausted, and it's been a damn long day."

"Wait!" Melanie burst out, shocked that he would leave her so abruptly. "Where are you going?"

Kent paused with obvious impatience. "Murphy's no doubt faxed me all the information she's compiled, and now I have to analyze it. Don't worry, Stannie'll take good care of you."

Before she could protest further, Kent turned and exited the room. Melanie felt as if she'd been totally abandoned...except for the comforting press of Loki against her leg.

"Don't fash yourself, lass," Stannie said. "He's a stubborn-headed man, but good-hearted for all of that, and smarter than the most of 'em. Maybe smarter than 'em all. Come along, then, and I'll feed you." She motioned for Melanie to follow, but Melanie hung back.

"I'm really not very hungry, thank you. If you don't mind, I think I'd like to just sit here for a while, beside the fire…."

Stannie studied her with those dark, forceful eyes, then nodded in a brusque fashion, the same way Melanie imagined this woman did everything. "Aye then, lass, I'll bring you a tray, and you can stay right here. It's a good and restful place, it is. I don't blame you a bit for wantin' to set a spell after the terrible day you've had."

She stomped from the room, and Melanie let her pent-up breath escape as she collapsed onto the couch, grateful that Loki chose to wriggle up beside her. "Oh, Loki," she said, closing her eyes and leaning into the dog's warmth. "You're just what the doctor ordered."

Stannie returned sooner than Melanie would have thought possible, interrupting her exhausted soul-searching and bearing a tray heaped with enough food to last a week, along with a carafe of red wine. "I hope you likes the meal, lass," she said gruffly, laying the tray on the table in front of the couch. "I'll put another log on the fire for you, and when you're ready for bed, I'll show you your room. There's a bathroom just down the hall to your right, should you have a need. And if you keep on long enough you'll come to the kitchen, which is where I'll be."

Stannie turned to leave and Melanie stood so abruptly that Loki nearly fell off the couch. "What about Dr. Mattson?"

"Oh, I expect he'll be working all night long, he had that look in his eye."

"His wife…is she here?"

Stannie's expression turned to stone. "Wife?"

"He mentioned that Loki was more his wife's dog…."

The housekeeper stiffened. "His wife is dead. Susan was her name."

Melanie was moved by the stark pain shining in Stannie's dark eyes. Might she be Susan's mother? "I'm sorry. I didn't know."

Stannie paused, then said softly, "I worked for Susan, before she was taken by the Lord. She was killed, you see. Seven years ago."

"Then he is raising their children alone?"

"Their children?"

Melanie realized it must have sounded like she was prying. "Um, yes. Earlier he mentioned some boys?"

At this the woman's face softened almost imperceptibly and she gave a wry chuckle.

"No lass, not 'their' children, though I would say they belonged to Susan in a way."

At Melanie's confused expression, Stannie continued, "Susan worked with children—a real gift she had. After she died, some of them followed Dr. Mattson here. A few even stayed. For all the devilment they can cause, I believe they were a gift from God."

Melanie's overtired mind did not know quite how to respond to this, but she was spared the effort when the housekeeper excused herself with a quick nod and left the room, leaving Melanie to her tray of food, the flickering firelight and the ugly dog with the beautiful heart who snored gently on the couch beside her.

KENT WAS SLUMPED at his desk, looking through the notes and staring at the photographs with scratchy eyes, exhaustion dulling his wits. Stupid to try and make sense of this now, but there was something strange, something that didn't fit the pattern of a typical serial killer. The motive...the motive was the key. Neither victim had been raped or sexually molested in any way, and both victims had apparently known their killer. Both victims had also known Victor Korchin. Both victims also knew Melanie Harris, a fact, he was forced to admit, that did not cast her in an altogether favorable light.

His phone rang, and he glanced at his watch as he reached for it—10:00 p.m., but it felt much closer to midnight. "Mattson," he said.

"It's Murphy. Thought you'd want to know that we're having the spicy shrimp dip and the cat analyzed. T. Ray's handling the cat himself and says the animal definitely braved the spices to eat some shrimp. Its stomach contents proved that out. The lab is analyzing both the cat's last meal and the dip, we'll have the results as soon as they know anything."

"What about Victor Korchin?"

"Korchin isn't saying anything about anything. He contacted his lawyer, who happens to be one of Hollywood's biggest guns, and they're holed up at his estate together. My gut instinct tells me that he's definitely involved and he's definitely withholding information. He's my primary suspect, but to prove anything first we need to know how these women were killed."

"And why he might have killed them," Kent commented. "He seemed genuinely concerned about Ariel."

"I've seen cold-blooded murderers weep convincing tears, Kent," Murphy said in a cynical voice.

"What about his wife? Did you question her about where Ariel might have gone?"

"Not home. He says she travels a lot, and doesn't always tell him where she's going. He can't recall when he saw her last, they have separate bedrooms and different schedules. Korchin has no alibi whatsoever for the entire weekend. He says he never left the estate, and on his days off he spends all his time in the gardens."

"Did the security guard at the gate verify that?"

"Apparently he was given the weekend off to attend his best friend's wedding, but even if he'd been on duty, there's a boat house and dock located in the cove right below the mansion, and no one keeps tabs on that."

"Convenient." Kent rubbed the band of tension gathering between his eyes.

"Very. We still need to locate and question his wife, of course, but meanwhile, Ariel Moore and her baby are still missing. We have an all-points bulletin out and all the hospitals are being contacted, along with the airlines. I've ordered every garbage hauler in the damn city to check their dumpsters very carefully, and search-and-rescue dogs have been deployed at the landfills—"

"Shit, Murph. Isn't it possible she's in Hawaii, resting up for a few weeks?"

"Maybe, but if she is, she didn't walk there and so far none of the airlines have produced her name on their passenger manifest. The Coast Guard's keeping an eye on the waters around the estate for floaters. It would have been just as easy for him to toss them both off one of those cliffs."

"Did Korchin happen to mention a party held at the estate on Saturday night to celebrate the birth of Ariel Moore's baby girl? A party that both Rachel Fisher and Stephanie Hawke attended?"

There was a moment's pause. "No. He must have forgotten all about that," Murphy said. "How very interesting."

"Even more interesting is the fact that his wife made the

spicy shrimp dip that was served at that party. The bowl on Melanie Harris's counter that the cat got into was left over from that party and was delivered to her the following day by Stephanie Hawke."

"It just gets better and better," Murphy mused. "We need to find Anatanyia Korchin and see if *she* remembers the dinner party…if she's still alive."

"Seems like a lot of 'ifs,'" Kent said.

"We're working on it. Sometimes the wheels don't turn as fast as we'd like, but they do turn. We should know a lot more by morning. Get some sleep, Kent. It's been a long day."

"It's been just as long a day for you, Grandma." No matter what, he could never resist that dig.

"I may have two grandchildren, sonny, but I can run circles around you any day. See you tomorrow."

Kent went back to studying the preliminary case notes, nagging thoughts chasing around in his head. If Victor Korchin turned out to be the killer, this was the easiest case they'd ever cracked. Something just didn't jibe. Motive… A tap at his office door several minutes later roused him a second time. Stannie entered without waiting for an invitation, bearing a fresh pot of coffee. She set it down on the desk and whisked up the cold pot.

"Your young lass is sittin' by the fire," Stannie said as she left. "Won't go to bed. Just sits starin' into it right sorrowful like, thinking about her friends, no doubt, and her missing sister."

Kent gave up on the notes and photos and carried a fresh mug of coffee into the living room. Sure enough, Melanie was curled on the couch gazing into the fire, Loki snuggled next to her and a half-empty glass of red wine cradled in her lap. She looked sad and ethereal in the soft, muted light. "Stannie told me you were still up. You should try to get some sleep."

She sighed, pushed her hair back from her forehead, tried for a smile and failed. "I'm afraid of the dreams I might have if I go to sleep."

Kent sat down beside her and slouched back, extending his feet toward the fire and resting his mug on the flat of his stomach. "There are no bad dreams at Chimeya. Stannie says the jasmine keeps them away."

"Then it must be pretty powerful stuff," she commented and sighed. "I was just thinking about Ariel and the next movie Victor was scheduled to direct. *Celtic Runes*. He told me he had just cast Ariel in the lead role."

"When did he tell you that?"

"This afternoon. I'm sorry," Melanie said, interpreting the unspoken criticism in his sharp glance. "I would have told you earlier, but it didn't seem significant and I guess I forgot."

Kent let his head tip back and closed his burning eyes. This enigmatic woman was definitely driving him insane, in more ways than one. "Melanie, it's important for you to realize that every little detail in a murder investigation is significant, and what you just told me is *extremely* significant."

"I'm sorry, Kent," she repeated in a small voice.

Being this near to her was torturous, and Loki wasn't helping one bit. Every time Melanie's slender fingers stroked his ugly head, the damned dog either moaned or sighed with pleasure. Kent opened his eyes and got up to tend the fire—anything to keep his mind off her. He gave a log in the fireplace a nudge with his booted toe, watched as the flames leapt higher, then turned to face her.

Before Kent could say another word, the hacienda's main door burst inward with a resounding bang.

"Señor Kent!" a boisterous voice called out, and Kent turned to look at the young man Susan had befriended. Some days he couldn't believe that Julio Estevan had been living at Chimeya for almost as long as Susan had been dead.

Julio stepped into the room, the lamp light illuminating his smooth, handsome features, and those dark, wicked eyes that flashed with surprise and pleasure when he spotted Melanie on the couch. "Ha! I can see that I've come at a bad time, but I have news that cannot wait."

"What news, Julio?" Kent said.

"The black mare gave birth to a new foal!"

Kent smiled. "And…"

"And all went well. I did not even have to call the vet," Julio said with no little amount of pride in his voice. He turned to Melanie. "No doubt Kent has already told you that I'm the very best when it comes to handling the horses," he announced, lifting his chin and squaring his shoulders. If cymbals had crashed and drums rolled, Kent thought, Julio would not have been the least bit surprised.

"As a matter of fact, no, he didn't," Melanie responded, rising to her feet and extending her slender, delicate hand toward the young man who, if not for Susan's intervention, would have been, at the age of twelve, turned over to the juvenile authorities and placed in a system that created more lifelong criminals than it rehabilitated. All for being in the company of an older illegal immigrant who held up a convenience store and shot the owner dead over the forty-six dollars and twenty cents in the cash drawer. "I'm Melanie, and what I've been told is that you were a gift from God."

"*Sí*, I like that," he said with a grin that only seemed to widen. "That is me—just ask Kent what a gift I am."

Kent snorted. "Gift? Some gift. First gift I ever had that ate me out of house and home. I wonder if God offers refunds on his gifts."

Julio laughed. It was clear, in spite of his grumbling, that Kent was very fond of the young man. But that fondness obviously had its limits and after a half hour of Julio's restlessness, during which the lad told and retold all the details surrounding the birth of the foal, he none too subtly suggested Julio get to bed. This was met with good humor and he bowed to Melanie—who half expected him to take her hand and kiss it—before he exited the room.

As soon as the young man was gone Kent stood, picked up his coffee mug and excused himself, saying he still had a ton of paperwork to go through. Melanie was again left alone with Loki and her thoughts.

CHAPTER SIX

MELANIE DIDN'T KNOW if it was the jasmine or not, but when she opened her eyes the next morning, it was after a sound and mercifully dreamless sleep. She stretched her legs as her eyes adjusted to the semidarkness of the unfamiliar, but comforting room. Bright sunlight glinted through a crack in the curtains and she could hear the sound of flowing water outside in the not too far distance. Her mouth was in midyawn when she became aware of something heavy on the bed beside her. Startled, she sat up and could just make out Loki stretched out on his back, all four paws in the air. She smiled, but as she reached over to scratch the dog's belly the events of yesterday cascaded through her mind in a fast-forward montage: The awkward visit to Kent's office, the discovery of Stephanie's body, the death of Rachel and the disappearance of Ariel and her baby. She shut her eyes to block out the terrible images, both real and imagined, and tears slid down her cheeks.

Loki rolled over and moved closer to Melanie, putting his head on her shoulder. She threw her arms around the dog's neck and allowed the tears to flow into his fur. It was all just too much. Hard as she tried, she just couldn't believe Stephanie was gone. Stephanie and her love of cookies with milk at 2:00 a.m. Stephanie, who always remembered everyone's birthday or anniversary and other special events. Stephanie, the truest friend Melanie had had. Why would anyone want to kill that gentle soul? And Rachel, too? Though not nearly as close a friend, Rachel's death hit almost as hard, coming as it did so close to the loss of Stephanie.

She had been on the brink of tears for most of the previous day and had come close to breaking down last night, sitting with Kent in front of the fire. She probably would have if not for the abrupt arrival of Julio.

Now, as much as she would have liked to, Melanie could not hide from the day forever. Also, she was anxious to see if Kent had uncovered anything new overnight.

As she slowly got herself under control she heard something outside the bedroom door—faint rustlings and soft voices.

"Shh, you're going to wake her up!"

"I am not, you're the one making all the noise."

"I am not, move over and be quiet."

Puzzled and more than a little curious about who was lurking outside while she slept, Melanie threw back the covers and quickly realized her clothes were not on the chair where she'd left them.

She got up, pulled on the robe draped over the foot of the bed, cinched it tight and opened the door. Peeking out, she saw nothing until she looked down into two pairs of the widest, brownest eyes she had ever seen. Two small boys appearing to be no more than eight years old were seated cross-legged and side-by-side on the floor in front of the door.

"*Buenos días,* señorita," the two said in perfect unison as they stood up and formally extended their hands.

"Good morning to you." She shook each hand automatically and looked around for Kent, Stannie or any other adult. Loki bounded out of the room and sat down next to the boys, tongue lolling.

"I'm Miguel and this is my brother Tito," the boy on the right said.

"Twin brother," the lad named Tito stressed.

That they were twins was obvious. They were perfect copies of each other, right down to the straight black hair, olive complexion and the faded flannel shirts and jeans in which they were dressed.

"We were told to look out for you," Miguel said.

"Look out for me?"

"*Sí,*" Tito said. "Señor Kent told us this morning to get you anything you need…."

"Take you anywhere you want to go on the ranch…." Miguel said.

"And not bother you," they finished in unison.

"We're not bothering you, are we?" Tito asked, and Melanie had to laugh in spite of herself at his serious expression.

"No, no, not at all," she said, shaking her head. "But boys, can you tell me where Dr. Mattson is?"

"Oh, he's not here," Miguel said.

"Not here?" Melanie felt a pang.

"No," Tito replied. "He flew away early this morning. But not before he told us to look out for you."

Melanie wasn't listening. Kent gone? Flown back to L.A. and leaving her here? Without even taking the time to say goodbye or explain? The first stirrings of anger were starting to overshadow her initial disappointment.

"…anything?" Tito was asking.

"I'm sorry, what did you say?" she asked.

"Can we get you anything?"

"Well, actually, would you have any idea where my clothes from yesterday are?"

"Señora Stannie," they both said, looking at each other.

"Would you like us to go find her?" Miguel asked.

"Yes, please," Melanie said, but before the boys could scamper off, they all heard footsteps coming down the hall.

"What the devil are you two doing here?" the house-keeper asked as she rounded the corner.

Tito, Miguel and even Loki all shrank against each other.

"Scat, the lot o' you and let this woman be!"

The two boys and one dog began sidling against the wall around Stannie, who was dressed in the same utilitarian manner this morning as last night except the meat thermometer in the tight bun of hair had been replaced by what looked like a metal skewer.

"Oh, Stannie, the boys weren't bothering me. In fact, they were telling me it was their duty to take care of me today."

The older woman snorted. "Take care of indeed. Get on with ye, git down to the kitchen and give the young lady some privacy. She needs to get dressed before breakfast."

All three made their escape and Melanie could hear them clattering in what she could only assume was the direction of the kitchen. At the mention of the word breakfast, Melanie suddenly realized how hungry she was. Then she noticed that Stannie carried her clothes, obviously freshly laundered and folded, as well as a pair of jeans and a flannel shirt that she assumed were classic ranch attire.

"Nice boys," Melanie said as she backed into the room.

"Nice enough when they're not up to mischief," Stannie said, "which is most of the time." The housekeeper set the clothes on the edge of the bed. "Them two are Julio's brothers. As far as the boy knew, they were livin' safe and fine in foster homes. That was until two years ago, when out of the blessed blue Dr. Mattson gets a call from some high talkin' government official from Taos sayin' he has the boys and they had been gettin' in trouble—stealin', lyin', that sort of thing and the foster parents wanted to get rid of them. Them folks at the foster agency had Dr. Mattson's phone number in case they had to contact Julio here, so here is where they called first."

Melanie nodded and waited for Stannie to continue.

"Well, the minute Julio heard about them needing a home, he was at Dr. Mattson day 'n' night beggin' him to let them come live here. Not that it took much. Next thing you know, Dr. Mattson is makin' a passel of phone calls and suddenly I have two more mouths to feed and two more bodies what to clean up after."

"Where do they go to school?" Melanie asked, thinking of yesterday's bird's-eye view of Chimeya, which did not include anything resembling a school.

"Closest school's a two-hour drive down the valley. So Dr. Mattson schools them here."

Melanie was flabbergasted. The last thing she had expected of Kent was to learn he was a schoolteacher. Although she was quickly becoming aware there was much more to the doctor than simple good looks.

"That's right, miss," Stannie went on. "He's a right smart man, for all of his foolishness with planes and horses. He plans out their lessons every weekend, gives them to the boys on Monday and several times a week they sit down after supper to go over them. Why, if they was in public school they'd be in fourth grade but Dr. Mattson has them figurin', writin' and readin' two or three grade levels above that." This last was said with a great deal of pride, as if she, not Kent, were personally responsible for the boys' education, which was probably partially the case, as Melanie imagined Stannie was the type who was more than able to make sure two small boys were attentive to their studies.

"Aye, they're good lads fer all their devilment. Now you get yerself dressed and come have something to eat. I've kept breakfast and those two stubborn mules you found outside your door refused to eat until you did."

At those words Melanie found herself wondering what time it really was. She glanced at her watch and was amazed to see it was just past 11:30 a.m. She couldn't remember the last time she'd slept this late.

"And Dr. Mattson told me to tell you to call him. The number is by the phone there." Stannie motioned to the bedside table, and with that she swept out.

THE PHONE was picked up on the third ring.

"Mattson here," came the curt, masculine voice. Melanie could make out sounds in the background: phones ringing, what sounded like doors slamming and lots of voices.

"Kent? It's Melanie...."

"Well, good morning, or should I say good afternoon," he said, his voice warming several degrees. "How'd you sleep?"

"I'm ashamed to say, wonderfully."

"No shame there. You needed it. Best medicine for what

you have been through is plenty of rest. Now, I bet you're wondering why I rushed off and abandoned you to the wild Estevan brothers."

"The thought crossed my mind."

"The thing is, not only is Chimeya the perfect place for you to recover from yesterday's multiple shocks, it's by far the safest place for you to be."

"You don't really believe I'm in any danger, do you, Kent?"

"I don't want to think so, but we have to be realistic," he said, the tone of his voice becoming quite serious. "I don't mind telling you I am a lot less worried about you knowing you're tucked safely behind Chimeya's walls. This case is still very much unsolved."

"You still haven't found any leads on where Ariel and the baby are, have you?" Melanie said.

"We're doing everything we can. There's an army of police officers out there searching. We're going to find them. I promise you that." He sounded tired and distracted, for all his apparent concern for her well-being, and she felt a pang of guilt for bothering him at work.

"There's something else, isn't there?" she said.

There was a moment's hesitation, then she heard him expel a weary sigh. "Victor Korchin's wife is missing and Korchin can't or won't explain her whereabouts. At the moment we're treating her absence as part of this case and there's an APB out on her. We'll find her."

"Kent, I can't just stay here cooped up. There has to be something I can do to help find Ariel and her baby."

"What you can do is rest and let Chimeya work its magic on you. I understand about wanting to help find your sister, but trust me, we have that covered."

"And just how long do you intend to keep me prisoner?"

"As long as this takes. Please trust me and, for God's sake, please don't consider yourself a prisoner!"

"All right. I suppose there are worse places...."

"That's the spirit. If you'll recall, I also offered you Big Bertha and a hotel room. You were wise to choose Chimeya."

"And I appreciate you bringing me here, I really do. But Kent, I only have the clothes I was wearing yesterday. I can't expect Stannie to wash them every day."

Kent laughed. "Believe me, she would, too. But don't worry, I'm one step ahead of you there. Fax a list of everything you need to my office. Stannie will give you the number. Your place is under surveillance and I'll ask a female plainclothes detective to go in and pack a bag for you. I'll bring it back with me tonight."

Something outside the bedroom window caught Melanie's attention. What on earth? There were Miguel and Tito, side-by-side as usual, Miguel holding three fishing rods and Tito a large picnic basket. Behind them, three horses stood saddled.

"Kent?" she said. "Don't be alarmed, but I think I'm about to be kidnapped."

Two HUNDRED miles away, after Kent was satisfied Melanie was not in any real danger other than having her ears talked off by the chatty team of Miguel and Tito, he had bid her goodbye and wished her a good day of fishing. Truth be told, he was more than a little envious. What he wouldn't give to be in the boys' place, spending a day on a clear lake with Melanie. Instead, he was here in L.A. coordinating multiple searches and examining crime scene photos. Now there was the mysterious absence of Anatanyia Korchin to factor in. The case was getting more convoluted by the moment.

He sighed and his eyes caught the stack of newspapers on his desk. While concern for Melanie's safety was the primary reason to keep her at Chimeya, he had also wanted to shield her from the predictable feeding frenzy. The media, as Kent had fully expected, was having a field day with the case. The double murders had made the front pages of all the L.A. papers and was the lead story on the news, both TV and radio. It was a sad fact there were murders every day in and around Los Angeles and most were never even mentioned. But let anyone connected at all to the film industry get gunned down or killed and it was a different matter entirely. It was nonstop coverage, and experts and anyone with any connection at all to the dead, no matter how tenuous, were trotted out, interviewed and analyzed. Kent had run the press gauntlet this morning. Murphy confessed to having sneaked in through the basement parking garage.

Luckily, there were no newspapers at Chimeya and poor television reception, so Melanie would never have to read the speculative and inflammatory headlines. It wouldn't take the media vultures long to connect the dots between the two dead women, the missing Ariel and her baby, and Melanie Harris.

Kent did his best to push all thoughts of Melanie out of his head. He had to concentrate on the matters at hand. Information was coming in fast and furious from the crime scenes. Photographs, notes, interview transcripts—copies of everything were automatically forwarded to Kent. And if he wanted to get any kind of productive handle on the whole thing, he had to start breaking down the information into manageable chunks.

He swiveled around to examine the corkboard behind him. Murphy had already turned one of the department's conference rooms into an incident room. He knew her superiors were breathing hard down her neck on this one but he preferred to keep his own information close by. One never knew when a fresh idea or solution to the puzzle would surface.

Earlier that morning he had pinned photographs of the two dead women on opposite ends of the corkboard. Between them, he put up every scrap of information available, drawing lines connecting them. For now, the missing Ariel Moore had her own corkboard with her photo tacked at the top. As the case evolved, he would create a master chart in the incident room. By the time he was done breaking down the forensic information his chart would look like a giant family tree. Where the lines overlapped, another connection between the victims would be established. So far, there was already a fair number of connections, the most glaring of which were the relationships with Victor Korchin and Melanie Harris. Given the profiles of the victims, Kent did not believe he was being overly cautious in insisting Melanie remain sequestered at Chimeya.

But what about Ariel and the baby? If one or both of them had been kidnapped, why no ransom note? And there was the letter she'd left Melanie at the guest cottage, saying she was going away for a few weeks. But where?

Processed forensic evidence and information were arriving in a constant stream. For the next three hours he was completely absorbed in reading, organizing and prioritizing that information for Murphy and her team of homicide detectives.

Just after 3:00 p.m. Murphy walked into his office and tossed an inches-thick pile of file folders on his desk.

"Figured I'd deliver these in person," she said.

"What are they?" Kent asked, opening the top folder and glancing at the first page.

"The latest reports from the victims' apartments and offices."

"That was quick. You just got started last night."

Murphy nodded her head in disgust and walked over to the half-full coffeepot on Kent's window ledge. "There's going to be a lot of overtime logged on this one," she said.

She refilled her cup, took a sip, grimaced and added a generous portion of sugar. Kent wasn't insulted—rare indeed was the individual who could stomach his brew un-diluted. Murphy sank down in the chair across his desk and looked at him over the mountain of paperwork.

"Talk to me, Kent."

He noticed she was wearing what he always referred to as her standard detective garb: dark slacks, blue silk button-down shirt, suede blazer and black leather boots. Not for the first time he thought that Carolyn Murphy had to be the hippest grandma in South Central.

Out loud he said, "I can't remember a case when we had this much information this fast from so many separate crime scenes."

"I don't have to tell you, the D.A. is breathing down my neck on this one. Needless to say, this case has become his top priority, which means it is *our* top priority. Never mind we have two open murders from east Encino and at least a half-dozen rapes from down on the strip," she said, unable to mask the bitterness in her voice.

Kent was all too aware of the pressure being exerted on

his boss. Los Angeles County District Attorney Trent F. Brannigan III was a man with lofty ambitions. He was also the bane of Murphy's existence. Brannigan loved the cameras and he loved the ink. He gave at least one press conference a week, whether he had anything to talk about or not. In his mind, and through the persona he showed the public, he was a true anticrime crusader committed to protecting the safety and interests of the public. In reality, Brannigan was arrogant, vain and committed to his own interests, which at the moment centered on furthering his political career. It was no secret he had his eyes on a run for the governor's mansion in three years. Kent had little to do with him but Murphy was forced to attend biweekly departmental meetings at the D.A.'s office. Kent and the rest of her team knew from experience her dark moods following those meetings and would give their captain a wide berth for at least a day.

Kent could easily envision Brannigan basking in the media spotlight shining on the double homicide. Crackheads, hookers, gangbangers and runaways were not known for their political involvement, much less exorbitant campaign contributions. Hollywood movie moguls, executives and the other rich and famous in and around Beverly Hills, on the other hand, were. Brannigan knew which side his political aspirations were buttered on. If he was going to make it all the way to Sacramento, it could only be with the support of the city's powerful movers and shakers. And if the movers and shakers did not feel safe in their beds at night, District Attorney Brannigan could not map out his upwardly mobile future with any degree of certainty. So, let the downtrodden and lower classes police their own. Brannigan had much larger and wealthier fish to fry this week. Kent often consoled himself with the thought that if Brannigan did become governor some day, it would mean a new D.A., and anyone would be an improvement.

"I take it his highness is riding your ass?" Kent asked.

"Riding it ragged," Murphy said. "I have a meeting with him at 4:30 to brief him on our progress before his 5:30 press conference…scheduled just in time, you will note, to make the six o'clock newscast."

"You'll have what I have before you leave here, I promise," Kent said.

"Give me a preview."

Kent picked up his notepad. "All the evidence, which is largely circumstantial at this point, is pointing to Victor Korchin as our doer, but two things are missing—a motive, and his wife. No matter how convenient this might be for Brannigan, I haven't found one solid reason to explain why Korchin would kill two women in his employ. And where the hell is his wife? If, in fact, she made that spicy shrimp dip, and if that's what killed the two women, wouldn't *she* be our prime suspect, if we could find her? I'd give anything to talk one-on-one with Korchin. For all we know, they could be in on it together. Or he could have killed his wife, too. I wish I had more, but it's going to take some time to analyze all this," Kent said, gesturing toward his bulletin board.

"I know, and I'm not asking you to rush it." Murphy was looking at the board. "Have you factored in the other connection between the two victims, the missing woman and baby?"

"I'm not sure I follow," Kent said.

Murphy looked back at him. "Melanie Harris."

Kent rubbed the band of tension at his temples. "Of

course I have. That's why I placed her in something of a protective custody."

"That's not what I'm talking about, Kent," Murphy said.

"Then what are you—" He stopped abruptly and stared at his boss. "Oh, c'mon, Murph, you're not suggesting Melanie had anything to do with all this?"

Murphy just stared back at him, sipping her coffee.

"It's *her* sister and niece who are missing. One of the murder victims was her best friend, the other was a well-liked colleague. I mean, you were there. You saw the look on her face and her reaction when she saw her friend's body. She was shocked almost out of her mind." But even as he was saying this, the first flickering of doubt was creeping into his mind. Had he allowed his obvious attraction to Melanie cloud his judgment?

"Let's look at that a bit closer, shall we?" Murphy said. "You told me Melanie Harris was engaged to the man who fathered her sister's baby, isn't that right? And that she discovered this on her wedding day, and dragged her sister to the altar and flung her at the feet of her fiancé? A fiancé who, need I remind you, died just over a week ago in a fiery accident on the set where he was working? And didn't you also tell me that Melanie's best friend, Stephanie, had befriended Ariel Moore, had accompanied her to the hospital for the birth of Mitch Carson's child and had begged Melanie to attend a dinner party at Blackstone that was being given in honor of the birth of that same child?" Murphy was ticking things off on her fingers as she spoke. "Did I forget anything? Oh, yes, you yourself told me she was able to access the estate easily, which would have given her plenty of opportunity to plant evidence against her boss, the man who introduced her to Carson. As for

Rachel Fisher, I haven't figured that connection out yet, but don't worry. I will."

Kent was thunderstruck. He could only stare.

Murphy leaned toward him. "Kent, a lot of people have been killed in this town for a lot less than that. You have to at least consider the possibility that Melanie Harris had motive."

All day long Kent had been struggling to pin down the elusive third element in the investigative tripod; motive. Now Murphy was handing it to him on a silver platter, only it was connected to the wrong person...or was it? Had Melanie been playing him last night? Could she be faking concern over Ariel and her niece? Could her grief over Stephanie's death be contrived? Kent didn't believe it. Damn it, there *had* been a genuine bond between them. He'd felt it, if only briefly, the previous evening in front of the fire at Chimeya. But he couldn't deny the facts as outlined by Murphy.

Kent realized Murphy was waiting for him to say something. "You're wrong about her. She had nothing to do with those murders."

"I hope you're right," Murphy said. "But she has a lot more explaining to do, and she can start with what she knows about Victor Korchin and his wife, two people she somehow forgot to mention the first time around. I trust you'll pass this request for another official statement along to her?"

"But, Murph—"

Murphy held up her hand. "No buts. When I go to the D.A.'s office this afternoon he's probably going to ask about Melanie Harris. Should I tell him you're keeping her in hiding up at that ranch of yours? I guess I don't have to tell you how bad that might look."

Kent pushed out of his chair and paced to the window. "You okayed it yesterday."

"I know, and I'm already regretting it. If he asks, I'm going to tell him she's in protective custody. Nothing more. But that will only keep his mouth shut for the time being. The press is already clamoring for a piece of Melanie Harris, and Brannigan plays to the press."

"Murph, give me some time. Let me talk to her. I agree she probably knows more than she's let on so far, but she's still in a state of shock. My gut instinct tells me she's an innocent bystander in all this, and she could be in real danger from the actual killer."

The captain weighed his request.

"Okay," she said. "I'll give you some time on this one. Get your ass back into the mountains and talk to that lady, but know this. The taxpayers aren't footing the bill for your gut instincts. I expect you to play this one strictly by the books, no matter how you might feel about Ms. Harris." Murphy glanced at her watch. She got up and tossed her empty cup into the waste basket. "I'll need whatever you have as soon as you can get it to me. I'm leaving to see Brannigan in under an hour and I'll hold him off as long as I can."

Kent heaved a sigh of relief. "Thanks, Murph, I owe you one."

"Yeah, no kidding. I don't have to tell you this could blow up in both our faces pretty damned fast." She was almost out the door when the detective dispatched earlier that day to gather the items on the list Melanie had faxed came in carrying a suitcase.

"Hey, I'm glad to find you both here," Detective Lynn Cabot said.

"What do you have?" Murphy asked.

Cabot set the suitcase down on the floor just inside

Kent's office and pulled a small notebook from her hip pocket and flipped it open.

"While I was at the Harris residence I spoke to a beat cop who spent the morning canvassing the neighborhood. He told me several neighbors reported seeing a woman who matches the description of Anatanyia Korchin arrive at Ms. Harris's condo three days ago. From witness accounts, Korchin stayed about an hour and then was seen driving away in her Lexus with a female passenger."

"Melanie Harris?" Murphy asked.

Cabot shrugged. "No one got a good look at the passenger. The Lexus had privacy glass all around. But the folks the beat cop talked to assumed it was Ms. Harris in the car."

"Did anyone see her come back?" Kent asked.

"Nope, but neighbors reported seeing lights on in the apartment that night."

"Thanks, Lynn, good work," Murphy said and dismissed the young detective before addressing Kent. "So, Melanie Harris was apparently the last person to see Anatanyia Korchin." She tapped the face of her watch. "Talk to her, Kent. The clock is ticking."

CHAPTER SEVEN

WHILE MELANIE would rather have been helping Kent find her missing sister, there was no denying the appeal of the twins holding the fishing rods and the picnic basket. And though Melanie had never ridden a horse before, and was worried that she might not be able to keep an adequate eye on Tito and Miguel, Stannie shrugged away her concerns as she cleaned off the kitchen table after breakfast. "They might be young, but they know horses and their way around this ranch. Don't you be worrying about them. Just mind you don't let them wear you out with their mindless chatter. I never did hear such ones as them twins for talkin' a person's ear off."

The boys beckoned to her when she finally stepped out of the ranch house. Melanie had not anticipated a fishing trip when she'd dressed the day before, but Stannie had come to the rescue. She had on one of Kent's too big but wonderfully soft flannel shirts and a pair of jeans, rolled up at the ankles and cinched around the waist with a belt that had once been Julio's. "Hurry, señorita, the fish don't bite so good when the sun is high!" Tito said. "We've got food, lots of food, and a very fast horse for you! Hurry! Please?"

"We've got a very gentle horse for you," Miguel corrected, casting his twin brother a disapproving look. "His name is Turtle."

Melanie laughed in spite of her anxiety. "That's a promising name, if he lives up to it. I've never been on a horse before."

Tito was jumping up and down with impatience. He unlaced Turtle's reins from the hitch rail and led the quiet animal forward. "All set. Climb aboard."

"Easier said than done, I'm sure," Melanie muttered, hoisting her leg and stabbing the toe of her boot through the stirrup as her hands clamped around the leather saddle horn. She hopped several times on her right foot, pulled mightily with her arms and swung into the saddle with a feeling of triumph. "Wow. I feel like I'm on top of the world!"

"You're not, señorita," Miguel informed her. "Turtle is a very little horse."

"Well, I'm a whole lot taller than I was," Melanie said, gathering up the reins while the boys vaulted onto their horses as if born to the life of a daring vaquero.

"Don't worry. Turtle won't let you fall off," Tito said, riding up beside her with a younger version of Julio's handsome grin. "He promised me he'd keep you safe."

"Tito thinks he can talk to the animals," Miguel scoffed. "He's crazy that way."

"I'm not crazy," Tito said. "I *can* talk to the animals. You're just jealous."

"Where's this high, pretty lake of yours that we're going to picnic at?" Melanie said to interrupt the brotherly squabble as Turtle started off at a slow, easy walk.

"Up there." Miguel pointed to a pass behind the ranch. "Not very far. Maybe a mile."

"It's two miles, easy," Tito corrected, kicking his horse

up on the other side of her. "Unless we take the short cut…."

"The short cut is too steep, Señor Kent doesn't like us to use it." Miguel frowned. "Besides, it goes past his shooting place, and he says for us not to go there."

"His shooting place?" Melanie echoed.

"Where he practices with his guns," Tito said. "He's a very good shot. Sometimes he lets us watch."

"He never lets us watch," Miguel corrected. "He tells us to stay away from that place, so sometimes we spy on him. We hide in the trees."

"But if he's shooting live ammunition, that could be dangerous. He might hit you accidentally. That's probably why he doesn't want you there," Melanie explained.

"Kent would never hit anything accidentally," Tito said. "Besides, we're behind him when he's shooting. It's fun to watch because when he starts the big generator up, that's what makes all the people move around so he can shoot at them."

"What do you mean?" Melanie said. "What people? Who is he shooting at?"

"Tito!" Miguel said, scowling.

"We could show you his shooting range," Tito said. "I know how to start the generator."

"Tito!" Miguel reined his horse in. "I'm telling Kent if you do this."

"Go ahead," Tito challenged. "You're the one who taught me to start the generator."

Melanie was intrigued. "I'd like to see it, but I don't want you boys getting into trouble. Maybe we should just ride up to the lake."

But a lake full of fish didn't hold a candle to visiting

the shooting range, in the boys' opinion, so fifteen minutes later Melanie was sliding out of the saddle and tying Turtle up to a small tree while the boys opened the door of a run-down shed that sat on the edge of what looked like a demolition site. Tall heaps of scrap lumber were piled here and there, several old trucks on flat tires baked in the sun and a heap of fifty-five gallon drums and piles of tires completed the junkyard look of the clearing, which was such an affront to the beauty of the valley that for a moment Melanie could scarcely believe that Kent could have anything to do with this. Then a muted rumble came from the shed as the boys got the generator running, and as the motor smoothed out and gained power, she caught a flash of movement out of the corner of her eye.

She cried out, startled, as the profile of a man jerked up from behind a stack of lumber then vanished almost instantly from view. A head and shoulders flashed briefly up from the other side of the nearest truck. Metal cut-outs of human profiles jumped and twitched from behind every pile at random intervals, one after the other, a startling blur of motion that could hardly register on the mind before another took its place.

Melanie had never seen anything like this. She couldn't imagine that anyone would have time to get off a shot, the action was so fast paced, and some of the figures barely showed any target at all. While the show went on, the boys flung a constant and furious barrage of small rocks at the targets, but neither hit anything. Ten minutes later, when the generator was shut off, she stood for a moment, dazed, as the boys joined her. "Neat, huh?" Tito said.

"Does Dr. Mattson get used to the pattern so he can anticipate his shots?" she asked.

"There are twenty different programs," Tito said, shaking his head. "They're all different so he can't memorize them. He always hits the right targets, though. Every single time."

"He must be quick."

"He's *very* quick," Miguel said.

"But sometimes, he's not quick enough," Tito amended. "Once, he got shot when he was working in the big city, and the police called and said he wouldn't be coming home to Chimeya that night. He didn't come home for ten nights after that, because he was in the hospital. That was a very bad time."

"But that wasn't his fault," Miguel said. "There were too many of them and he was trying to protect his captain."

"Captain Murphy?" Melanie asked.

"*Sí*. Yes." Miguel nodded. "These very bad men had her and they were going to kill her, but Kent, he shot the man who was holding her, and then he shot three others, only while he was doing this, he got shot, too. Twice!"

"But he saved his captain," Tito said. "And he got all kinds of awards for that. He even had to go to Washington to get one of them. Kent is real brave."

"When did this happen?" Melanie asked.

"Two summers ago. We had just come here. I remember when the police called, Stannie cried and cried. She stayed in the kitchen and cooked lots of food and cried for days."

"Julio cried, too," Miguel said. "He doesn't know I saw him, but I did. He was out in the stables. Julio never cries, but they both thought Kent was going to die."

"Kent is too tough to die," Tito said. "Besides, he knows how much we need him, so he can't die. Not ever."

Melanie felt a cold quiver of fear run through her at the

boys' words. "I think we should ride to the lake now, and see if the fish are still napping," she said. She was glad to leave the shooting range behind, and the dark side of Kent Mattson that it represented.

KENT WAS TRYING to keep his mind on his work and off the image of Melanie fishing in the cool clear waters of the mountain lake while the twins gave her all kinds of sage angling advice, but he wasn't having much luck. Murphy strode into his office for the second time in less than an hour and found him staring into space. She laid a sheet of paper, fresh off the fax, in front of him.

"We have our poison. You were right, it was in the bean dip that was allegedly left over from the dinner party at Korchin's estate," she announced. "The lab identified it as ricin, a by-product in the manufacture of castor oil, which is made from castor beans. Apparently this plant grows everywhere. Blackstone has a veritable plantation of castor bean bushes."

"Ricin, huh?" Kent picked up the fax and began to scan it.

"Anatanyia's Mexicali shrimp dip was loaded with the stuff. Ricin isn't very tasty, but nobody would have noticed it in that dip, which was so full of hot peppers I don't know how that poor cat managed to swallow any of it. Apparently, if the ricin is concentrated enough, it doesn't take much to kill a person."

"How does it do that, exactly?"

"It prevents the cells from making proteins, and without protein, cells die. The symptoms of ricin poisoning are similar to food poisoning. Initially, the victim would suffer from vomiting and diarrhea within six hours of ingestion.

This is typically followed by dehydration and falling blood pressure, and eventually the major organs shut down, causing death. It's not instant by any means, but by the time the victim realizes how seriously ill they are, they might be too weak to summon help."

"And T. Ray couldn't pick this substance up with any of his lab tests?"

"No. It isn't detectable in the blood, and the stomachs of both victims were empty. But analyzing the Mexicali shrimp dip provided the information he needed to verify that ricin was responsible for the symptoms that caused the deaths of Stephanie Hawke and Rachel Fisher…and the cat still had traces of that same substance in its stomach."

Kent leaned back in his chair, still scanning the fax with a dubious frown. "Anatanyia may have made that dip, but anyone could have put the ricin in it."

"True. And Anatanyia might have eaten some."

Kent jerked his gaze up to Murphy's face. "What if she did? Where the hell is she now? Dead in some hotel room?" He had already mentally added her photo to the board with Ariel Moore.

Murphy straightened up and sighed. "So far we don't have a clue, and if Victor knows, he isn't saying. But get this. He confirmed that there was a dinner party at the estate, and that Rachel Fisher, Stephanie Hawke and Ariel Moore attended. He also confirmed that Anatanyia had made her special dip. He said that both Stephanie and Rachel were fond of the dip, but because Ariel was breast-feeding the infant, Anatanyia told her she couldn't eat any because the spiciness would get into her milk and make the baby sick. When asked if he'd had any of the dip himself, Victor said he couldn't eat spicy foods."

Kent blew out his breath and tossed the fax onto his desk. "Murph, Victor Korchin was just nominated for best director. This isn't the most logical of times for him to be knocking people off at a dinner party with some poison he whipped up in his garden shed. It just doesn't make sense."

Murphy paced to the window. She turned to scan Kent's evidence board. She looked at the pictures of the two dead women pinned at either end and sighed again, running her fingers through her short hair. "The detectives found a manuscript at Rachel Fisher's apartment."

"That's not surprising. She's a screenwriter."

"This particular manuscript has nothing to do with screenwriting," Murphy said. "Apparently she was working on Victor Korchin's biography."

"No kidding?" Kent rocked forward in his chair. "Anything juicy in the manuscript that might give him a motive to kill her, along with Stephanie Hawke, his wife of thirty-odd years, and possibly Melanie Harris, Ariel Moore and her newborn infant?"

Murphy raised an eyebrow. "The crime team only just found the manuscript. You'll have to stay tuned for the contents. I'm not that fast a reader when I'm working twenty-four hours a day, but I do have the experts analyzing it even as we speak. In the meantime, we need to find out from Melanie Harris how close Stephanie and Rachel were."

Kent leaned back in his seat. "Right."

"There's a big cardboard file of research materials that was taken from Rachel Fisher's apartment. The contents seem to go along with the biography. I'd like you to go through it when you get a chance after it's processed and also review the manuscript when the guys in documents are done with it. It might help you to profile Victor Korchin."

Murphy stared out the window and sighed for the third
time. "I'm meeting with Brannigan in ten minutes, and I'm
going to announce Korchin's being brought in for questioning. Officers have already been dispatched to pick him up."

"You're throwing Brannigan the bone he's been
drooling for just to get him off your ass," Kent observed,
lacing his hands together behind his head and stretching
to ease a muscle cramp in the small of his back.

His captain gave him a challenging stare. "I'll admit
there are holes in this investigation big enough to drive a
dump truck through, and yes, I want Brannigan off my ass,
but I also want the right person behind bars. Talk to
Melanie Harris, Kent. Try to feel her out without overstep-
ping any legal boundaries. I'm not saying I think she's
directly involved in any way, but I do think she's the key
to helping us solve this case. I need you to remain objective."

After Murphy left his office, Kent pushed out of his chair
and paced back and forth in front of his corkboards, his
mind systematically sorting through the latest barrage of information Murphy had dredged up. Melanie couldn't have
had anything to do with the murders. He was convinced of
that, objectivity be damned. But he felt the same gut-deep
instinct that Murphy did: Melanie knew more than she was
telling. Why? Who was she protecting? And where the hell
were Ariel Moore, her baby and Anatanyia Korchin?

MELANIE LAY in the lulling warmth of the sun, listening to
the waves lap against the gravel shore, and watched Tito
and Miguel ply their skills against the canny trout that
lurked in the cold depths of the high mountain lake. Stannie
had packed enough food in the hamper to feed the three of

them for a week, and Melanie, after the short but strenuous ride, was famished to the point that she'd devoured a lion's share of the delicious cold fried chicken and potato salad. The boys seemed far more interested in proving their fishing skills to her than in eating, and when she tried to lure them back to the picnic by holding up Stannie's apple pie, she was unsuccessful. She ate half the pie all by her lonesome, and it was wonderful. Best pie she'd ever eaten.

Now, however, after this enormous meal, she was ready for a long nap, and already the sun was slipping toward the towering wall of mountain peaks to the west. Soon they would have to start back for the ranch. She propped herself up against the log Tito had laid a blanket on and closed her eyes.

Melanie felt guilty for feeling so relaxed. She had wept herself to sleep the night before, mourning Stephanie's death and the loss of Shakespeare. Now, she tried to focus her thoughts on Ariel, but it was difficult. As much as she wanted to put the past behind her, she still couldn't accept the fact that Mitch was the father of Ariel's baby, yet she knew she must. She loved Ariel, in spite of everything that had happened between them, and if Ariel were in trouble, wasn't that partly her fault for shutting her sister out? It was Mitch who'd been at fault, for playing around with both of them. Mitch had been sexy, dangerous and irresistible. She'd fallen for him in an instant. Could she blame Ariel for doing the same?

She edged closer to sleep, her thoughts drifting. Ariel's voice on her answering machine, distraught after Mitch's death, saying that Rachel thought it was suspicious, too.

Rachel…

She bolted upright, the sleepiness gone. Kent had left her behind because he'd thought she would only complicate things, get in the way of his investigation. Well, he was more than halfway right. She was lounging here beside this glorious mountain lake when she should be trying to figure out why a dinner party held to celebrate the birth of her sister's child had become the staging ground for the murder of Stephanie and Rachel. She should be trying to figure out what had happened to Ariel, and where Anatanyia was. Victor was innocent of involvement, she knew that.

Melanie frowned, brushing the hair back from her face as another memory surfaced. Several years ago she'd been at Blackstone, discussing locations for one of Victor's movies. He'd sent her upstairs to find Anatanyia, and walking down the hallway Melanie had passed a room, door ajar, that was unmistakably furnished as a nursery. She had peeked within, feeling a twinge of guilt at doing so, and wondered at the fairy-tale beauty of the room. Mentioning it later to Victor had been a mistake. He had leaned forward in his chair and dropped his head into his hands with a groan of despair.

"She will not let this go, this dream of giving birth to a child," he told her, his face mirroring his torment. "The doctors have told her she cannot, and that we should adopt. But she thinks that it will happen if she prays hard enough and is good. She thinks the child must be of my blood. Nothing I say to her can change her mind. I tell her we should adopt, she would be so good a mother and she wants it so much, but she believes she can only have *my* child, and until she can do so, she will be a failure as a woman and a wife."

The nursery at the cottage had looked very similar to what Melanie had seen at Blackstone. Had those furnishings come from Anatanyia's own shrine to motherhood? Yes, of course they had! They were identical. Anatanyia had decorated the little study at the cottage for Ariel using all the furnishings from the nursery at Blackstone. Perhaps she'd finally relinquished her dream of motherhood when Ariel became pregnant. But then a second, more disturbing thought struck her. Melanie wondered now if this obsession with having a child had somehow turned more sinister. Could Anatanyia have had designs on Ariel's baby? Could that explain the absence of all three?

Melanie knew Victor doted on his wife and, in deference to that, she had always done her best to try to get along with the older woman. Something not always easy and rarely reciprocated. But until now, she had never considered Anatanyia particularly dangerous. Except... Melanie's eyes opened wide. Through the lens of the previous day's revelations, an incident with Anatanyia some days earlier was now cast in a very different light.

Melanie reflected on her last meeting with Anatanyia. Anatanyia had come by the apartment to ask her once again to attend the party for Ariel, and once again Melanie had refused.

"Even though Mitch is out of the picture, I'm just not ready to make amends," she'd told Anatanyia.

The older woman had seemed indifferent to Melanie's feelings. "If Rachel can face your sister, why can't you?" she said.

Even now, Melanie felt the shock that Anatanyia's words had generated. "What do you mean?"

Anatanyia shrugged. "You of all people should know that Mitch could never be satisfied with the same woman for long."

While Melanie could take no real satisfaction in the knowledge that Mitch had played Ariel in the same way he'd played her, it confirmed her theory that for Mitch it was all about the conquest. But Rachel? She would have given Rachel more credit. It was possible that Anatanyia was just trying to stir up trouble, but why?

Anatanyia, unaware of Melanie's emotional turmoil, had asked her to check out a couple of locations for the party she was planning to throw for Victor, win or lose the best director award. Melanie had agreed with reluctance. She could think of better ways to spend her morning, but she also wanted Victor to have the best party possible, in the best location. He deserved it. And so they shared a ride in Anatanyia's car to the first country club. Melanie stared out at the passing scenery, thinking about Mitch and Rachel, Mitch and Ariel, Mitch and herself....

"...would change all that," she heard Anatanyia comment from the driver's seat.

"What?" Melanie said.

"The baby. Ariel thought fatherhood would settle Mitch down. Of course none of that matters now."

"Ariel thought that Mitch's death was suspicious."

"Suspicious? Mitch Carson was arrogant and careless. He got what was coming to him."

Looking back on it now, Anatanyia seemed almost satisfied that Mitch had died the way he had. There had been a cold, triumphant gleam in her eyes as she spoke those words. Not an hour after that conversation, Anatanyia was showing her the cliffside restaurant in Malibu as the second potential site for Victor's party. She'd been so keen for Melanie to see the view from the cliffs, even though Melanie, with an innate fear of heights, had held back and voiced her misgivings about holding a party in a place where people under the influence of too many drinks could easily plummet into the frothy, rock-studded surf below.

"Nonsense," Anatanyia had said, putting her arm through Melanie's and escorting her onto the ledge high above the pounding waves. "This view is what they will remember. It is what makes the site so spectacular." And then, just as they were nearing the edge of the dizzying drop-off, Anatanyia had stumbled into Melanie, throwing her off balance. Melanie remembered crying out as she slipped, snatching blindly for a spindly shrub growing from a crack in the rocks. She didn't remember the following events very clearly, but she did remember that it hadn't been Anatanyia who had reached to pull her to safety. It had been the groundskeeper, hidden behind the hedges he was trimming, who had heard her cry out; a man with swift reflexes, strong hands and faded blue eyes. Badly shaken, Melanie had asked Anatanyia to drive her home. She'd dismissed the frightening incident in the aftermath of Rachel and Stephanie's deaths. But now she wondered.

Had Anatanyia's stumble into her been accidental? And had Mitch and Rachel been having an affair? She had to talk to Kent as soon as possible.

"The fish are all asleep," Tito announced, startling her back to the present as he trudged up wearily and dropped cross-legged beside her, laying the fly rod on the ground. "I knew they would be. They only wake up early in the morning and after the sun sets. We were too late getting up here."

"It's my fault," Melanie said. "I wanted to see the shooting range. I'm sorry."

Tito shrugged, his large brown eyes philosophical. "There will be other days. We can come again, right?"

"Yes. I'd like that."

"Next time, you'll fish?" Miguel said, joining his twin brother and reaching for another piece of chicken.

Melanie laughed. "I'd like to try that, too."

They heard the rapid staccato hoofbeats of a horse approaching at a gallop and as one body they turned. "Julio," Tito said with no little disappointment. "I knew he'd show up."

Julio drew near, reining his fiery black horse in at the last moment and skidding to a stop as he flung himself out of the saddle with the lithe grace of a born horseman. "Señorita Harris," he said with that broad handsome grin, pushing his hat off his forehead to reveal his glinting eyes. "Stannie sent me to rescue you from the twins."

"She did not." Miguel scowled. "You're supposed to be working on the line fence near the landing strip. The cows got in there and Señor Kent couldn't land his plane too good last week."

"All fixed," Julio said, dropping down beside Melanie and resting his forearm on one knee. "Have they been driving you crazy?"

"They've been wonderful company," Melanie said. "But I'm afraid I can't say the same for myself. I think the fish have the right idea, napping in the sun. This is such a peaceful place I nearly fell asleep."

Julio's white teeth flashed. "*Sí*, yes, it is peaceful here." He looked at his brothers. "Have you done your lessons yet today?"

"We can do them tonight," Tito said. "After supper."

"Stannie wants them done *before* Kent gets home."

Julio's voice had become as stern as his expression and both Tito and Miguel squirmed uneasily. "Get your horses." While the boys went to saddle the grazing horses, Julio plucked a piece of grass and chewed on it, gazing out across the sparkling lake. "You went to see the shooting range, didn't you?" he said. "I saw your tracks."

Melanie encircled her knees with her arms. "Yes, the boys showed me. I was expecting tin cans on a log, but it was a very sophisticated setup."

"Yeah. Kent spends hours there." It looked to Melanie as if Julio wanted to say more. Instead, he shook his head, reached for the trailing reins of the black horse and vaulted effortlessly into the saddle. "I'll escort you back to the ranch, señorita," he said, taking Turtle's rein from Tito and handing it to Melanie.

Tito and Miguel rode ahead at a jog, but Julio held back his fiery black horse beside the steadily plodding Turtle. "Kent has never brought a woman to the ranch before," Julio commented.

"Never?"

"He must really like you."

Melanie felt her cheeks flush and she smoothed Turtle's long glossy mane with her free hand. "He brought me here because he felt I might be in danger in the city. He was just being nice."

Julio glanced sidelong at her. "The city is a dangerous place, isn't it? But you like it."

"I work there. I've never really thought about living anywhere else."

"Would you live in a place like this if you could work here?"

Melanie looked around her and drew a deep breath of

the clean mountain air. "Of course I would, Julio. Anyone would."

Julio pulled his hat down lower and made no reply.

CHAPTER EIGHT

IT WAS AFTER 7:00 p.m. when the wheels of the plane touched down on the grass landing strip just south of Chimeya and Kent taxied to the little shed with the pick-up truck parked beside it. He was tired after another fourteen-hour day, and he wasn't looking forward to his talk with Melanie. He'd rehearsed over and over on the flight home how he was going to broach the conversation without offending her.

He cursed as he started up the truck for the last leg of his journey. His stomach was in a knot of tension and his head was pounding. Sooner or later he was going to have to tell her that he hadn't made any progress in locating Ariel or the baby, and that if she'd eaten any of the dip from that dinner party, she'd be dead, too, just like Stephanie and Rachel. Why hadn't she eaten any of the dip when Stephanie had dropped it off the morning after the dinner party? Was it really that she didn't like it, or was Murphy right? Did Melanie know something she wasn't telling?

No matter what angle he approached it from, this wasn't going to be a pleasant conversation. He parked in front of the gate and carried the suitcase containing Melanie's clothes with him as he entered the courtyard. The scent of night jasmine rode the currents of the mountain air as the twilight deepened.

He exchanged a few words with his housekeeper as he passed through the kitchen, placing Melanie's bag on the floor. "You'll find the lass in there," Stannie said, indicating the door leading to the living room. Kent found her reading a book in front of a crackling fire.

"Oh, Kent, I had the most wonderful day," she said, marking her place in the book and setting it on the arm of the couch as he walked in. "Being here in this place somehow erased all the awful things that happened yesterday, at least temporarily."

"Stannie tells me the twins took you fishing," he said. To avoid staring at her he walked to the fireplace and nudged the log with a poker, sending a shower of sparks up the chimney.

"They did, and on the way to the lake they taught me how to ride a horse."

Kent tried to keep his eyes on the fire, but Melanie was so compellingly beautiful he couldn't help but watch her while she spoke. She glowed from within as she told him about her day at the lake. "They're wonderful boys, all three of them. And this place…" She raised her hand in a graceful, all-encompassing gesture. "I can see why you love it so much, and why you choose to commute back here every night, no matter how long and grueling a day it's been. You can almost forget how cruel and violent life can be in the city when all this beauty surrounds you."

Her eyes locked on his. For a long moment she was silent, and he felt the tension build. "*Almost,* but not quite," she added quietly. "Are you going to tell me anything at all about the investigation, or do I have to ride Turtle into town, wherever that might be, and buy myself a newspaper?"

He turned in the pretense of tending the fire, staring into

the flames. "We haven't found your sister or the baby yet, but we will."

"Of course you will."

"There's a female police officer staying at your apartment in case Ariel calls there. The answering machine is on, and we're prepared to tap the line and trace any incoming calls…with your permission, of course."

"All right," Melanie agreed slowly. "I'm pretty sure she'll eventually call unless…unless for some reason she can't."

Kent glanced at her over his shoulder at the trepidation in her voice. "She's your sister. She'll call."

"But what if—" Melanie stood abruptly and moved to stand beside him. Her eyes were dark with unspoken doubts and fears. "Kent, what if she never went anywhere? What if the same terrible thing happened to her? She had to have known about Stephanie's death, if she was the one who took the baby from the hotel room. She had to have known she was in danger. What if Ariel's dead?"

Kent cast around for words that could offer some comfort. But the best he could do was a feeble, "We're doing everything possible and—"

"There's something I have to tell you," Melanie interrupted. "Something I know now I should have told you right away. Please don't be angry…it's about Anatanyia and Rachel. I think it could be important."

"Oh?"

"The last time I saw Anatanyia, she told me she thought Mitch deserved what he got."

"Can you blame her for saying that? No offense, but he didn't exactly treat you or your sister very well."

"She claimed that Mitch was having an affair with Rachel Fisher."

Kent felt a jolt to the soles of his feet. "And you're just telling me this now?"

Melanie's face flushed at his words and her chin lifted. "I'm sorry, but the past few days have been such a blur and where Mitch is concerned, I try to block things out entirely. And, well, there's more. Something that happened the last time I saw Anatanyia."

Kent forced himself to speak evenly. "I'm sorry. I didn't mean to jump on you. I know this has been hard on you, but this is important. And if there is more, you have to tell me everything. Take your time, but try not to leave anything out. Can you do that for me?"

She drew a deep breath, then nodded. "Yes. Of course." Slowly, and with great deliberation, she told Kent about Anatanyia's obsessive desire to have a baby and about the visit to the seaside restaurant.

"At the time, I really did think it was an accident," Melanie said finally. "But now, with everything that has happened, I just don't know…."

Kent was nodding. "You were right to tell me all this," he said, thinking, *but I wish to hell you had told me earlier. Murph's going to have a field day with this.* Out loud he said, "And try not to worry about your sister. We'll get her back safely."

"Ah, there you are, admirin' that beautiful fire!" Stannie interrupted as she swept into the room, startling them both. "Supper be served, if yer ready to eat. It's not fancy, but there's plenty of it."

Melanie stood and looked at Kent questioningly.

"You go on ahead," he said. "I want to make some notes about what you just told me."

"But you have to eat," Melanie said.

"I'll grab something and eat while I work. I do it all the time."

"That he does," Stannie said in disgust. "Can't count the number of fine meals gone cold in that office. But never you mind, lass." She turned to Melanie. "You and I will enjoy a meal together."

"There," Kent said. "You're in fine hands. Stannie will make sure you're well fed." He added softly, "And thank you for telling me everything. I think it's going to be a real help." With that, he walked off in the direction of his office.

"Coming, lass?" Stannie was standing on the threshold leading from the room. "I hope you like roast pork. We've a mountain of it!"

"As a matter of fact, I do," she said, and joined the housekeeper in walking to the kitchen and waiting meal.

SAFELY BEHIND his office door, Kent slumped into his chair and replayed the earlier conversation with Melanie in his mind. It certainly painted a new and very sinister picture of the case. Unfortunately, it also created more questions than it answered. How far would Anatanyia Korchin have gone to secure a child for herself? It was obvious from what Melanie had said that the woman had little love for the late Mitch Carson, or for any of the women in her husband's life, for that matter. But was it enough to add up to motive and murder? Kent shook his head; he had the feeling the unpublished biography of Victor and Anatanyia Korchin by Rachel Fisher could very well hold the key to this puzzle. Hopefully the document analysts would be done processing it by tomorrow and he could have a crack at it. He sat up and reached for a pen and paper and began transcribing Melanie's revelations from this evening while they were still fresh in his memory.

Some hours later, as he was rereading his notes, he heard a soft tap on the door. Without waiting for an invitation, Stannie walked in carrying a pot of fresh coffee and a plate laden with cold meat sandwiches.

"Stannie, you're an angel," he said, as she set the food and coffee on a side table next to the desk.

"Aye, and don't you be forgetting it."

Kent tossed down his pen and picked up a sandwich. "How's Miss Harris doing?" he asked, reaching for the coffeepot with his free hand.

"Fine," Stannie said, wincing as Kent added the fresh coffee to a mug half-full of cold, stale brew left over from the morning. "In fact, we had us a right nice time, even without your company."

"Well, glad I wasn't missed."

Stannie looked serious for a moment. "We talked quite a bit, she and I. There's a good heart in her. She's a good lass."

Kent raised an eyebrow. This was high praise, coming as it did from the taciturn housekeeper. "And where is she now?"

"Off to bed. She insisted on helping with the dishes," Stannie said. "Those two young fools ran her ragged today." Stannie looked at him.

"Yes…"

"Well now, don't go flyin' into a rage, but your Miss Harris told me the boys took her to see your shooting range. She wanted me to tell you before you found out some other way. She doesn't want the boys to get into trouble. She feels responsible seein' as they was with her and all."

Kent nodded. "Well, she's not and those two should know better. I'll have a talk with them in the morning. I've told them a hundred times to stay away from there."

Stannie looked as if she had more to say. "Well, I'll leave you to your work, then," she said and swept out, closing the door behind her.

After she left, Kent sat staring into space, his sandwich all but forgotten. That damned shooting range. It was both his sanctuary and his curse. And his shield when the memories became too much. Memories of Susan. Susan, the one person Kent had ever known who truly believed no matter how bad a person was, somewhere inside of them there was goodness, too. He even grew to think she was right, up until the day she was killed. The tragedy that changed the whole direction of his life. Seven years. It seemed both like an eternity and like yesterday....

Susan had been his high school sweetheart, and they had continued dating throughout their college years and were married by the time Kent began his doctoral program at the University of New Mexico. To make ends meet and stretch Kent's limited fellowship dollars, Susan had gotten a job at a small but respected private counseling clinic in Taos. It was there she was drawn to youth intervention. She was good at it and within two years of starting, she was the center's chief staff clinician.

Kent completed his doctoral work in the then somewhat obscure but promising field of forensic psychology in record time. Thanks to some lucky contacts he made during his research, he was offered a lucrative professorship at the university. Since the field was a relatively new one, there were few opportunities other than teaching, so he took it and was soon on the fast track for tenure and an endowed chair. They were young, they were successful, they were in love.

Of course, there were compromises. When aren't there? Kent's university position carried with it some political baggage. He knew that to make it, to *really* make it in the world of higher academia, the right people had to be stroked, coddled and wooed. This meant, among other things, a continual round of social engagements. Departmental suppers, professional conferences, symposiums, weekend retreats and so on. Married professors were generally expected to attend these events with their spouses.

Susan hated these functions, so Kent never pressed her. By an unspoken agreement, she would accompany him no more than three times in any one month. He left it up to her which ones she attended and she could usually tell which of the endless invitations contained a hidden command performance for her. He knew these outings were a huge sacrifice on her part and he loved her all the more for it.

When the invitation to the annual meeting of the National Association of University Teaching Scientists arrived, Susan had known there was no getting out of that one. UNM was hosting the black-tie affair and Kent was up for one of the group's top honors. One of those rare awards that carried prestige *and* cash.

The evening of the banquet fell on the same day of the annual review at Susan's clinic. Since she would be tied up there all day, they had agreed ahead of time to meet at the hall. Kent knew it was a hell of an imposition.

He had arrived at Darling Hall first. No surprise there. He knew that Susan, after finishing up with the review team, had to shower and change at her office. He figured she'd be at least a half hour late. When she hadn't shown by the time dinner was announced, he tried to reach her on her cell phone. When the waitstaff was collecting the salad plates to make room for the entrees and her seat was still empty, he began to get worried. Dessert was just being served and Kent was heading out to try and reach her on the cell again, when he saw two uniformed New Mexico highway patrolmen talking to the dean of his department at the doorway to the banquet room. Dean Block scanned the room, caught his eye, looked quickly away and then back again. Slowly the older man walked over to Kent, who remembered thinking, "If I sit here and don't move, then he can't find me and tell me the bad news."

He had known instantly it was about Susan, and it was going to be bad. Kent had felt 200 pairs of eyes on him as he walked back to the troopers. They went into a small room off the banquet hall where, in the blink of an eye, Kent's promising, well-ordered, perfect world was wiped out.

"We're very sorry to have to tell you this, Dr. Mattson," one of the young troopers was saying. He only caught snippets after that. "She was alone... Not sure how they gained entrance... Single gunshot to the head... No sign of assault..."

The subsequent investigation turned up two young criminals that were high on crack. For some reason, they thought Susan's clinic stored narcotic drugs and they went looking for them. They caught Susan just as she was walking out the door, dragged her back inside and demanded she give them the drugs. When she couldn't, they shot her and ransacked the place.

For no reason other than that they were stoned out of their minds, they had killed the most beautiful, kind and loving person Kent had known. Racked with grief from the loss and with guilt from the knowledge that if she had not had to hang around to change for his stupid banquet she would have been long gone by the time the punks arrived, Kent had retreated to his childhood home at Chimeya.

Here he had stayed and managed to reach some sort of truce with himself. He had always enjoyed target practice and on days when the world seemed like too much to face, he would go to the old gravel pit behind the ranch and shoot at paper targets. Over the years his range had expanded into one that would be the envy of many law enforcement training centers. It was there, amid the din of high-powered rounds and consistent bull's-eyes, that he was able to punish Susan's killers. There, under the tall, fragrant Douglas fir trees, she was not alone in her moment of greatest need and he arrived in time to save her.

It was silly, irrational and juvenile. Kent knew that. And since the arrival of Miguel and Tito, he had toyed with the idea of taking it down. Practicing with live ammunition anywhere near where young children could happen by was never a good idea. And no matter how many admonishments they received to the contrary, the twins could not resist the pull of the range. Susan was dead. It was a fact Kent accepted, no matter how badly it hurt. Tito and Miguel were alive and needed him. That, too, was a fact. The range had served its purpose. Once this case was over, Kent vowed, he would disassemble the whole damned thing.

That promise made, he went back to his notes.

CHAPTER NINE

MELANIE HAD OPTED not to close her curtains the night before to allow the fresh breeze to flow in unimpeded through the open window. But it also allowed in the early morning sunlight and she found herself wide awake by six o'clock. Once again, Loki had kept her company through the night and was snoring softly, his wiry head on the pillow next to her. Anxious to see if Kent had gleaned any more information after leaving her the night before, Melanie hopped out of bed and headed for the shower with the intent of sharing breakfast with him. But as she was toweling off, she heard the now-familiar sound of the turboprop rev and then fade into the distance down the mountain. Disappointed, she dressed and wandered down to the kitchen where she found Stannie flipping through a box of recipe cards.

"Good morning," she said. "Was that Dr. Mattson's plane I heard?"

"And a good mornin' to you, too," Stannie said. "Aye, that was himself. Was up and out of here right quick saying he wanted to get an early start on things. Help yourself to the coffee."

Melanie poured herself a cup from the pot on the counter and turned to look out the window over the sink.

The view was expansive. In the distance rose majestic mountains, colored a deep, cool blue in the morning light. In between the ranch house and those peaks were the deep valleys and rolling hills of Chimeya. From her vantage point, Melanie could also see the barn set back from the road leading to the airstrip. Movement caught her eye and she saw Miguel and Tito ambling toward the barn, Loki tagging along behind.

Now, what am I supposed to do today?

As if reading her mind, Stannie spoke up. "Once you've had breakfast, Dr. Mattson asked me to ask you if you could read some notes he left behind."

"Oh?"

"He said it was something about background information or some such thing. But once you're done, he wants you to fax them to him at his office," Stannie said, pulling a felt-tip marker from her hair bun and making some notations in a cookbook open on the counter.

It sounded very much like busywork to Melanie, but if it would help locate her sister and niece in some way, she would do it.

"Before I have anything to eat, I think I'll just enjoy my coffee on the porch for a bit, if that's okay?" Melanie said.

Stannie waved a hand without looking up. "You go right on. If I'm not in here when you get back, I suspect you can find your way around to fixing something to eat?"

During their supper of roast pork, potatoes and garden greens the night before, Melanie had come to appreciate and like the housekeeper's direct style, something sorely missing among the people of the film industry.

"Don't worry about me," Melanie said, taking her coffee and stepping out into the chilly mountain air. She

sat down in a weathered Adirondack chair and let the vista
before her fill her mind and soul. Not long after, she heard
a door slam from somewhere inside the house. Stannie
must be about whatever business she had for the morning,
Melanie thought. Her coffee mug long drained, Melanie
was thinking about fixing herself a light breakfast when
she heard a crash and shouts coming from the barn.
Startled, she stood up and saw Tito and Miguel rush out
of the old building and head up to the house at a dead run.

"What on earth?" she said and walked down the porch
steps to meet them. As the boys neared, Melanie was
startled to see they were crying.

"Please, you have to help!" Miguel yelled.

"Come to the barn, hurry!" Tito cried.

They each grabbed her by a hand and fairly dragged her
off the porch and down to the barn.

"We didn't mean to do anything bad, honest," Miguel
said.

"We only wanted to see the new colt."

"Boys, calm down," Melanie said, as she trotted along
with them. "What happened?"

With a mighty sniff, Miguel said, "We came to see the
new colt. He was sleeping in the straw so we couldn't see
him over the stall. So, we opened the door…."

"We didn't see Loki behind us, honest," Tito said
through a sob. "But he ran in right after us."

"The mother horse got scared and—and…"

"Go on," Melanie said, her heart sinking.

"She kicked at the sides of the stall and it made Loki
bark. We tried to pull him out but before we could, the
horse kicked him!"

By this time they were at the barn. Slowly, Melanie and

the boys walked into its dark interior. It was quiet. Too quiet. "Where is he?" Melanie whispered.

The twins pointed to a corner stall, its door yawning open. Melanie could just make out a dark form lying on the straw. "Where are the mother horse and colt?" she asked, a slight tremor in her voice.

"After she kicked Loki, she and her baby ran outside into the pasture and I closed the gate behind them," Tito said.

"Okay, you boys wait right here," Melanie said. "Loki?" she called softly, walking to the stall. "Oh, Loki!" she breathed.

The scruffy dog was on his side, mouth open and tongue lolling out. She could see he was breathing, but it was very shallow. His eyes were half open and looked glazed over. A bloody scrape on his side indicated where the mare's hoof had made contact. Dropping to her knees at his side, Melanie gently ran her hand over the dog's body.

At her touch, Loki's eyes opened a bit more and he managed a thin whine. His bushy tail did its best to approximate a wag, but he didn't have the strength to lift it off the ground. "Stay still, boy. Just stay still. It's going to be all right." There was a lump in Melanie's throat and she felt hot tears rising in her eyes. Remarkably, in a matter of two days, this funny-looking dog had completely won her heart. Like so many dogs, Loki gave his loyalty and love, asking little in return. Well, she was not about to let him just lie here in pain. Pulling herself together, she called out to the twins.

"Boys, how far is the nearest vet?"

Slowly, Miguel and Tito crept to the edge of the stall.

"Is Loki going to be okay?" Tito asked.

"We're going to do our best," Melanie said. "Now, where is the vet?"

"Down the mountain in Gunsten," Tito said. "We know the way, we could show you!"

Kent's pickup would be a mile down the road at the airstrip and there was no way they could carry the poor dog that far. She was contemplating running down to get the truck, hoping the keys were in it, when Tito said, "We could go in Julio's truck."

Melanie looked up at him. "Julio has a truck?"

"*Sí*, it's behind the barn."

"Could he drive us to town?"

"No," Miguel said. "He left early to check some cows in the high meadow. But I know he wouldn't mind if you drove his truck."

"Fine, Julio's truck it is." Melanie stood up and looked around. "I want you boys to take those blankets over there and spread them in the back of his truck, make a nice, soft bed for Loki. I'm going to tell Stannie what's happened and ask her to call the vet and tell him we're on our way."

As the twins rushed off, Melanie gave one last look at Loki and then ran back up to the house to break the news to Stannie that the beloved pet of Kent's late wife was seriously wounded.

JULIO'S TRUCK turned out to be an ancient Ford Bronco. But it appeared in good running order and, thankfully, its keys were dangling from the ignition. Stannie had accompanied Melanie back down to the barn and together the two women had gently eased Loki onto a makeshift stretcher of horse blankets and into the back of the Bronco. The housekeeper had said little, only that she would call Dr. Belknap and alert him they were on the way.

With Miguel in the front seat to give directions and Tito sitting in back to comfort Loki, Melanie was able to navigate the old truck down the winding mountain road to where it met the pavement of the highway. From there, it was a forty-five-minute drive to the clinic of Dr. Hank Belknap.

When they arrived, Melanie saw the doctor and his assistant on the clinic's front porch waiting for them. Wasting little time on words, Dr. Belknap listened intently while Melanie described Loki's accident before he whisked the dog away into the operating room.

"Well, boys, I guess all we can do now is wait," Melanie said, forcing a smile and sitting on one of the clinic's waiting area's plastic chairs. Silently, Miguel and Tito took seats on either side of her. It was a long wait. At one point, the technician came out to say Loki had sustained several broken ribs, a punctured lung and possible additional internal injuries, before again disappearing into the operating room. The twins said little, just held on to Melanie's hands and stared at the operating room's door.

Finally, Dr. Belknap came out.

"Loki's going to be fine," he said, and Tito and Miguel let out whoops of joy.

"Oh, thank you, doctor," Melanie said. "Thank you so much!"

"He's going to need some direct care for a while, given his age and the seriousness of his injuries. So I'm recommending he spend a couple of nights here. But, all in all, it could have been much worse." He looked pointedly at the twins. "I assume you two have learned an important lesson about getting too close to new mothers and their babies?"

The twins nodded.

"Can we see him?" Melanie asked.

"Of course, follow me."

Loki was lying on a bed of soft blankets in an open kennel. A thick layer of white bandages was wrapped around his rib cage and an IV snaked from his front leg to a bottle containing clear liquid hooked to a rack above him. He appeared to be sleeping, but his eyes opened when he heard the twins whispering and his tail gave a small wag.

"Easy, boys," Dr. Belknap said as the twins rushed up to the dog.

Gently, Tito and Miguel patted Loki's head and ruffled his fur. Melanie had a hard time keeping her tears back and noted the vet was wiping his eyes.

After a moment, she said, "Okay, boys, that's enough. What do you say we let Loki get some rest?" Before following them out, Melanie knelt down beside the dog and gave his ears an affectionate rub. "Get better soon, you darling thing," she whispered. In return, she was rewarded with a small lick to her outstretched fingers before Loki shut his eyes and fell into a deep doggy sleep.

It was late afternoon when Melanie and the boys stepped out of the clinic. Before leaving, she had made arrangements with Dr. Belknap to have him or his assistant call Chimeya the next morning with an update on Loki's condition. She had also given him her credit card number to cover the expenses. As she was walking to the Bronco, she saw Miguel and Tito dash around the side of the building. What on earth were they doing now?

"Miguel, Tito, come on. I really don't want to do that drive in the dark and…"

Before she could say anything else, the boys reappeared, each holding a bunch of colorful wildflowers plucked hastily from the field adjacent to the clinic. Solemnly, they handed her the bouquets.

"You saved Loki," Tito said.

"We're glad you were with us," Miguel said.

Openmouthed, Melanie accepted the flowers as the boys, now looking a bit embarrassed by their display, hopped into the Bronco with no further encouragement. Smiling, Melanie followed.

IT HAD BEEN another long, frustrating day in a case that was producing far more in the way of questions than solutions. Predictably, Murphy had pounced on the romantic liaisons between Mitch Carson and Rachel Fisher, and Melanie's encounter with Anatanyia Korchin, a woman seemingly obsessed with, yet unable to have a baby. Murphy had immediately dispatched detectives to the restaurant described by Melanie to interview the groundskeeper and anyone else who may have noticed anything suspicious the day Melanie either was almost pushed or slipped off the cliff.

"Do you think she's still leaving anything out?" Murphy asked, sitting behind her desk as Kent stood at the window.

"I wish I knew," he said after a moment's reflection. "This is a woman who has been through a lot. It could be she's still in partial shock or…"

"Or?"

"Or, yes, she's deliberately holding something back. But I have to tell you, Murph, I just don't peg her as a killer."

Murphy considered a moment, and then nodded. "Okay, fine. The document guys delivered the Korchin bio first

thing this morning. There's a copy on your desk. I'm going
to work on running down the information your houseguest
provided. I want you on that bio. Read it, pick it apart and
let me know what you find. And Kent…"

"Yeah?"

"You know you are going to have to bring Melanie Harris
in for official questioning sooner or later, don't you?"

"Yeah, I know," he said as he walked out. *I'm just
hoping it's later.*

The Fisher manuscript was indeed on his desk. He poured
himself a cup of coffee, flipped it open and began reading.

Two hours later, he was done with his first read-through
of Victor Korchin's biography. The draft was roughed out
and there was no way of knowing how much more Rachel
had intended to include. There was a major lack of information when it came to Victor's youth, or how he came to
be involved in the movie industry. The manuscript began
with Victor's recent nomination for best director, then
jumped back to his arrival in Hollywood, fresh from Russia
and struggling to learn English. Struggle was the key word
for those early years, for though the man had talent, Hollywood proved a tough nut for him to crack. But Victor had
an asset that proved more valuable than his directing
talents: his young wife, Anatanyia.

Early on in the biography it was evident that Victor
openly credited his big break to the talented adolescent
figure skater that the world still remembered from the
Olympics, the little Russian girl with the big dreams that
everyone had hoped would win the gold. Anatanyia's
dreams still clutched at their hearts, and her acting at
Victor's direction had launched both of their careers. Their
story unfolded like a fairy tale. In the biography, Victor was

depicted as the hero who had rescued Anatanyia from the prospects of a squalid life in poverty-stricken communist Russia after an injury ended her skating career, but here the biography faltered. Once Rachel had opened the Russian door for a peek into Victor's earliest years, his past became very murky indeed.

Kent reread those critical pages several times, but could glean only that Victor was twenty-five years old when he first met Anatanyia Komeninski, who was barely sixteen. He was apprenticing with a Russian director, but there were no details as to the movies this director worked on, or what Victor had done with his life before this apprenticeship. Five years later, with no explanation whatsoever of those in-between years, Victor and Anatanyia were husband and wife, setting up housekeeping in a low-rent district outside of Hollywood and preparing to conquer the movie industry. To Kent's way of thinking, this was a huge omission if one was writing a biography. A person's life didn't begin at the age of twenty-five. An LAPD interoffice note clipped to the front of the biography said an entire box of notes and clippings had been logged in as evidence. Currently, the document experts were indexing the items. Kent hoped when he finally got his hands on those, they would fill in some missing pieces.

In the meantime, he turned back to the first page of the Fisher manuscript and prepared for a second reading and to start profiling both Victor and Anatanyia Korchin.

He was on reread number three when Murphy stuck her head in his door. "How's it going?"

Kent looked up and rubbed his eyes. "Slow. Very slow. Anything new on your end?"

"A few leads. We're chasing them down. Frankly, I'm

hoping you find something in there to point us in the right direction."

"Well, nothing conclusive yet," Kent said. "Certainly nothing worth killing over."

"Fine, keep on it. I'm on my way to meet with Brannigan. He wants to form a task force on this one—can you believe it?"

"Sadly, yeah, I can," Kent said. "Good luck."

He didn't see his captain the rest of the day and, with little new information coming in, Kent decided to head home a bit early. Truth be told, he was more than a little anxious to see how Melanie had fared on her second full day at Chimeya.

Driving up from the landing strip, Kent was surprised to see Julio's Bronco parked at the front gate. That was odd. Julio never took his truck out without first checking with Kent. It was a deal they had struck when the young man had begged to take on the aging truck after Kent had bought his newer pickup. Walking up the front steps, he was even more surprised to see a welcoming committee of sorts waiting for him. Melanie, Miguel, Tito, Stannie and Julio were all sitting on the steps or chairs on the porch.

Melanie, he saw, looked exhausted. Julio looked grim while his young brothers looked downright fearful. Stannie, as always, was unreadable.

"Something I should know about?"

They all looked at each other.

"Well?" he said.

"Kent," Melanie said, "Tito and Miguel have something to tell you. We're going to leave the three of you alone."

Melanie, Stannie and Julio shuffled into the house, leaving Kent looking at the young twins.

"All right, fellows. Who's going first?"

A half hour later, Kent found Melanie sitting by the fire in the living room. The front of his shirt was still a bit damp from where he had held each tearful boy in turn after they had poured out the day's events. Judging they had been scared badly enough by the accident that no further punishment was warranted, he had sent them to the kitchen for a bite of supper and with strict instructions to go right on to bed.

Kent walked around to the front of the couch and saw that Melanie's eyes were closed. In her hand was a glass of red wine. He smiled and shook his head as he reached for the bottle of wine and the extra glass on the table in front of the couch. She looked up at him as he sat down beside her, an eyebrow raised in question.

"They told me the whole story. Sounds like you've had one hell of a day," Kent said.

"I guess we all did," Melanie said.

"I want to thank you. I mean it. That dog, well, he means a lot to the boys, you know. Would break their hearts to lose him."

"Just the boys' hearts?"

"Well, I guess I've gotten kind of used to having him around."

"You know what I think, Dr. Mattson?"

"No, what?"

"I think you are a big phony."

Kent laughed. "Guilty as charged. Seriously, what you did today took guts. I don't know too many people who'd risk that drive on their own."

Melanie shrugged and took a sip of wine. "I really had no choice."

This woman a killer? Kent thought. No way. He poured himself a glass of wine and sat back, watching the fire.

"I wish I had some better news for you tonight," he finally said.

"You still don't know where Ariel and the baby are, do you?" Melanie said softly.

"I wish to hell we did, but no. There's no reason to think we won't find them, so please don't give up hope. In fact, new leads are coming in all the time."

Melanie looked unconvinced and Kent cast around for something encouraging to say. Unfortunately, his captain's words kept echoing in his brain: *Question her, Kent. Bring her in if need be. But find out what she knows.* He knew he had to, but not tonight; not after what she had done that day.

Instead, he gently changed the subject. "The boys really appreciated what you did. I think they've taken a real shine to you."

Melanie smiled. "I think it's mutual." She tried unsuccessfully to stifle a yawn.

Kent took her glass from her. "Why don't you make it an early night? I have to be in the office first thing again tomorrow, but you can sleep in."

She shook her head. "Thanks, but I just feel so helpless here and, well, I could use a few more things from my apartment I forgot to ask for."

"Listen, I'll call you tomorrow to keep you up to date on what's going on and where the investigation is headed. And as for your things, write them down and I'll have the detective pick them up, just like last time. But only if you promise to take it easy—deal?"

"Deal. But please let me know what's going on."

"Don't worry. You'll be the first to know."

CHAPTER TEN

KENT WAS INDEED long gone by the time Melanie entered the kitchen for breakfast the next morning. She helped herself to the coffee and then went to look at the open cookbook resting on the counter.

"Ah, there you are!" It was Stannie coming in the back door. "I've just seen those two wild twins off to start their chores and thought you and I could have a proper breakfast."

At those words, Melanie suddenly caught a whiff of something delicious.

"Blueberry muffins," Stannie announced, removing a pan from the oven. "With berries supplied by Tito and Miguel, who actually got themselves up early to pick them."

Melanie was as impressed as she was touched. "They smell heavenly," she said.

"And they'll go perfectly with some of this peppercorn bacon I've been saving for a special occasion. Now set yourself down while I fix us up."

As the woman began frying the bacon, the phone rang. Stannie looked up and motioned for Melanie to answer. It was Dr. Belknap, reporting that Loki had spent a peaceful night and managed to eat some solid food that morning. "He should be able to come home in a couple of days," the doctor said. Melanie thanked him and hung up.

"Those boys will be some relieved to hear that," Stannie said, as she plunked down a basket of hot muffins, a platter of crispy bacon and a pitcher of orange juice on the table. "Eat before it gets cold."

The food tasted every bit as good as it smelled and, over the meal, the two women continued the process of getting to know each other.

"I'm from Labrador, born in Goose Bay," Stannie said, reaching for a muffin. "I married an Air Force pilot who was stationed there at the time. We moved all over throughout his career, and I raised up three boys. Then he was transferred to Luke Air Force Base and got himself killed in a plane crash. Our boys were all grown and gone, thank the Lord, but I had no skills, no way to survive, and the military doesn't pay a widow much, not these days. I took a seasonal job in Taos, working as a housekeeper at a mountain resort. Then I was offered a better-paying job cleaning the private counseling clinic where Susan—that's Dr. Mattson's late wife—worked, and after a year or so she asked me to clean their house, too, and offered me an apartment over their garage. Treated me like family, she did. They had a big beautiful house that looked out over the mountains.

"Susan did good things at that clinic with youth intervention and such. She was the center's top clinician. Oh, she had a big heart, she did. She saved many of them kids from a terrible fate. All those lost and troubled souls she helped..." Stannie roused from her reminiscing and laughed self-consciously. "Listen to me blatherin' on."

"Stannie, what happened to Susan?" Melanie asked hesitantly.

Stannie was silent for a long moment, then she said, so

softly Melanie had to lean in to hear, "They killed her, they did. For no reason. Just killed her." Then she relayed the story of Susan's brutal murder.

"She was like an angel, aye, and like a daughter, too. I loved her," Stannie said. "Oh, Susan was dearly loved by many, she was. Kent brought her back here to bury her. She's in the graveyard behind the ranch, high on the mountainside. Well, he brought her here, no funeral in Taos, no chance for us to say our goodbyes, and went into seclusion. If it hadn't been for needing to take care of his mother, he probably would've died himself, the poor soul was that heartbroken."

Melanie could scarcely think of what to say in response, so she remained silent. Stannie was lost in her memories.

"I came just after Kent buried his father. His mother was failing then, and he needed help with her. After she died, the poor dear soul, he asked me to stay on. I been here ever since. Then the boys Susan helped came the same as I did, you see. Like a pilgrimage, they came to put flowers on Susan's grave. Oh, they weren't boys anymore, they'd grown up. Julio stayed, but most just came and helped out in the busy times. Branding calves in spring, rounding up beef cows in the fall. Haying and such.

"When the first of 'em came, Kent didn't know who was leaving the flowers. One day he caught one of 'em at her grave. He went crazy, he did, and nearly killed the boy. He thought they were all the same, those kids, the same as the ones who killed Susan to steal drugs from the clinic. But he was wrong. They were a part of Susan, you see. The ones who came all the way from Taos to put flowers on her grave were a part of who she was and what she cared about."

Melanie listened, feeling a strong wave of compassion

for the man who had loved his wife so deeply. "So he let them stay," she said.

"Aye." Stannie nodded. "The flowers, and the boys. If they came, hungry and homeless, he gave them food to eat and a job. Taught 'em about cattle and horses and hard work."

Melanie gazed out the kitchen window behind Stannie. "Thank you for telling me all this," she said softly.

"I just thought you should know," Stannie said. "Now, I'd best be about my business." She looked at Melanie. "Hard work can be good for the soul, you know. There's plenty to be done and if you don't mind an old woman bossing you around..."

"Stannie, I'd take orders from you any day. Just tell me what to do."

THE CAPTAIN had been less than thrilled when Kent had shown up with nothing new from Melanie. It didn't help matters much that Murphy was still seething from her meeting with Brannigan the day before.

"That's it, time's up," Murphy said, sitting across from his desk. "Korchin's coming in tomorrow for further questioning—most likely with a lawyer—but at least he's coming in. It's going to look damned suspicious if we don't have Ms. Harris do likewise."

Kent could only nod glumly.

"For cripe's sake, Kent, look at your own notes and case workups! Can you sit there and honestly say if Melanie Harris were a man, you'd be this hesitant to bring her in?"

Kent looked up. He wanted to say something in his defense. But in his heart he feared she was right.

"Now listen," Murphy said. "We have two dead women, two missing women and a missing baby. We also have two viable suspects, Korchin and Ms. Harris. One has already been brought in once for questioning. The other is ensconced at that ranch of yours. Well, that ends tomorrow. Bring her in. I don't care if it's in chains. Just get her here. Do I make myself clear?"

"Crystal," Kent said. "Anything else?"

"Yeah, Rachel Fisher's notes should be ready for you by the end of the day or first thing tomorrow. When you get them, I want them to be job one."

After Murphy left, Kent shut his door and asked the desk sergeant to hold all his calls. Safe in his inner sanctum, he cleared a spot on his table and laid out all his notes, photos and reports. He spent the rest of the day going over them all piece by piece in an attempt to find something—anything—he may have missed that could shed some light on the case. But by the end of the day, he was no further ahead than when he started. And nothing had magically appeared that would conclusively clear Melanie.

He looked up at the clock and was surprised to see it was past five. An hour earlier a uniformed officer had dropped off a bag of items from Melanie's apartment and he sat back looking at it. Kent had not kept his promise; he had not called her all day. What good would it have done? Her sister and niece were still missing and he was feeling like a failure.

"To hell with it," he muttered, closing the last file and turning his desk lamp off. "I'm going home." What he would tell Melanie when he got there, he had no idea.

KENT SHUT DOWN the plane's engines and swung down from the cockpit. He was surprised to see Julio, Tito and Miguel waiting for him by his truck.

"Loki's okay!" Tito yelled, as the two younger boys ran up to him.

"He can come home in a couple of days," Miguel said. "And Julio said he'd take us to visit if it's okay with you. It's okay, isn't it?"

"We'll see about that, boys," Kent said. "But that's good news about Loki." He threw his briefcase and Melanie's bag into the truck bed and climbed in the cab. Julio joined him on the passenger side and the twins clambered into the back seat for the short ride to the ranch house. Julio, Kent noticed, had an odd little grin playing at the corners of his mouth.

"What's with you?" he asked.

Julio's grin widened. "Stannie is making a special supper for you and Señorita Harris. She's set the dining room table for two, and there are candles."

Tito groaned. "That means we'll have to eat in the kitchen with Stannie. I hate it when we have to eat with her. She's mean to us."

"She's not mean," Julio said, turning to face his brothers. "She's trying to teach you little animals some manners."

"She stabs our hands with her hairpins and it hurts," Miguel complained.

"You shouldn't grab for things across the table," Julio said.

The rest of the squabbling was lost on Kent. A romantic supper? He had to get to Stannie before it went any further. When he got to the house he sent Julio, Miguel and Tito to the bunkhouse to wash up for supper and headed inside with a heavy step.

He opened the ranch house door and saw the fire crackling in the corner fireplace, the bottle of red wine and two glasses on the coffee table reflecting the golden flames, the cheese and crackers on the cutting board, the bright wildflowers in the blue glass vase.

"Stannie?" he called, moving swiftly toward the kitchen with a growing feeling of panic. "Stannie!"

"Hush, now, there's no need to be shoutin' at the top of your lungs," Stannie scolded from where she stood scrubbing a pot at the kitchen sink. "Are those Melanie's things? Ah, good. She's been needing them ever since she got back from taking another ride up to the lake with the younguns, the devil take 'em for slackin' on their lessons, but she soon sorted them out and set them to studying."

"Melanie got them to do their lessons?"

"Aye, she did. They started and finished in jig time. I've never seen the like, them two vying with each other for her attentions at the kitchen table, doin' their lessons like they loved the schoolin' more than the fishin'. She has a way with younguns. She'll make a grand sort of mother, that one will. When she wasn't with those boys she was all about helping me with chores around the house. Yes, a fine woman, she is. Here, give her satchel over, then, and I'll bring it to her room directly." She took the bag out of his hand and stared at him with a questioning expression. "Why, whatever is the matter with you?" Stannie frowned and pointed her finger for emphasis. "I'll not have any bad humor in this house tonight, Dr. Kent Mattson. Not with the fine meal I've fixed for the two of you. Go on now and get washed up."

"Stannie, I need to talk with Melanie in private."

"But of course you do, and you will, over a meal the likes of which the two of you won't soon forget."

The Harlequin Reader Service® — Here's how it works:

If offer card is missing write to: Harlequin Reader Service, 3010 Walden Ave., P.O. Box 1867, Buffalo NY 14240-1867

NO POSTAGE
NECESSARY
IF MAILED
IN THE
UNITED STATES

BUSINESS REPLY MAIL
FIRST-CLASS MAIL   PERMIT NO. 717-003   BUFFALO, NY

POSTAGE WILL BE PAID BY ADDRESSEE

HARLEQUIN READER SERVICE
3010 WALDEN AVE
PO BOX 1867
BUFFALO NY 14240-9952

Play the Lucky Hearts Game

and get...
2 FREE BOOKS
and a **FREE MYSTERY GIFT...**
Yes! YOURS to KEEP!

I have scratched off the silver card. Please send me my *2 FREE BOOKS* and *FREE mystery GIFT*. I understand that I am under no obligation to purchase any books as explained on the back of this card.

Scratch Here!
then look below to see what your cards get you... 2 Free Books & a Free Mystery Gift!

336 HDL EEZW   **135 HDL EEYM**

FIRST NAME   LAST NAME

ADDRESS

APT.#   CITY

STATE/PROV.   ZIP/POSTAL CODE   (H-SR-02/06)

Twenty-one gets you **2 FREE BOOKS** and a **FREE MYSTERY GIFT!**

Twenty gets you **2 FREE BOOKS!**

Nineteen gets you **1 FREE BOOK!**

TRY AGAIN!

Kent's headache worsened as Stannie fairly beamed with satisfaction. "You don't understand...."

She patted his arm with a snort. "Oh, I understand better than you think I do, young man. Now get along. It won't do to keep her waitin'. There's nothin' harder on a young woman's heart than waiting. Nothin' harder in the whole wide world." Before he could protest any further, she swept off toward the guest room with Melanie's bag.

Kent watched after her for a few moments, then groaned aloud and retreated to his room to fort up all his reserves. He took a fast and very cold shower, dressed in a fresh pair of Levi's and flannel shirt, and shaved off the five o'clock shadow. He felt guilty that Stannie had put so much effort into a meal that could only turn out to be a disaster.

Stannie was back in the kitchen when he reappeared, checking on something in the oven that smelled quite delicious. She gave him a swift glance and a curt nod. "Aye then, you'll do," she said, closing the oven door and straightening. "She's waiting for you in the living room. Supper will be ready soon."

"Stannie, there's something you should know—"

"And there's something you'd be forgettin' now, young man," she interrupted. "Never keep a beautiful woman waitin'."

Kent gave up. He turned toward the living room with a feeling of doom, a feeling that vanished as soon as he set eyes on her. Melanie was sitting on the sofa, legs curled gracefully beneath her. She was dressed in a pair of gray slacks, a white linen blouse and a pale pink cardigan. At his approach she raised her eyes, and smiled up at him. "Hello, Dr. Mattson. I trust Stannie has coached you on how you're supposed to behave tonight."

Kent couldn't help but grin. "As a matter of fact, she has," he said, reaching for the bottle of wine and the corkscrew Stannie had placed beside it. The wine might give him the courage he needed to pull this fiasco of Stannie's off. His job would be a whole lot easier if Melanie didn't remind him so much of Susan.

"She's determined that we should fall in love over this meal she's prepared," Melanie said. "She's so sweet and sentimental."

Kent removed the cork from the bottle and filled both glasses. "I don't suppose you'd believe me if I told you she doesn't normally behave like this," he said, handing one of the glasses to Melanie. The alluring scent of her perfume was making him feel far less the police investigator and much more the lovestruck fool. He took a breath. He had to stop this pretense of a romantic evening right now, before it became too painfully real. "Melanie…" he began, intending to get down to business and tell her about the ricin in the Mexicali dip and let things progress from there. But before he could, Stannie swept in to announce the first course was ready.

"Come along, now," she said. "I've lit the fire in the dining room, as well, so you won't be without the charm of it this fine evening."

Fighting against Stannie was like trying to turn back the tides, Kent knew. Better to go along for now. Stannie led the way in her brusque fashion and stepped aside as they entered the dining room, allowing the two of them to admire the candlelight glow that accentuated the dark wooden beams in the whitewashed ceiling and the simple mission table with its high-backed chairs. True to her word, a fire burned in the raised beehive fireplace, casting a golden light that mingled with that of the two candles in the center of the table.

It's going to be a long evening, Kent thought glumly.

"How lovely," Melanie murmured as Kent pulled out her chair.

Stannie had disappeared, but she soon entered the room bearing two artfully arranged plates of salad greens. "Mesclun, fresh from our own garden, this is," she said, placing them on the table. "Most of the meal tonight all came from this ranch. The dressing is a honey balsamic vinaigrette. I hope you like it."

"Thank you, Stannie," Kent said, giving his housekeeper a significant glance that Melanie interpreted as a mute request for privacy. She picked up her fork and squelched a smile as Stannie left the room, her spine stiff and her chin raised. Kent took a swallow of wine. "She'll be in here every two minutes making sure things progress the way she wants them to," he predicted with a wry grin.

"And if they don't?" Melanie asked.

"Heaven help the both of us." He set his glass down carefully and drew a deep breath as if about to broach a painful subject. "There's something we need to talk about." He paused and picked his glass back up, studying the contents as if trying to analyze what kind of grapes went into its making.

"What is it?" Melanie felt her stomach flutter with anxiety. He was withholding something from her. Something very unpleasant.

He raised his eyes and she saw the flicker of hesitation. "I…I want to thank you for helping the twins with their lessons."

She stared, her fork poised above the salad plate. She knew that wasn't what he intended to say. "I enjoyed that very much. They're very smart boys."

"Too smart, sometimes," he said gruffly, taking another swallow of wine. He set his glass down so abruptly that wine spilled onto the dark wood as he pushed out of his chair. Her eyes followed him as he paced to the fireplace, ducked his head and ran his fingers through his hair. "What more can you tell me about Anatanyia Korchin?" he asked as he swung to face her.

Melanie laid her fork down, her appetite gone. "Oh, God. Is…is Anatanyia dead, too?"

"No, but she's still missing. Can you think where she might have gone? Any relatives or friends she might have visited? Any favorite places she liked to hang out? Someplace that perhaps she and your sister might have gone together?"

Stannie chose that moment to come back into the room, holding two soup bowls balanced on plates and looking faintly puzzled as she set them on the table, no doubt wondering why Kent was on his feet. "Gazpacho," she announced. "I hope you like it, lass. Any night now we'll be gettin' a killing frost but we might as well enjoy the garden's bounty while we can."

"Thank you, Stannie," Kent said in a curt manner. Stannie gave him a brief but haughty stare before returning to the kitchen.

"Anatanyia can be very impulsive," Melanie offered when they were alone again. "She loves to shop for clothes. Sometimes she'll take spur of the moment trips to New York City just to buy a pair of shoes and she'll call Victor on the set or at the studio after she's already boarded the plane or checked into the Waldorf Astoria. Once she even flew to Paris for a fashion show without telling a soul."

Kent stared at her as she spoke, and while it was impossible to read his dark eyes in the flicker of the firelight, she sensed that he was waiting for something more. She picked up her wineglass and took another small taste before setting it back down. "Anatanyia is a very complex woman. I've known her for as long as I've known Victor, yet she remains very much a mystery. As far as I know, she has no close friends," Melanie said, her feeling of unease growing as Kent continued to stare at her.

"She immigrated here, obviously," Kent said.

"Thirty years ago, with Victor." Melanie nodded.

"Would you say they have a good marriage?"

"Victor worships the ground she walks on." Melanie paused. "Kent, why are you asking me all these questions about Anatanyia?"

Stannie stomped into the room wearing a forbidding scowl and carrying a great ironstone platter which she set on the table with a resounding thump. The roast on the center of the platter was browned to perfection and flanked with an equally perfect array of roasted vegetables. She spun around, sallied back into the kitchen, and brought forth a second baking dish holding a golden Yorkshire pudding. On her third trip she brought a tureen of gravy and a carving knife and fork, which she arranged carefully beside the big platter. She then turned to Kent, who remained standing by the fireplace, and placed her hands on her hips.

"And the *next* time I come into this room, Dr. Kent Mattson," she said in a threatening tone of voice, "the most of this food had best be gone, or the cook, nanny and housekeeper of this fine ranch of yours *will* be!"

Kent watched her leave and then ran his fingers through his hair with a defeated sigh. He returned to the table, dropped into his seat and picked up the carving utensils. "Dig in and eat," he said. "I sure as hell can't run this place without her. Besides, she's right."

"About what?"

"About this meal, and about your company." His eyes held hers for a long moment across the table. "I'm glad you're here."

Melanie felt an easing of the tension within her at his words. She breathed a silent sigh of relief and picked up her fork again. "Thank you. So am I."

THE REST OF THE MEAL was like a dream. Kent never once mentioned anything further about the investigation. He asked her a multitude of questions about her childhood and her job as a location scout. He seemed genuinely interested in getting to know her on a personal level, though she cautioned herself that he was probably just making polite conversation. She asked him an equal number of questions about his own childhood growing up here in the Sierras. He spoke with warmth and affection of his deceased parents, of the seven years that Julio had been living at Chimeya, and at the arrival of Julio's younger twin brothers. The only person he never mentioned was Susan, his dead wife. Throughout the dinner, Stannie made infrequent appearances, mostly to clear dishes and to bring a second bottle of wine, which Kent opened and poured.

Perhaps it was the influence of the wine, but Melanie began to feel as if the night was becoming more perfect by the moment. Kent's attentiveness, humor and sensitivity all conspired to completely destroy the protective wall she'd built around herself after Mitch's betrayal. When Kent related the fight he'd made to get legal custody of Tito and Miguel, she felt herself beginning to melt, and when he told her he was in the midst of adoption procedures of all three boys, she felt her eyes fill with tears.

"I think that's wonderful," she said.

"They don't know anything about it." Kent pushed back in his chair and stood, taking his glass of wine with him. "I thought if I failed, it was better they didn't know."

"How could you possibly fail?"

"They sent someone to the ranch to inspect the living conditions here. A woman in her fifties. She thought the place was remote and primitive, too isolated to socialize the boys properly. She didn't like the idea of home schooling, even though the boys all tested way above normal in every subject. I received a letter from my lawyer a week ago saying that the department of social services was reviewing the adoption application and the agency would be contacting me. All in all, it didn't sound too promising."

"They'd be crazy to take those boys away from you, Kent," Melanie said. "They love it here, they love you, and they're perfectly well-socialized. What more could they possibly need?"

"A mother, maybe," he said. "Maybe that's what the agency is looking for. A two-parent home."

Melanie watched him standing by the fireplace, gazing into the fire as if visualizing a long lost face in the golden light. "Stannie told me about your wife. I'm sorry, Kent."

He turned his head to look at her. "As bad as it was, I was lucky to have Chimeya to come back to," he said softly, and then slowly, haltingly, began to tell Melanie of those first awful years following Susan's murder.

Kent was welcomed home with open arms, and amid the trees, hills and streams of the Sierras and under the attention of his parents, he began to heal. Around the time Kent was coming out of the depression following Susan's murder, the LAPD was considering the idea of taking on a forensic psychologist. Kent put his name on the list of applicants and, following several interviews, a background check and a qualifying round at the firearms range, he found himself with a new career. He liked the job. He liked his colleagues and, most of all, he liked the idea of helping to put away the very kinds of people who had taken Susan from him. It was valuable work he found satisfying in a way university teaching had never been.

By the time the second anniversary of Susan's murder rolled around, Kent was beginning to believe life might, after all, go on. Right up until his father walked into the Sierra foothills for the last time. A search party found his body a week later at the bottom of a rocky gulch where he had fallen after slipping on some loose rocks.

His father was buried in the small family cemetery on Chimeya land. Six months later Kent stood again amongst the old grave markers and watched as his mother's casket was lowered into the ground. The doctor had said it was a heart attack that took her as she slept one night, but Kent knew better. She'd died of a broken heart.

From that point on Kent had thrown himself into his work. And a good thing, too. When his parents' estate had been settled there was something of a shock. Chimeya was in dire financial straits. Aggressive land development on all four abutting sides had driven property valuations up and, as a consequence, the taxes were going through the roof. The ranch was on prime real estate. Heavily wooded, it counted a good-sized lake, several smaller ponds, a river that was home to a healthy population of native trout and two designated mountains within its boundaries. Land developers from as far away as San Francisco and L.A. drooled at the thought of getting their hands on the property, envisioning high-end condos and gated communities for the rich and famous.

Over Kent's dead body.

An accountant friend of the family helped him restructure the ranch's not insignificant debt and he spent the next five years paying it down. As luck would have it, a former colleague from his teaching days had called Kent out of the blue several years ago. The colleague was in town for a conference and wondered if Kent wanted to hook up for lunch. Over tacos and beer at a sidewalk cantina, Kent listened while this former professor turned private clinician extolled the virtues of private practice. By the time the check came, Kent knew where his future was headed. Even if his friend had been exaggerating, Kent figured he could spend two days a week listening to and counseling well-heeled clients and easily triple what he made as an LAPD forensic psychologist and homicide detective.

The only thing absent in his life was Susan. He'd lived with that empty ache for so long he'd grown used to it…until Melanie Harris walked into his life and reminded him how much he'd been missing for the past seven years. He looked at her now, sitting in her chair and listening quietly as he paced the room, and came to a sudden stop. Once he'd started talking, he found he couldn't stop. There was something so compassionate about her, something that made him want to tell her everything about himself, both the good and the bad. And now, having done so, he felt better than he had in seven years. He gazed at her for a few moments and then uttered an abrupt laugh. "So, Dr. Harris," he said, "how much do I owe you for that session?"

LISTENING TO Kent talk, Melanie felt she'd been given a compelling glimpse of the past that had molded him into the man he'd become, and was more than a little humbled by his trust. She sensed that he was the sort of man who bared his soul to few, and that she, for whatever reason, was one of the few.

She rose to her feet and regarded him steadily. "Stephanie told me you were the best of the best, and now I understand why."

He picked the bottle of wine off the table. "Let's go sit in the living room," he said. "The couch is infinitely more comfortable than these chairs."

While Melanie settled onto the sofa, Kent put another log on the fire. The flames curled up from the deep bed of coals, slow and languorous, and she leaned back with a blissful sigh. She felt exactly the same way. When Kent sat beside her, she had to restrain herself from leaning against him and putting her head on his shoulder.

"Did you get enough to eat?" he said.

Melanie smiled. "I've eaten more in two days at this ranch than I have in the last two weeks."

"Good. You could stand to put on a little weight."

She tilted her head and studied him. "Thank you again for asking me here. Just a few days, and I feel like a new person…."

His eyes had become so dark they looked almost black in the muted light of the room. He stared at her for a moment that was filled with all sorts of sensual imaginings, then set his glass of wine on the end table, took her own glass from her hand and placed it beside his own. He leaned toward her and she felt her heartbeat flutter, and wondered if she should close her eyes or keep them open for their first kiss. Her thoughts raced wildly as she waited. *Please don't let me disappoint him.*

"Melanie," Kent said, resting his hand on her shoulder as if to steady her. "I'm sorry, but there's no easy way for me to tell you this. Victor Korchin is coming in for questioning and I've been ordered to bring you in tomorrow. You might want to bring a lawyer along."

CHAPTER ELEVEN

A BUCKET OF ICE water splashed on her face could not have shocked Melanie more. She stared at Kent, eyes wide, and saw his mouth moving, but could not hear a thing he was saying. His words were drowned out by a wind screaming through her brain. Slowly, two emotions fought their way to the surface: first, a deep shame at the manner in which she had been ready to throw herself at Kent, and second, the stirrings of the embers of anger that Kent could not only be so cool and detached about Victor's fate and her own, but that he had also played some twisted romantic game before making his startling pronouncement.

The betrayal sat heavy on her shoulders as she felt the sting of tears in her eyes and a hot lump forming in her throat. Ah, but there was a third emotion, too, wasn't there? As much as Melanie did not want to admit it to herself, she was disappointed.

How could I have been so stupid?

The embers of Melanie's anger were growing brighter and hotter by the moment.

"…it does not look good for him," Kent was saying.

"Pardon me?" Melanie managed to say.

"I said, given all the evidence, which, granted, is circumstantial, we are starting to build a pretty good case against Victor and we need you to fill in the blanks."

Melanie's anger was a bonfire now, and Kent could sense the change.

"Melanie, I know this is an awful shock, and I'm sorry, but you have to understand I'm just doing my job."

He was reaching out to touch her shoulder, but before that strong, callused hand made contact, Melanie slapped it away. For good measure, she followed that up with a slap to Kent's cheek. It echoed like a shotgun blast in the room, followed by the sound of breaking dishes. Stannie had entered the room carrying a tray on which perched an apple pie warm from the oven, a dish of vanilla ice cream, two dessert plates and serving utensils just in time to witness Melanie's actions. It was certainly the last thing the poor woman had expected to cap off her well-choreographed evening. Truth be told, it surprised Melanie almost as much.

Before Kent could say a word, Melanie was on her feet, standing so suddenly she knocked both wineglasses off the side table, and they landed on the floor, shattering and adding to the tenseness of the moment. In an instant, Kent, too, was on his feet, trying to grab Melanie by her shoulders.

"Don't you dare touch me," she hissed, and his hands dropped back to his sides in a helpless motion.

"Melanie, calm down."

"I'll do no such thing. You bastard! You bring me out here to the middle of nowhere with promises of peace and healing. You leave me alone for three days while you fly off to build a case against the closest thing I have to a father. Then you have the nerve to wine and dine me while the whole time all you want is to pump me for information. Tell me, *Dr.* Mattson. Is this how you treat all your houseguests?"

"Melanie, sit back down and let me explain, please."

Melanie made no move to sit but crossed her arms over her breasts, glared at Kent and said, "Go on." She was dimly aware of Stannie picking up the broken crockery, muttering darkly under her breath.

Kent took a deep breath. "I still believe you're in very real danger and that the safest place for you to be is right here. You're right," he continued, "I probably shouldn't have just up and left you here the past couple of days, but I honestly didn't know what else to do and figured you'd be happier here than under protective custody in the city. And yes, I should have made an effort to call during the day with updates on the investigation, but I got really bogged down." He hesitated, as if struggling to find the right words.

"I'm listening."

"All right, here's what we know. The criminologist team has determined Stephanie, Rachel and even your poor cat were all killed by the same thing—a poison in that shrimp dip Anatanyia Korchin made and served at a dinner party several nights ago at Blackstone. That poison was ricin, a derivative of castor beans, and the beans were found in Victor Korchin's shed."

"But you just said Anatanyia made the dip," Melanie pointed out.

"That's right and that's why I am not convinced Victor is our man. And *that's* why it's so important I question you so we can get to the bottom of this and you and Victor can be cleared of any suspicion. Given what you told me yesterday about Anatanyia, it's even more important that we find her."

Her thoughts spinning, Melanie did not answer right away. A horrific realization hit her, forcing her back down on the couch.

"Kent," she said, looking up at him, "Ariel was at that dinner party. She loved Anatanyia's spicy shrimp dip!"

"Victor told us she didn't have any because she was breast-feeding the baby and Anatanyia told her it would make the baby sick," he said.

Melanie felt a rush of relief, then frowned. "Ariel, breast-feeding? Somehow I can't imagine…" She was immediately struck with another horrible thought. "Do you really think Anatanyia was the one who put the poison in the dip?"

Kent hedged. That's exactly what he had been thinking ever since the poison and its source were identified, but he wasn't about to share that with Melanie, at least not yet. "At this point, speculation serves no purpose."

That seemed to satisfy, if not comfort her. "I was invited to that party. I should have been there, and if I'd gone…" Melanie shuddered.

Kent sat on the couch, but made no move to touch her. Stannie had finished picking up the broken dishes and had vanished back into her kitchen.

"That's why you have to cooperate, Melanie. Not only could you be in real danger, but… But there are some attached to the investigation who are questioning your involvement beyond being a possible victim."

Melanie had been staring unseeing at the fire. Now she lifted her head, anger burning once again.

"Do you honestly think me capable of murdering my best friend, a coworker, my own cat and maybe my sister and Anatanyia? Is that where this is going?"

"Of course not, but you have to look at it from a purely

investigative standpoint. It would have been better all around if you had told us everything from the beginning," Kent said, instantly on the defensive. "I mean, let's face it, it looks like you're withholding information."

"I have been nothing but honest with you, Dr. Mattson," Melanie said, "and look where it's gotten me."

"What do you mean?"

"I thought I could trust you, but you're as bad as Mitch, maybe even worse. You're both willing to use people to get ahead. I only hope you didn't use your own wife that way."

Melanie stopped, appalled at the words that had just come out of her mouth. She had never meant to say such a hateful thing. She started to apologize, but one look at Kent's face shocked her into silence. His eyes had turned icy and hard.

He was on his feet before she could say a word. "Stannie, could you please escort Miss Harris to her room. I have to get back to work. Thank you for supper."

Unheard and unseen by Melanie, Stannie had reappeared in the room. Both listened to Kent's footsteps fade away until they ended completely behind the slam of his office door.

Two HOURS LATER the office door opened and Stannie marched in. Kent was sitting at his desk, shuffling through a pile of faxes that had arrived that night, but might as well have been written in Greek for all the sense he was making of them.

He looked up as the housekeeper shut the door firmly behind her.

"What did you do to the poor lass?" Stannie demanded.

"Look, Stannie, I know you went to a lot of trouble fixing supper, and I'm really sorry. It was very good and…"

"Bother the supper!" she snapped. "This is more important than food. That young girl has been cryin' her eyes out
nigh on two hours. Now, I know I'm just an ignorant
country girl, but I know a thing or two and one thing I know
is a woman's heart, and that one is breaking."

"Stannie, I'm sorry. I'm sorry Melanie is so upset. I'll
talk to her in the morning. I promise. I just don't think now
is the right time."

"Now's the perfect time! That lass needs you, though
for the world, I can't think of why at this moment!"

Kent glared at her. "Look, this has got to stop. I appreciate what you are trying to do here, but I have a double
murder to solve, a missing persons case, maybe another
murder or two and Melanie may be right in the middle of
it. I have to stay objective."

"Don't get up on your high horse with me. I know what's
what here and if you're any kind of man a'tall, you'll march
right into her room and make your own amends."

He looked up. There was nothing he'd rather do. It
would be so easy. Just walk to her room, take her in his
arms, tell her everything would be all right and give in to
the powerful feelings that were almost painful whenever
he thought of Melanie Harris. But not now. Not when the
investigation was taking so many turns. He sighed and
slumped farther down in his chair.

"Stannie, please understand, that's the one thing I can't
do."

THE NEXT MORNING Kent waited until the very last minute
to go down for breakfast. He told himself he wanted to
avoid any more accusations from Stannie. What he really
feared was another confrontation with Melanie. He

planned to leave it long enough that she would have had
her breakfast and left the kitchen. When he walked through
the swinging double doors, it looked as if his plan had
worked. Julio, Tito and Miguel were sitting at the table,
eating bowls of oatmeal in silence. Stannie was at the
stove, stirring something in a large kettle, and Melanie was
nowhere to be seen. With a sigh of relief Kent sat down
and accepted the cup of coffee Stannie brought over.

"'Bout time," was all she said.

"And a good morning to you, too," Kent said. He had
no desire to squabble with his housekeeper this morning.
He had stayed up well past 2:00 a.m. studying police
reports and, moreover, the best he ever did in most argu-
ments with Stannie was a draw. He jumped at the yelp of
pain from Tito. The lad had tried to reach for the sugar
bowl that was in front of Julio by leaning halfway across
the table. Stannie, who missed nothing that went on in her
kitchen, had drawn the large knitting needle from her hair
bun, smacked Tito's grasping fingers and replaced it back
in her hair before anyone could see.

How *does* she do that? Kent wondered.

Kent decided he at least should attempt some kind of
breakfast conversation. "Sorry I didn't get to look at
your school work last night, we'll do it tonight," he said
to the twins.

All three Estevan brothers said nothing and continued
to eat in silence.

"Is that all right? Stannie told me you did it," Kent said.

"She's leaving," Tito said.

"She took her bags and went away," Miguel said.

"What?" Kent stared around the table. Was Tito sniffling? And did Miguel look on the verge of tears?

"Señorita Harris," Julio said. "She's outside sitting in your truck. I helped her carry her bags out this morning. She says she's going home."

Was that accusation in his voice?

"Did we make her mad?" Tito asked.

"We're sorry. Tell her we won't do it again. We promise," Miguel said.

It was all too much. Kent pushed back from the table and got up, his own breakfast untouched. He had once been jumped by a gang of drug dealers while working under-cover. They had tied him up, beaten him and threatened to kill him, all the while questioning him on what he had told the authorities. A repeat of that ordeal would have been in-finitely more endurable than this quiet interrogation by the young boys and Stannie. It was obvious all four of them had fallen deeply in love with Melanie Harris at some point during her time under protective custody at Chimeya.

"We'll talk about it tonight," he said and beat a hasty retreat, four pair of accusing eyes boring holes into the back of his head.

Kent walked out into the fresh dew of a mountain morning. He saw that Melanie was indeed sitting inside the truck, the passenger door was open and she was staring out at the mountains. Kent climbed into the driver's seat and slammed the door. Without a word, Melanie swung her legs in and shut the door.

Kent turned the key, put the truck in gear and shot down the road toward the airstrip. In the shower that morning he had rehearsed what he had wanted to say to Melanie, but now, in her presence, all the words left him. He wished she would break the silence but she was looking fixedly at the passing landscape. His false starts at conversation were met with brief, albeit polite, responses. After a few moments he gave up and resigned himself to a long , silent flight into the city. If only she didn't look so damned lovely and vulnerable sitting there! It was obvious she had slept as little as he. There were dark lines under her eyes which were red and puffy, indicating she had been crying. The knowledge that he was in no little way responsible made him feel miserable.

The flight in to Los Angeles was smooth and uneventful. In deference to Melanie's feelings Kent had held off on his normal morning flight music, which alternated between Pink Floyd and Jefferson Airplane. Instead, he left the radio off, hoping it would encourage her to say something. No go. He knew he should be the one to say he was sorry, to tell her that he would do everything in his power to help and protect her. In the end, he said nothing. To have done so would have been the quickest way to get Murphy to boot him off the case—his objectivity was already in question. No, to best help Melanie, he had to keep it professional all the way.

The plane barely had time to taxi to a halt before Melanie had unbuckled her seat strap, opened the cabin door and hopped out. Kent shut down the controls and reached behind to grab her bag. They met as she rounded the front of the plane.

"Look, Melanie—" he began awkwardly, handing the bag over.

She held her hand up, cutting him off. "Whatever I have to say to you, Kent, I will do so at the station. I think it was pretty obvious last night your interest in my involvement in all this is beyond casual. I plan on going in to check on Victor anyway. When I get home I'm calling my attorney and we will meet you at your office."

"Good," he said, more harshly than he intended, "saves us the trouble of sending an officer for you."

Melanie whirled around and marched off toward one of the two cabs that were always hanging around the airstrip in hopes of a lucrative fare. Without a backward glance, she got in and told the driver her destination. By the time Kent had driven out of the lot in his rental car—there was still no sign of his missing and presumed dead Audi—the cab had been swallowed up by the early morning commuter traffic.

MELANIE HONESTLY THOUGHT she had no more tears left. But she had spent the better part of the night crying into her pillow. After a few hours of fitful sleep, she had risen with one thing in mind—get as far away from Kent Mattson as possible. Her resolve had almost broken when she had seen him that morning looking more handsome and masculine than any man had a right to look. But his demeanor on the drive and subsequent flight gave her no opening to utter the words that could have healed the breach that had sprung up between them the night before.

Melanie cringed at the thought of it. The night should have turned out so differently. She could not remember wanting to be with a man more than she had wanted to be with Kent last night. She'd always prided herself on her inner strength and her independent spirit, but just now she would have traded both for one night of letting someone else shoulder all of her burdens.

The traffic was getting heavy by the time the cab driver took the exit leading to her neighborhood. But he made good time and all too soon they were pulling into her driveway. She paid the fare and as the cab drove off an overpowering feeling of desolation swept over her.

Melanie was feeling the lowest she had in years and there was no one to turn to. Her best friend was dead. Her sister was missing, and Victor was presumably even now in custody of the LAPD Even her dear little Shakespeare would not be there, rubbing his face against her legs in his incessant need for attention. It took a few moments, but she pulled it together enough to pick up her bag and go inside.

Once there, it was obvious to her the entire place had been searched. Professionally searched, but searched nonetheless. Whoever had gone through her belongings had obviously done so with the utmost care. Everything was in its proper place, but a woman knows when her things have been touched, examined and moved. It made her feel a little sick and violated.

A uniformed female officer was drinking take-out coffee and reading the morning paper at the dining room table. She looked up as Melanie walked in and dropped her bags on the floor. "We didn't expect to see you today," she said.

"I had some business to attend to and had to come back. Actually, I was wondering…"

"If I'd get the hell out," the officer said with a smile that was not unkind.

"Well, yes."

"No problem." She folded her paper and picked up her coffee. "You do understand we have to remain on site, but my partner and I can hang in the vehicle for a while."

Melanie looked out the window to the tree-lined street below. "I didn't see a police car."

"That's the idea. Actually, it's not a squad car. See that plumber's van down the way? That's us. Rig's got video equipment, a cooler of sandwiches, good seats and all the comforts of home. Well, all but a bathroom, that is."

Melanie had to smile in spite of her tumultuous emotions. "Feel free to use mine anytime," she said.

"Thanks. Name's Darcey. Francis Darcey. Partner's Frank Engles. See that radio there?" She pointed to a small handheld radio on the table. "Just push the numbers 4-1-5 and we'll come running." She turned her head to the radio mounted on her shoulder, "Base, this is 4-9-Charley. I'm 10-19 to your location. Be advised subject is on premises. Over."

Melanie walked Officer Darcey to the door and watched as she strolled across the street and, when there were no cars in sight, scrambled into the green van a block away. She turned back to look at the empty room. From the moment she got up that morning Melanie had wanted nothing more than to be alone to gather and organize her thoughts, but now that she was, she hadn't the foggiest idea how to begin.

CHAPTER TWELVE

NORMALLY KENT used the drive from the airstrip to his office as a time to focus his thoughts and plan his day. This morning, he spent it trying to banish all thoughts of Melanie from his mind. It was a losing battle and her face was as fresh in his mind when he got to the station as it had been when they had made their hostile farewells that morning.

Murphy was already in her office when he walked by, and she motioned for him to come in. She was reading something and told him to sit down. As he did, she pointed to a large cardboard box on the floor.

"What's that?" he asked.

"Research notes for the biography of Victor Korchin, courtesy of the late Rachel Fisher," Murphy said. "Everything's been indexed, but not read. That's your job."

"Lucky me," he said.

"I need you to separate fact from fiction in all this," she said, indicating the full box of notes. "Did you get anything from Melanie Harris that could shine a light on any of it?"

Kent shifted uncomfortably in his chair.

"You did question her, didn't you?"

"Well, Murph, it's a bit complicated," Kent said, stalling. "I mean, I did get some pertinent information."

"So you asked her about Rachel and Stephanie's relationship…?"

"Well, not exactly."

"Kent, I'm not in the mood. Did you question Melanie Harris or not?"

Taking a deep breath he told Murphy the entire story, starting with the romantic dinner gone awry of the previous night and ending with Melanie's promise to appear at the station that afternoon, lawyer in tow.

He was spared any further discussion of the events by the ringing of Murphy's phone.

"Murphy," she snapped into the receiver. "What? You're kidding. Okay, make sure at least two uniforms stay on it. I'll get a crime-scene team over there right away." She hung up and looked at him. "We'll discuss your handling of this later, Kent. Right now it looks like we may have caught a break. A patrolman at LAX found Ariel Moore's car in the back of the long-term lot."

"Great," Kent said, "I'll head right over."

"You'll do no such thing. As of this moment, you are no longer a primary on this case. You'll continue to run support from here, but that's it. I was willing to give you some leeway in this, but I'm reeling it in. I want you at your desk preparing a complete workup of Melanie Harris. Then I want that diagnostic workup on Anatanyia Korchin and Victor Korchin based on the Fisher manuscript and those notes."

"Then what?" Kent asked.

"Then we hit both Melanie Harris and Victor Korchin with what we have. We shake them good and hard and see what falls loose."

Kent grimaced. "I'm not sure I'm the one to talk to Melanie…."

Murphy barked a humorless laugh. "You got that right. I don't want you anywhere near her when she comes in. She can give her statement to another detective, but definitely *not* to you. In fact, I might take it myself. I have a few questions I'd like to ask her. Now get to work."

MELANIE HAD NO REASON to be nervous, but her stomach was full of butterflies as she walked into the police station to give her second official statement. As she reached to open the door she regretted very much her decision not to hire a lawyer on her behalf, but her threat to Kent had been an empty one. She *had* no lawyer, nor did she really know how to go about getting one she could trust. Then, too, if she arrived with a lawyer in tow it might make her look like she *needed* legal representation, and cast a shadow on her innocence…something she really didn't want to do. Something she shouldn't even be worrying about, since she had nothing whatsoever to do with any of this.

She approached the desk sergeant and drew a steadying breath. When he looked up and gave her a questioning glance, she dove in before he could speak.

"I'm here to give an official statement to Kent Mattson," she said.

"And your name?" he countered, keying into his computer screen.

"Melanie Harris. He's expecting me."

The desk sergeant grunted and picked up his phone. He gave his name and spoke briefly, then hung up and nodded toward the bench across the hallway. "Have a seat, please, Ms. Harris. Someone will be with you shortly."

Melanie sat on the hard bench, feeling very much out of place. She wondered where Victor was, and how he was holding up. She knew if she were in his shoes, she'd be a nervous wreck. She was a nervous wreck now, and no one had accused her of anything.

Yet.

The way Kent had spoken last night, there were people here who believed she was involved in the deaths of Rachel and Stephanie, and her sister's disappearance. What if this was a trap? What if she had been asked to come give a statement so that they could trip her up somehow, make her look guilty, put her behind bars?

Melanie stood, taut with anxiety. She'd die if she were caged up, locked away from the sunshine and sea breezes. She glanced toward the door, her heart rate accelerating. She was being foolish, she knew. Nobody was going to lock her away.

And yet, Victor was under suspicion and maybe they were getting ready to arrest him, and he was innocent. Couldn't the same thing happen to her?

"Ms. Harris?" A cool, slightly reproving voice at her elbow startled her. Melanie looked around to see Captain Murphy standing beside her, trim and efficient, looking elegant enough to grace the cover of a fashion magazine. "I'm ready to take your statement now."

"Oh, I…" Melanie stammered, feeling the heat rush to her cheeks. "I thought it would be Kent…I mean, Dr. Mattson."

Captain Murphy's smile was thin and humorless. "Dr. Mattson is busy. If you'll follow me, please?" Without waiting for a response, the captain turned and walked briskly down the corridor, leading Melanie to a room with a large pane of glass—one-way viewing, she was sure. She was also sure this was similar to the room they'd interrogated Victor in. Melanie paused in the doorway. The chairs, the table, everything inside was just like a scene out of a cop show.

"I…" She couldn't bring herself to follow Captain Murphy, who had turned and was giving her a questioning glance.

"It's all right, Ms. Harris. This won't take long. If you like, I'll have another officer sit with us."

"No. No, that's okay," Melanie said, taking the first step and crossing the dreaded threshold. Visions of handcuffs danced in her head as she sat at the table and placed her purse in front of her, cradling it between her hands as if gathering strength from its mundane familiarity.

Captain Murphy laid a small tape recorder on the table and pulled out her notebook. She flipped it open and clicked her pen into action. "Please, try to relax. Tell me about your last contact with Anatanyia Korchin."

Melanie bit back a nervous laugh. Telling her to relax at a time like this was about as effective as the gynecologist telling her to relax in the midst of an internal exam. She drew a deep breath, and began to speak. She told the captain everything. And when she was done, Murphy watched her the way the hawk watches a mouse, waiting for it to stray from cover. "Is that all?" she said.

THE FILE BOX containing Rachel Fisher's research notes was on Kent's desk where he had dropped it after carrying it from Murphy's office. Piecing together the tangled story of the Korchins was going to be tricky based on this secondhand information, he knew. There was one person who could shed some light on that, but was it worth losing his badge over? Then again, Murphy had only told him hands off when it came to Melanie giving her statement. She had said nothing about questioning her regarding the contents of the Fisher file. A fine hair, but one he was willing to split. Telling himself he was calling her only to check her memories against some of Rachel's vague references to Victor's past, he picked up the phone and dialed Melanie's home number.

No answer. She'd promised to come in to the station to give her statement, but she couldn't have left her apartment already. Maybe she'd stopped to see her lawyer…

He began sifting through the file box of research notes. After an hour Kent pushed the papers aside and rubbed his temples. His headache was worsening by the moment. He reached for the phone and dialed Melanie's home number again. Still no answer. Damn the woman! If she had caller ID she was probably not answering just to spite him. He dropped his head into his hands, wondering how he could ever bridge the distance that had opened between them, and wondering why it mattered so much. But the hell of it was, it did. It twisted him up inside when he remembered how she'd looked at him last night when he told her about the suspicions surrounding Korchin.

Kent lifted his head and stared unseeing at the opposite wall. Victor Korchin could clear a lot of things up, if only he would start talking. Some of Rachel's manuscript read as if she'd been conducting a personal interview, and there was information about Victor that he guessed few people would have been privy to, personal stuff, details that a good writer and researcher would have ferreted out only in personal conversations and through intimate knowledge of the person being profiled.

Maybe Rachel had uncovered something that she felt

was too questionable to include in Victor's biography? What were all those illegible notes scrawled in the margins and all those heavily blacked-out lines? Murphy had said that Victor Korchin hadn't volunteered much information at all since he'd been taken into custody, and maybe that was why. Maybe Victor didn't like the idea of a biography being written about him because he was trying to hide something in his past. Rachel must have stumbled onto something or hit a big roadblock, otherwise her manuscript wouldn't have faltered so badly in that one spot. And what—if anything—was Stephanie Hawke's connection to the whole thing? Could Victor have a reason for wanting her dead, too? The clues he needed to fill in the blanks might very well be in her research material…if he was lucky.

Kent pushed out of his chair and refilled his coffee cup. Then he resumed the slow, arduous process of scanning every single scrap of paper that was tucked within. The file was thick. There were countless newspaper and magazine clippings, sheets of paper with illegible notes scribbled on both sides, which he set aside for the team in analytical to decipher if they could, and a couple of CDs labeled as Academy Award presentations for the past two years. He was halfway through The Victor Files when he came to a thick envelope with a Russian postmark. He withdrew several old newspaper clippings wrapped inside a piece of lined white paper. On the paper was a brief note written in a woman's handwriting.

Dear Rachel,
    I have thought a great deal about our conversation. Perhaps you are right. Perhaps by telling this story

people of all nations might look differently at the terrible stress we put upon mere children to compete in world-class competitions. These newspaper articles prove that during the time you are researching, A. was working for the same Russian film company that employed V., and the company produced the sort of sordid films you suspected it might. All of the articles basically lament A.'s fall from grace after her skating injury and hint at some dark manipulation of her fate by the Russian mafia, who financed the majority of her Olympic training, with token help from the Russian government. I can personally vouch for this, as we were on the same team and in the same boat. The fact that A. managed to elevate herself above her terrible circumstances and escape that awful fate gave us all hope. We still talk of how V. risked his own life to rescue A. and her entire family and bring them to America and a life of freedom. Given your fondness for V., and my undying friendship for A., I trust you will treat this information with the greatest sensitivity.

Regards, Petra.

The newspaper clippings were from several different Russian tabloids, but each had the same head shot of a smiling and very beautiful young girl. Kent sifted through the magazine clippings for one that showed both Victor and Anatanyia attending some social gathering. He studied the mature woman on Victor's arm, and compared her to the young lady shown in the newspaper articles. They were undoubtedly one and the same.

Interesting.

He sat back in his chair with his mug and took a swallow of cold coffee, analyzing this latest information. In that murky time period, Anatanyia and Victor had apparently worked for the same Russian film company, a company that might not cast such a flattering slant on Victor and Anatanyia Korchin's earlier years…but then again, not all fairy tales had good beginnings or happy endings, and sordid films and the Russian mafia did not a happy fairy tale make. He called Murphy on her cell phone to relay the information to her.

"Hold on, I'm in the interrogation room," she said, and there was a long pause while she exited to a more private location. "Well, I'll be damned," she said after Kent had finished. "We may have just found our motive."

"Did you find out anything in connection with Ariel's vehicle being left at the airport?"

"She wasn't on any of the commercial flights. Privately owned aircraft fly in and out on a regular basis. We're checking into those as well, but they aren't required to report a passenger manifest, just file a flight plan. And Kent? She definitely had a baby with her in that car."

"Did you question Victor about where Ariel might have gone to spend two weeks?"

"Tried to, but Marquette is advising him not to volunteer any information whatsoever." There was another pause on Murphy's end, and Kent pictured her pacing restlessly with that stony frown.

"I'd like to question Victor about this information, Murph," Kent said. "I have a feeling that showing him these clippings might get him talking. But even if he never says a word, this stuff's bound to get a reaction out of him, and I'd like to see it."

"All right," Murphy agreed. "I'm just finishing up with Melanie Harris's revised statement. Why don't we break for lunch and I'll schedule Victor for an interrogation at one o'clock. He's with his lawyer now."

"Melanie's *here?*" Kent sat back in his chair, astonished and relieved. He'd been half afraid she wouldn't show, and her absence would have cast her in an even more suspicious light.

"She's been here for over half an hour, which is about how long it took her to tell me all the things she forgot to tell us the first time around. I imagine we can expect another official statement from her tomorrow, as more of her selective memory returns."

"Go easy on her, Murph. She's had a rough couple of days."

"I still think she's the key to this investigation, but getting information out of her is like pulling teeth."

"Must be your technique." Kent reached for the yellowed newspaper clippings and folded them back into the envelope. "See you at one o'clock."

THE DOOR to the interrogation room opened just as Kent was walking by. He glanced inside and came face-to-face with Melanie, but any pleasure he might have felt from seeing her was instantly washed away by the expression on her face. She looked drained, heartsick and not at all happy to see him. Kent was at a loss for the proper line to use when meeting up with a woman fresh from a police interrogation. On impulse, he said the first thing that popped into his head.

"Melanie. I'm just on my way to lunch. Care to join me?"

She regarded him a moment with wary skepticism and

made no effort to hide the sarcasm in her voice. "I've already told your captain everything I can think of."

Kent couldn't really blame her for feeling used and abused. So far he'd done nothing right when it came to her. "Look, can we call a truce and forget the investigation for a while?"

Melanie hesitated, but finally her features softened and she nodded, albeit reluctantly. "All right," she said.

Kent offered up a silent thanks and fifteen minutes later he was ushering her into the bright interior of Midday Deli, a small family-run soup and sandwich shop several blocks from the police station that was beginning to fill with lunchtime patrons.

"Kent!" a short, balding man in a white apron called from behind the counter and over the heads of waiting customers. "Thought you'd gone AWOL. Haven't seen you in here for three days. You been cheating on us?"

Kent laughed as he guided Melanie to the chrome-and-Formica-covered counter. "No way, Howie. I wouldn't dare. Things have just been a bit crazed at work. Melanie, meet Howie Levitson, the best-kept culinary secret in all of Southern California."

"Pleasure, miss," Howie said, extending a beefy hand over the counter for Melanie to shake. "This is a first, Kent bringing a date along instead of a bunch of files."

"We're on kind of a tight schedule here, Howie," Kent said, turning to Melanie. "Trust me to do the honors?"

"This is your territory, go for it," she said.

"Good deal." He turned back to Howie. "Can we get two specials to eat in?"

"With horseradish and kraut?" Howie asked.

"Is there any other way?" Kent said, and took Melanie

by the arm to lead her to a table near the window but partially hidden by a large plant.

"Sorry about that," Kent said as they sat. "Didn't mean to put you on the spot."

"That's all right," Melanie said. She was looking around at the forest of hanging plants, posters promoting long past rock concerts and an odd assortment of coffee mugs, which occupied floor-to-ceiling shelves tucked in a far corner.

Kent followed her gaze and grinned. "That's how you tell when you've become a regular. You get to keep your own mug here," he said.

"And I suppose one of those up there is yours?"

"You bet. Between what I drink here and what I take out, they could stay in business on my coffee orders alone. Ah, here we go."

A tall, slender youth had materialized at the table bearing a tray with two plastic baskets on it. He flashed a wide grin and set one basket in front of each of them, sliding a chipped blue mug sporting the LAPD logo full of black coffee in front of Kent. "Something to drink?" he asked Melanie.

"Green tea would be lovely," Melanie said. She was still staring at the massive corned-beef sandwich when the server returned with Melanie's tea and two bowls of sauerkraut, which he plunked on the table before dashing off to attend to another order.

Melanie picked up her fork and poked suspiciously at the newest addition.

"Sauerkraut," Kent said around a mouthful of sandwich. "They make it here. Try it, it won't bite back. At least, not much."

"I'm sure it's delicious," she said. "I've just never been a big fan."

"Chicken," Kent said good-naturedly. "Look, I'll trade you my coleslaw for it. You won't get a better offer than that, I guarantee it."

Melanie smiled for the first time as she pushed her bowl toward him. "Help yourself." She concentrated on tackling the sandwich. It was thick, messy and spicy with the freshly made horseradish and Kent knew once she took a bite she'd be hooked for life on lunch at the Midday Deli. For a while, silence reigned as they ate, and then Kent drained the last of his coffee, tossed his napkin on the table and leaned back.

"So, what's the verdict?" he said, damning his choice of words as soon as he'd spoken. "I mean, you only ate half your sandwich. Howie'll think you didn't like it."

"Oh, it was delicious. I'm just not that hungry."

Kent glanced at his watch. "I still have some time before they need me back at the station, and it's a beautiful afternoon. How about we walk back through Ocean Park?"

OCEAN PARK was a popular spot for lunch-hour walks. As they headed in the general direction of the police station, Melanie found herself gradually relaxing in Kent's presence in spite of her determination to keep her guard up. The sunshine felt good and the anger and bitterness she'd harbored toward him were rapidly banished by the bright beauty of the day. Across the busy road lucky people with leisure time on their hands basked on the white strip of beach next to the blue Pacific Ocean. They walked along in silence, each step taking them closer to the station house. They passed an empty park bench and Kent paused. "The last place I want to be on a day like today is inside that damn police station. Want to sit for a while before I have to head back in?"

Melanie nodded her agreement and they sat side by side in the shade of a yew tree. She breathed the fragrance of flowers blooming in wooden planters surrounding the benches and felt a rush of melancholy. "It's such a lovely day. It seems so wrong to be enjoying any of it."

"It's been a helluva past couple of days for you," Kent said. "I wish there was something I could say to make things easier."

Melanie said nothing, not trusting her voice or what would come out of her mouth. She could not look at him, she knew that much. She felt tears coming and squeezed her eyes shut, willing herself to pull it together. She felt Kent's arm encircle her shoulders in a comforting gesture and to her absolute mortification, his tenderness caused her to lose control. Hot tears burned and she couldn't quite stifle the sob. In response to this, he put his other arm around her and held her against his strong, broad chest.

"It's going to be all right," he said, one hand rubbing her back. "Your sister left you a note. She was planning to go somewhere, we just have to figure out where, and when we do, we'll find her."

Melanie took several shaky breaths, then nodded and straightened, wiping her cheeks with the palms of her hands. Kent placed a finger under her chin and tilted her face up until they were looking into each other's eyes. "You okay?" he said.

To Melanie, the moment was so reminiscent of the disastrous one at Chimeya she couldn't breathe. She wanted to look away, but couldn't. In no way did she want to acknowledge, much less act upon, the feelings welling up unbidden inside her. She felt betrayed by her own emotions. She was fully aware that any interest Kent had in her was largely professional. For that very reason she knew she had to remain on her guard around him, but why did it have to be so difficult? Why was her heart telling her that she should trust him when he didn't trust her?

She nodded again and his hand dropped away. "I'm all right now. I just feel so helpless. I want to be able to tell you what you want to know, what you seem to think I *do* know, but I can't, because I don't. I'm not hiding anything from you."

"I know that."

"Kent, how can I help you?" Melanie said. "Anything I can do to get Ariel and her baby back and find the killer, just tell me."

"There is something," Kent said. "This afternoon Murphy and I are going to interrogate Victor Korchin together, but so far he's given us nothing. Anything you could tell me that would give me some idea of how to get him to open up would not only help me, but go a long way in getting your sister and niece back safely."

Melanie felt her whole body tighten up. Hot anger bubbled up inside her, but almost immediately was extinguished by a feeling of overwhelming exhaustion. She was so tired of it all. Tired of looking for ulterior motives in Kent's questions and actions, tired of worrying about Ariel and her baby, but most of all tired of not knowing what to do or who to trust. It was all too much for one person to deal with. She'd been sincere in her offer to help, but the only help Kent wanted was help in nailing Victor. How could she be party to that? Weariness had indeed replaced the anger but now it was giving way to a steely resolve. Resolve to do whatever she could to protect her sister and to keep Kent at arm's length. With that she squared her shoulders and sat straight up, looking Kent in the eye.

"I've already told Captain Murphy everything I know. There's nothing more I can tell you that would help you soften Victor up," she said. "Besides, you know how I feel about Victor. I believe he's innocent. How could you even expect I would betray him?"

"I'm not asking you to betray him," Kent said. "We need him to cooperate with us if we're going to find who *really* killed those two women, and where your sister and his wife are. But he won't talk. We need his help. We need to know what he knows. His silence is just digging him a deeper hole."

"And you want me to tell you that if you just click your heels together three times, he'll suddenly spill his guts? You think I have some secret trick up my sleeve to get Victor to talk? Sorry to disappoint you, but I don't."

Kent settled back on the bench with a frustrated sigh. "Did you know Rachel Fisher was writing a biography of the Korchins?"

"It was common knowledge," Melanie said. "With Victor and Anatanyia, it was never a matter of *if* they would get a book written about their lives, but *when,* and by whom. It made sense it should be Rachel. She worked on several of Victor's movies and had known them about as long as anyone. And, more importantly, they liked her."

"Did they trust her?"

"That's an odd question."

"Well, did they?"

Melanie thought for a moment. "I suppose so. I mean, there had to be a degree of mutual trust. A biography is pretty personal."

"So, it would be safe to say that if Rachel had dug up anything scandalous the Korchins would have the ultimate veto power?"

"That would definitely go without saying, though I can't imagine that she did."

"I know I've asked you this before," he said, "but how much do you know about the Korchins before they came to America? I don't mean the stuff about Anatanyia's short-lived skating career and Victor's involvement in independent filmmaking. I mean more personal details, like where they grew up, how Victor got into filmmaking, how they got to this country in the first place. Really think, it could be important."

"I *have* thought about it, Kent, honestly, but their lives back in Russia are as much a mystery to me as they are to you," she said. "Wait a minute, you found out something about their past in Russia, didn't you? What?"

He shook his head. "I'm sorry, it's an open investigation and I can't tell you any details. But does the name Petra ring a bell?"

"Petra…" Melanie murmured. "That name is familiar. Let me think a moment…."

Kent remained silent while Melanie concentrated. Finally, her face brightened. "A couple of years ago there was a cocktail party at Blackstone. I can't remember exactly what the occasion was, a birthday or something, doesn't matter. There had been a lot of champagne and we were all feeling pretty loose. For some reason, Anatanyia started talking about her skating career and growing up in

Russia. Nothing specific, just some fond memories of her favorite games and that sort of thing. But more than once she mentioned her best friend, Petra Chechkova was her name, and wondered what had ever become of her."

"Were Rachel and Stephanie at that cocktail party?"

Melanie thought a moment. "Yes, both of them were there."

"Can you remember anything else Anatanyia might have said about Petra?"

"That night Anatanyia had pulled out some of her old skating awards—medals, trophies and letters of congratulations from the Russian government. There was a team photo with one of them, signed by all the skaters. Petra Chechkova was one of them. Afterward, I remember Rachel and Anatanyia talking alone and looking at that photograph. I remember thinking that Anatanyia must have had a lot of champagne to bring up all that at a party," Melanie said. "She was usually so reserved."

"Did Stephanie know about the biography?"

"Before Stephanie got her big break writing for the Hollywood papers, she was an investigative reporter. She's really good at getting to the bottom of any story and I wouldn't be at all surprised if she had been helping Rachel out on the research end of it."

Kent sat back, narrowed his eyes and rubbed his jaw. "Huh."

Melanie felt a surge of impatience. "When can I see Victor? I'm worried about him. His health hasn't been at all good."

"Look, Melanie, I realize the two of you are close, but right now the only people who should speak with Victor are police interrogators and his lawyer."

"All I want to do is say hello, and let him know he has a friend."

"I understand, but it's really not a good idea."

"Then I'll wait at the police station until you're done questioning him."

"Melanie, the media's been camping out in the station house. You should keep your distance."

"Why? Are you afraid I might tell them how wrong you were to have questioned a frail old man who also happens to be innocent? If you really suspect Victor of murder, then I must be right up there on your list as well. I'm surprised you haven't locked me up in a cell. Your Captain Murphy would love to see me behind bars. Well, you know what?" Melanie was standing now and not bothering to lower her voice. "To hell with Captain Murphy! To hell with the Los Angeles Police Department and while we're at it, to hell with you!" Melanie reached behind her and snatched up her purse. "Furthermore, I don't care about your police rules and regulations or what does or does not look good. I demand to see Victor as soon as possible. He needs to know he has someone on his side!"

Without another word, Melanie began swiftly walking back in the direction of the police station, attracting more than a few curious stares from people nearby enjoying some lunch-hour fresh air.

CHAPTER THIRTEEN

MURPHY LOOKED UP and called out to Kent as he walked past her office. He paused, hearing the tension in her voice, and then reluctantly glanced through her open door, eyebrows raised.

"Come in, close the door and sit down."

"Can it wait? We're due in the interrogation room in a few moments. We don't want to keep Mr. Korchin waiting…."

"This won't take long." Her eyes were unreadable. Kent sat, bracing for the storm while she folded her hands on her desk. "So. Did you have a nice lunch?"

"Midday Deli is always a sure bet for a great sandwich."

Murphy leaned forward and looked Kent directly in the eye. "Have you completely and totally lost your mind? Did I not, this very morning, tell you that you are hands-off when it comes to Melanie Harris?"

Kent nodded and shifted uncomfortably in his seat.

"And did I not, also this very morning, order you to cease any contact with her as far as this investigation went?"

Again, Kent could only nod, with a growing sense of his own doom.

"Then tell me, lieutenant, how is it two of my plain-clothes detectives, and God knows how many civilians, saw the two of you involved in a loud argument in the middle of Ocean Park not fifteen minutes ago? An argument during which I was told the name 'Korchin' figured more than once and quite prominently."

What could he say? His captain had him dead to rights. Maybe he should just get it over with and plead insanity.

"I'm waiting," Murphy said. The silence stretched out. "Kent, I don't want to see your career go down in flames. Especially not over this woman. I don't believe she can be trusted. She's given two statements and I still think she's holding something back. Am I wrong?"

Kent didn't answer right away. There was little doubt in his mind that Melanie was lost to him for good as anything other than a subject in the investigation, and yet he'd asked her to lunch in direct defiance of Murphy's orders because he'd wanted to see her on a personal level, not because he'd wanted to question her about Victor or Rachel or Stephanie or Petra. But afterward, he had, and he'd blown it all over again, with both Melanie and Murphy. Damn it! What was the matter with him? Murphy was right. He was losing his mind.

"You're wrong about her holding back information deliberately, but you're right about her knowing things we still need to know." Kent gave his boss a quick account of Melanie's recollection of Rachel's involvement with the Korchins and the probable identity of the mysterious "Petra."

Murphy listened with a critical expression. "That may prove useful," she conceded. "But I'm warning you, Kent. Step out of line one more time on this in any way that jeopardizes this case and I am going to be forced to kick the entire matter upstairs. I'm telling you this not just as your boss, but as your friend. You and I go back a long time but

I can only protect you so far. I would really hate for Internal Affairs to get their hooks into you."

"I understand."

"Make sure that you do." She stood and grabbed a stack of files from the top of her desk. "Now, as you said. Mr. Korchin awaits."

VICTOR KORCHIN sat in the interrogation room with a cup of black coffee in front of him and a look of dazed hopelessness on his distinctive but time-ravaged face. His lawyer, Daniel Marquette, a man close to Victor's age, sat across from him, his own expression one of great weariness. Marquette's hair was rumpled, his jacket was off and his tie was askew. When Kent and Murphy entered the room, he pushed back in his chair with a loud sigh of frustration. "Look," he said, splaying his hands on the tabletop, "my client has told you everything he's going to tell you. He's exhausted and he's not feeling well. Let me take him home. You have no reason to detain him any longer."

Kent ignored him, pulled out another chair across the table from Victor and dropped into it. He leaned forward on his elbows and studied the legendary director's face. "Mr. Korchin, I'm not going to feed you a line of crap about how all this'll go easier on you if you just help us out," he said. "Obviously you've decided that silence is the best policy, which it very well might be…if what you're trying to do is protect your wife." Victor's eyes flickered briefly to meet Kent's as he spoke, then dropped again. "I'm a lieutenant with the LAPD, Mr. Korchin, but I'm also a trained forensic psychologist. I profile criminal minds for the police department. We have all sorts of complex tests we conduct on suspects to give us an idea of their thought processes and motivations, but I think both you and I would agree that in this particular instance, administering those tests would be a complete waste of time…unless Anatanyia was the one taking them."

Victor Korchin's hands tightened around the coffee cup but he kept his eyes fixed on the tabletop. His breathing had become shallow and rapid.

"This is nothing less than inhumane," Marquette burst out. "First you bring Victor Korchin in for questioning on murder, a mistake on your part of grotesque proportions, and now you're casting disparaging shadows on his missing wife. Need I remind you that both Anatanyia and Victor Korchin are wealthy and highly respected citizens of this community?"

"Of *this* community, perhaps," Kent said. "But how much do you know about your client's past in Russia?"

Marquette pushed to his feet. "My client's background has no bearing whatsoever on his life in the United States. If you don't watch your step, *Lieutenant,* I'll file a lawsuit against the LAPD for defamation of character and ethnic discrimination." He leaned over the desk, conservative tie dangling and face flushed with anger. "You know what I think? I think you don't have a clue who killed those two young women. I think you're trying to appease that arrogant blowhard of a D.A., Brannigan. I think you're throwing him the most convenient bone you can find to help him look good, and it just happens to be Victor Korchin. Well, *know this.* I'm a senior partner in one of the most powerful law firms in this country. You drag this man through the dirt, and I'll drag your department through the fires of hell. You can count on that."

Murphy, who'd been standing near the wall, arms

crossed in front of her, stepped forward and leaned over the table, palms braced, squaring off against Marquette. "We've done everything by the letter of the law as far as this interrogation is concerned," she said. "By protecting his wife, Victor Korchin is opening himself to charges of aiding and abetting. If you really want to help your client, Mr. Marquette, you'll advise him to cooperate with us."

Marquette straightened to his full height and refastened his tie to the clip. "If you want to avoid a nasty lawsuit," he countered, his voice like flint, "you'll drop this now." The lawyer looked at Victor. "Come on, Victor, we're leaving."

"Not so fast," Kent said and pulled the thick envelope with the Russian postmark from his jacket pocket and laid it on the table, his movements smooth and deliberate. He withdrew the folded sections of newspaper from the envelope and flattened them on the table, turning them so that Victor could see the pictures and read the text. "These clippings came from Rachel Fisher's apartment. They were in a box of research material she'd compiled while working on your biography. But my guess is, you already knew that."

Victor lurched to his feet. Both men stared at the newspaper clippings for a few long moments, and then Marquette glanced at his friend with a puzzled frown. "Isn't that Anatanyia? What do these articles say?" Victor shook his head and sagged at the knees, bracing one hand on the table to support his weight while the other moved to his chest. His face had become the color of wood ashes and he struggled audibly for each breath, his eyes still fixed on the old newspaper articles.

"Victor, are you all right?" Marquette said, alarmed.

Murphy was summoning medical help from the interrogation room phone when Victor collapsed completely,
slumping forward onto the table and knocking over his cup
of coffee. She hung up the phone and helped Kent lower
him onto the floor, laying him flat on his back. Kent knelt
beside him and loosened the top buttons of Victor's dress
shirt, checking for his pulse. His own heart was thumping
wildly in his chest, but Victor Korchin's had stopped cold.
Kent broke into a sweat as he immediately began CPR.
"Get me the defibrillator!" he said to Murphy, who dashed
out of the room to retrieve the automatic external defibrillator hanging behind the door in the processing area.
"Come on, Victor, don't do this to me," he said as he continued the chest compressions. "You can't die on us now.
You're the only one who can tell us where Anatanyia and
Ariel are."

He was out of breath and counting his compressions out
loud by the time Murphy returned with the AED. She knelt
beside him on the floor, unzipping the red cordura case and
opening the two plastic leads while Kent ripped Victor's
shirt open, tore aside his undershirt and attached the
adhesive patches to the proper positions on Victor's chest.
He activated the defibrillator, not surprised when the sophisticated machine detected no heartbeat and began to
charge for immediate defibrillation. Kent watched the
blinking light and listened for the tone. "Stay clear," he said
before triggering the electrical charge to Victor's heart.

He checked for a pulse again even as the AED's electronic voice informed him that no further action was necessary. Victor's heart was beating once again, but the
rhythm was weak, rapid and erratic. To Kent's relief, two
EMTs arrived with a rush of swift footfalls down the

corridor. He moved aside as they reconnected the portable defibrillator's leads to their own heart monitor and took over. Within minutes, a stretcher was wheeled in and lowered. Victor was shifted onto it and he was whisked down the corridor, out of the precinct house and into a waiting ambulance.

After this brisk and efficient flurry of lifesaving activity, Marquette's face was nearly as gray as Victor's. He reached for the suit jacket draped over the back of his chair and paused at the door to jab his finger at them. "You'll be hearing from my law firm, Captain Murphy," he said. "I guess I don't have to tell you that the city will be footing all of his medical bills, and if Victor Korchin dies because of the uncalled-for abuse and harassment he suffered at your hands over the past thirty-six hours, believe me, you'll both live to regret it."

He slammed the door of the interrogation room behind him when he left, and in the silence that followed Murphy blew her breath out and ran her fingers through her hair. She moved to the table and glanced down at the newspaper clippings, shifting them away from the spreading pool of spilled coffee and studying the photographs of a much younger Anatanyia framed within the columns of foreign text.

"Well, you definitely got your reaction out of Victor Korchin," she said. "We can only hope he doesn't die on us before he can start talking." She glanced up at him with a cryptic expression and shook her head. "Nice going, Kent."

Kent was dazed—never in his wildest imagination had he figured on a suspect having a heart attack under his questioning. The realization of what had just gone down sickened him. He collected the newspaper clippings, thankful the EMTs had arrived so quickly, and wondered how he was going to break this latest shock to Melanie.

Walking out of the interrogation room, he saw a knot of people huddled at the end of the corridor. The show was over, but they were busily telling and retelling the events to each other and anyone who had missed the action. He started when he saw Melanie standing against the far wall, staring down the hall where Victor had been wheeled past moments earlier.

He hurried over to her, but before he had a chance to say a word, she whirled on him, her eyes snapping.

"What happened? My God, what did you do to him?"

Kent shook his head. "I'm sorry. He had a heart attack. I…"

"You should have left him alone! He's a good and gentle man. You had no right to arrest him and no right to keep him in this place." She pulled away from his touch. "Where are they taking him?"

"City General. I'll give you a ride…."

But Melanie was already moving down the corridor toward the main entry doors, a sob catching in her throat. Kent watched her go. If Victor died, he knew, Melanie would never, ever forgive him. For that matter, he'd never forgive himself.

THE EMERGENCY ROOM at City General was always busy, but seldom were there uniformed police officers guarding the doors. Melanie resented their presence and paced restlessly, watching medical personnel enter and leave through the swinging doors, listening to everything and anything for some clue as to Victor's condition, since the woman at the admission desk was most unhelpful. When Kent and Captain Murphy arrived together, Melanie put as much distance between them as she could but Kent immediately crossed the room toward her.

"Melanie, I'm sorry this had to happen," he said.

"It didn't have to happen," she said. "You *made* it happen. If Victor dies you'll have to find someone else to interrogate. No doubt I'm next in line."

He ducked his head and ran his fingers through his hair in a gesture of frustration. "Look, you have to understand that this is a police investigation, and we're doing everything we can to find three missing people, two of whom happen to be related to you."

"And you think Victor knows where they are? Why wouldn't he tell you if he did? He has nothing to hide!"

"Maybe not, but he has a wife he loves very much. A wife who might be involved in two deaths, and who might have already tried to kill you. A wife he might be trying to protect."

Melanie turned her back on him, blinking back the sting of tears. "Just leave me alone," she choked out. "We have nothing left to discuss." She was saved from further discussion by her cell phone ringing. Moving out through the exit doors to give herself some space from Kent, she dug the small cellular phone out of her purse, wiped her cheeks with the palm of her hand and cleared her throat.

"Hello?" she said.

"Melanie, oh, thank God! You have to help me."

Melanie was too stunned to answer. It was the last voice she'd expected to hear.

"Melanie, are you there? Please talk to me, I don't know what to do and I'm really scared."

Melanie finally found her voice. "Ariel? Oh, Ariel. Where have you been? Are you all right? Where are you?"

Five minutes later, Melanie drove her Mercedes sports coupe out of the hospital parking lot and headed for the interstate. "Hang on, Ariel," she said under her breath. "I'm coming."

As MELANIE drove south down the coastal highway, one eye on the speedometer and the other peeled for cops, she kept reviewing her brief and emotional conversation with Ariel outside the E.R. waiting room, trying to remember every small detail. Twice she had reached for her cell phone to call Kent and tell him that Ariel had contacted her, and twice she'd put it down again. She was still seething at the way he'd treated Victor, questioning him relentlessly about Anatanyia and causing him to have that heart attack. For all she knew, Victor was dead, which could only mean that she truly was next in line. Captain Murphy believed she was somehow involved in the murders of Rachel and Stephanie, and the disappearance of Ariel and Anatanyia. She hadn't said as much, of course, but during the questioning the captain had plainly exuded her distrust of Melanie.

Leaving the hospital without telling Kent about Ariel's call had been an impulsive move—and it was a move that she was beginning to regret as the coastal miles blurred past. Her anger had been steadily watered down by an increasing sense of foreboding, and she questioned the logic of attempting to rescue Ariel on her own. The phone conversation with Ariel had rocked her to the core, just as Melanie's revelations about the deaths of her two friends had shocked Ariel.

"How can they both be dead?" she'd said. "Oh, God, Melanie. I'm so scared. Anatanyia's acting so strangely. Please come."

"I'll come, of course I'll come," Melanie had replied. "Just tell me where you are!"

"That's just it, I'm not sure. It's a big place with a red tiled roof on the water in Mexico, in a very isolated spot with no neighbors. The sun sets over the water, so I think we're on the Pacific side of the Baja. Anatanyia told me about this place after the dinner party at Blackstone but never said where it was, just that it was on the water and very peaceful. She said she and Victor sometimes came here to get away from the Hollywood scene, and that it would be a good place for me to spend a week or so resting up before starting the filming of *Celtic Runes*."

Melanie could sense her sister fighting to keep control.

"She made it sound so beautiful that I agreed," Ariel said. "I wanted to spend one last night out on the town before leaving. Stephanie volunteered to babysit for me at the Beverly while I met with friends. And then, oh, God, she called me and told me she was feeling really sick, and when I got back to the hotel it was just after midnight and Stephanie was lying on the floor and my baby was in her crib crying. I couldn't wake her, Mel! I called Anatanyia. I didn't know who else to call. It was stupid, I know…I should have called 911 right off. She told me not to, that she'd call for medical help and I should get out before the ambulance arrived. She said the press would be sure to find out if I was there and the publicity would be really bad for me and could hurt the studio. Then she said she'd send her plane to pick me up right away. So I got the baby and drove to the airport and met it there. I know it was stupid to run off like that, but Anatanyia was so insistent and the baby was crying and I was so scared…. Oh, Mel, what have I done!"

Ariel's voice had become so hysterical that Melanie

could barely understand her. "Okay, Ari. Stay calm. Tell me who else is at the house with you," Melanie said.

"There's nobody but Anatanyia and me, and a servant or a bodyguard dressed in black, I'm not sure what he is but he's creepy. I flew here in the dark and all I know is that the flight wasn't more than an hour—less, even—and the house is very near the airstrip. Everything seemed fine, but then more and more she started taking Kathleen away from me, which I didn't mind at first. She was so much better with the baby, and Kathleen was so fussy, crying all the time and driving me crazy. Now she only lets me take the baby to feed her. But Mel, when I asked Anatanyia where we were, she just said that we're in heaven. She's acting more and more strangely, and when I told her I wanted to go home, she said I *was* home." Her voice lowered to a whisper. "I have to go, she's coming. I'll try to find out where we are and call you back."

Kathleen. Ariel had named her baby girl after their mother, Kathleen Julienne Harris. Melanie felt a stab of pain and regret that she hadn't gone to the hospital when Ariel had given birth to her niece. Oh, God. Anatanyia had already killed two people and the woman was obviously dangerously unbalanced. Dozens of questions whirled in her head. How did Anatanyia lure Ariel away in the first place? What if she did something to the baby, or to Ariel? And where *were* they? What was she to do until Ariel called again? Just keep driving south? Cross the border and stop at every private waterfront house facing the Pacific? *What was she to do?*

She reached for her phone a third time and dialed Kent's number. The phone rang and rang, and then the automated voice mail picked up. Melanie listened as the instructions

were given on how to leave a message for Dr. Kent
Mattson, and then when the beep came she blurted, "Kent,
it's Melanie. I'm…" She stopped, at a sudden loss for
words. What could she possibly tell him? She had no idea
where Ariel was. If she told him she was on her way to
rescue her sister, who was being held at an unknown
location, he'd think she was as crazy as Anatanyia. She
ended the call and laid the cell phone on the seat beside
her. She'd have to wait until Ariel called again with more
information.

Ten long minutes later, the phone rang, and she nearly
went off the road in her frantic haste to answer it. She
pulled over onto the gravel shoulder, throwing up a cloud
of dust, and put the car into Park. "Ari? Is that you?"

"Melanie. Ariel tells me that you are coming to visit
with us." The voice that responded was smooth and well-
modulated, with a hint of Russian accent.

"Anatanyia?" Melanie's mind raced in panic. "Where
is Ariel, and Kathleen? Are they all right?"

"Oh, they are fine. They are doing well, and they are
happy."

"Where are you, Anatanyia? Tell me where you are.
Ariel was so vague, you know how she can be. She
couldn't give me good directions." Heart pounding, mouth
dry, fingers clenching around the tiny cell phone, Melanie
held her breath.

"*Cielo,*" Anatanyia announced with great satisfaction.
"Heaven. I have prayed to God to be able to stay here and
never leave, I have prayed all my life, and we are here,
finally, only this time, I don't have to go away ever again.
This place is so beautiful. So very beautiful."

Melanie closed her eyes, cold sweat springing onto her

brow. "I'm sure it is, Anatanyia. Ariel told me it was. I can't wait to get there. I'm near the border crossing at Tijuana. Where do I go if I want to be with you in that beautiful place?"

There was a pause that lasted so long Melanie was sure the answer would never come. "You must only come if you can be here with us in peace," Anatanyia said.

"Peace sounds like just what I need," Melanie said.

"I have been praying all of my life for peace." Anatanyia's voice was pensive.

"We all pray for that," Melanie said. "Peace, and happiness."

"They are both here, in this place."

"Can you tell me how to get there? I need to find that, too. I need peace and happiness."

There was another long pause, during which three cars whipped past, southbound, and a seagull flew over, clamoring loudly in the bright afternoon sunshine. The air wafting through the open window smelled of hot tar and cool salty ocean. "How do I know that you deserve such things?" Anatanyia said, her voice suspicious now, challenging.

"How do any of us ever know if we deserve peace and happiness?" The woman was insane. Somehow, Melanie had to convince her to divulge her whereabouts. "Victor is so worried about you, Anatanyia." She managed to keep her voice even, speaking carefully through numbed lips.

"*Victor.*" Anatanyia fairly spat the name. "He worries only about his own career. He does not worry about me. He no longer loves me."

"You're so wrong. He loves you very much."

"Once, perhaps. But I could not give him what he wanted."

Melanie's grip on the phone tightened. "Tell me how to find you. We can talk about this when I get there."

"It was your sister Victor wanted. Ever since he first saw her. She is who he wanted, but I won't let him have her. He will never have her."

"Where on the Baja is this special place of yours, Anatanyia? Tell me."

"Ariel gave Victor what he wanted, but she is not a good mother. I don't want her here with us anymore. She does not belong."

"Tell me where you are, and I'll come and take her away from there."

Another long pause. "If I tell you, will you take only your sister, and leave the baby here with me? She is not good with the baby. She is not a good mother."

Melanie didn't hesitate. "I will leave Ariel's baby in a peaceful, happy place."

"Do you promise this to me?"

"I promise, Anatanyia."

"You will come to this place alone?"

"Yes. I'll come alone."

Two more cars sped past as Melanie waited, her body tense with anxiety. "I don't believe you," Anatanyia said. "You are just like the others."

"Please, Anatanyia." Melanie tried to keep the desperation out of her voice. "I'm alone. There's nobody with me."

"No. If you come, you will take the baby away. You do not belong here, either. If you try to find us, that would be a big mistake."

"Wait!" Melanie cried out, but the line had gone dead. She slumped forward, her forehead on the steering wheel, and burst into tears. Her life had become a twisted parody of a suspense thriller, and she felt very much like the helpless hand-wringing woman as she wept tears of frustration and fear. Movie credits ran through her tortured mind. She could almost hear the sinister music in the darkened theater as the crowd of moviegoers rose to leave.

Movie credits...

Melanie lifted her head. The credits of every movie that Korchin Productions produced always contained four people with Anatanyia's maiden name of Komeninski. It was common knowledge that they were relatives that Victor had hired and trained to fill various roles. One was a gaffer, one worked grips, two were gofers. Melanie knew them in the most casual of ways. They never visited Blackstone. Their lives, apart from the studio, were very mysterious. But several weeks ago, she had run into Stephen, the youngest of the Komeninskis, while leaving Victor's office. Not wanting to talk to anyone—she had only come in to sign some contract papers—Melanie had smiled politely without stopping, but the young man stepped in her path, pulling a letter from his pocket, a letter that held a picture of a baby boy. It was his first born, and he was beaming with pride. Stephen had shown her the picture of the newborn baby and she had made all the proper admiring noises, then asked where his wife and baby lived, so she could send a card of congratulations to the new mother.

Happily he had torn off the corner of the envelope with the return address and handed it to her. At the time, Melanie remembered thinking that it had probably been sent from Russia, but the return address was someplace in Mexico. When she mentioned that to Stephen, he had said,

"Yes, they are in Mexico, we are hoping that soon their papers will be good so they can move here, to be with me."

Melanie remembered stuffing the address into her purse and had not given it a thought since. Now she emptied the bag's contents on the passenger seat and rummaged through them. There! Triumphantly, she held up a wrinkled piece of torn paper. She turned it over and read, "Casa de Cielo, 3209 Bahía de Bonita Vista, Ensenada, Mexico." Ensenada was sixty or so miles south of the border, on the Pacific side of the Baja. It wasn't unusual that Victor and Anatanyia had never mentioned having a place in Mexico. They were extremely private when it came to their getaways, and who could blame them? They were dogged by paparazzi and fans every step they took. When they wanted to escape the Hollywood scene, they simply said they were going on vacation for a few days or weeks and disappeared. No one had ever questioned that behavior before, but now Melanie wished that she'd paid more attention. That's where Ariel had to be. Melanie fumbled for a tissue to wipe her eyes and blow her nose. Her stomach was in knots. Were Ariel and the baby still alive? She had no way of knowing. Could Anatanyia possibly hurt them? No!

And yet…hadn't Anatanyia already tried to kill her twice, once at the cliffs, and then a second time by sending Stephanie to her apartment with some of the poisoned dip? Would she try yet again when Melanie arrived at the villa with the red tile roof? Why would Anatanyia want her dead? Why had she poisoned Stephanie and Rachel? Had all this been leading up to the kidnapping of Ariel's baby? Melanie's heart was racing and her palms were damp as she pulled back onto the road. She couldn't possibly rescue

Ariel all by herself, but what sort of jurisdiction did the LAPD have in Mexico? Should she go to the local authorities and beg for their help?

No. Alone, she might stand a chance. Anatanyia might talk to her if she arrived by herself. She couldn't risk Ariel's life, or baby Kathleen's, by bringing the law into this. Somehow she was going to have to pull this off on her own. Maybe then, Kent would believe she had spoken the truth about what she'd known…and hadn't known. As much as she tried to convince herself that his opinion of her didn't matter, Melanie knew in her heart that it did. It mattered so much that she hadn't slept at all the night before, at Chimeya, even with Stannie's jasmine standing guard to keep her dark dreams at bay.

CHAPTER FOURTEEN

KENT GLANCED at his watch and fidgeted impatiently outside the emergency room. What was taking the doctors so damn long? He needed to question Victor about Anatanyia's whereabouts, but he was beginning to fear that he'd never get the chance. It seemed as if every few moments another doctor, nurse, or technician trotted into the E.R., and the two nonchalant badges stationed outside of the double doors seemed oblivious to the screaming tension of the situation, causing Kent's anxiety levels to rise ever higher. Where the hell was Murphy? She'd left fifteen minutes ago to hunt up a couple of cups of real coffee. And after taking that call on her cell phone from a friend over thirty minutes ago, Melanie had said she had to go to the ladies room and hadn't returned. How long did it take to powder a pretty nose? No matter. He wasn't going to worry about Melanie leaving the hospital, not as long as Victor's life hung in the balance.

He rounded his shoulders, shoved his hands into his jeans pockets and paced. He hated hospitals. Just being inside them reminded him of Susan's death, and the awful, endless days he had been laid up in the intensive care unit the time he'd botched two easy shots.... He walked out of the emergency room doors and stopped on the sidewalk.

He pulled his cell phone from the holder on his belt and started to call Murphy when he noticed the phone was off. He'd forgotten that he'd silenced it before entering the interrogation room. He activated it and checked his messages. There were three, the latest from his office, a change of appointment for a client the following week. One from Stannie. Bring home some Colman's dried mustard for the marinated pork loin she was grilling for supper. The third and final message nearly landed him on a stretcher beside the unconscious Victor Korchin with a heart failure of his own.

"Kent, it's Melanie. I'm…"

That was all, but that was enough. Melanie wasn't in the hospital.

He listened to her brief, heart-clutching message again, cursing her for not continuing to speak and cursing himself for speaking too much the night before and saying all the wrong things.

"Kent, it's Melanie. I'm…"

Her voice had been taut with fear. He knew Melanie was in trouble the same way he knew that she was deeply angry with him, the way he knew he was more than halfway smitten by her, and the way he knew that his life just wouldn't be the same without her, now that she'd broken through the walls he'd built around himself after Susan's death.

He called the cell phone number on the message screen and slumped with relief against the wall when Melanie answered on the second ring. "It's Kent," he said. "Are you all right? Why did you leave the hospital without telling me? And where the hell are you?"

"I can't tell you that, but Ariel's alive and I'm going

down to get her. I know you don't trust me, Kent, but I'm going to bring her back with me, her and the baby both. Maybe when you hear what Ariel has to say about Anatanyia, you'll start believing that I knew nothing about what happened to Stephanie and Rachel."

"Was it Ariel who called you on your cell phone while you were at the hospital?"

"Yes."

Kent ducked his head and pinched the bridge of his nose hard to keep from shouting into the phone. "Listen carefully," he said, speaking as calmly as he could. "If your sister is with Victor's wife, she could be in real danger. Do you understand?"

"Of course I understand!" Melanie cried out. "That's why I'm going to get her. Ariel is so scared. She says Anatanyia has her baby, and won't let her leave."

"Melanie, I want you to pull over," Kent ordered. "Pull the car onto the shoulder and stop driving." The long silence that answered him chilled his blood and cramped his fingers around the cell phone. He waited for what seemed like an eternity. "Talk to me, Melanie."

"I'm stopped," she said, her voice marginally calmer.

"You need to think carefully about the situation you're putting yourself into. You can't do this on your own."

"I don't want to, Kent, but I can't risk anything happening to Ariel and the baby." There was a definite tremble in her voice.

"You'll be exposing yourself to the same dangers if you go there alone. We have professionally trained police units who are experts at hostage situations. Just tell me where they are, Melanie. Tell me where you are."

"Why? So you can grill me, too, the way you did Victor?"

"Damn it, Melanie, I don't want you getting hurt. I'm sorry about what happened last night, and I'm sorry about what happened to Victor. Don't let the fact that you're mad at me cloud your judgment. I trust you and I care about you very much."

"I wish I could believe that, Kent. I really do."

He cursed as the line went dead, and was about to redial her cell number when he saw through the glass doors a lean, gray-haired doctor in wrinkled green scrubs come out from the E.R. By the time Kent reached him, the doctor had filled a paper cup at the wall-mounted water dispenser, drained it three times in quick succession and was turning back toward the E.R.

"Wait," Kent said, moving to intercept. "I need to question Victor Korchin. He has critical information that could help in an official police investigation."

The doctor shook his head. "I'm sorry. He can't be questioned now."

Kent blocked his way. "You don't understand. Innocent people's lives are at stake."

The doctor nodded with a hint of impatience. "I do understand, but right now, *his* life is at stake. He's not even conscious. We'll be moving him up to the critical care unit as soon as we get him stabilized and I'll be able to tell you more when the preliminary test results come back, but the way things are looking he's going to need an emergency shunt. We've scheduled him for immediate surgery, and…"

The E.R. door burst outward and a nurse, dressed in identical baggy green scrubs, came through and said, "Doctor, he's gone into arrest again."

The doctor shouldered past Kent and dove back into the E.R. The doors swung shut, but not before Kent caught a glimpse of Victor Korchin being furiously worked over by a team of medical professionals. He stood watching the drama through the small window high on the door, willing Victor's heart to beat, and was filled with a helpless rage as he spun from the window, exited the hospital again and retried Melanie's cell number. Her phone rang and rang but she stubbornly refused to answer his call. He tried Murphy, and his boss answered on the first ring.

"I'm standing in line at the Starbucks counter. How's Victor?" she asked.

"Alive, at least for the moment." He told her about Melanie leaving the hospital and about the brief but emotionally charged conversation he'd just had with her.

"So she sneaked off on us. Sweet," Murphy said with disgust. "I'll put an APB out on her vehicle. We should have kept her under strict surveillance or better yet, house arrest."

"She's not involved in any of this," Kent said. "What we should have done is kept her in protective custody."

"Your professional judgment has hit an all-time low, Kent. I wish you'd never invited that woman out to your ranch. No, strike that. I wish you'd never met her, period. If she were a mass-murdering serial killer, you wouldn't see it. Stay with Victor. If you get a chance to question him, do so. I'll put a triangulation tap on Melanie's cell phone number to try and find out where she's heading. We have the list of private aircraft that flew out of LAX between 2:00 a.m. and 8:00 a.m. on the morning in question and I have all the people I can spare working their way through it, but it's extensive."

"Narrow it down to commuter flights within driving distance of here," Kent said. "Melanie's going by car to rescue her sister and I doubt she's driving clear across the country."

"That's a given, but it's going to take some time. Victor might still be our best bet."

"Don't count on it," Kent muttered, looking back inside at the closed doors behind which the gray-haired doctor was still frantically working on Victor Korchin.

EACH MILE that Melanie drove closer to the border raised her anxiety level another notch. If her hunch was correct, and Ariel was somewhere south of Ensenada, it could take her another two hours to reach her. A lot could happen in two hours. Her cell phone rang and she picked it up to scan the screen. Kent again. He'd tried to reach her seven times. Would he never give up? She felt her throat cramp and tears sting her eyes as she turned the cell phone off and kept driving. Was she ever going to learn that men were not to be trusted? Kent had used her to further his own investigation, and she had blindly fallen for his tactics. She'd *wanted* to fall for them. She'd deliberately ignored all the warning signs because she'd wanted to believe in him. She'd wanted to believe that he truly cared about her.

What a fool she had been!

When Melanie approached the border crossing she began to tense. Surely the stern, uniformed man would take one look at her and think she was some sort of criminal. But to her surprise, she was whisked right through. Apparently leaving the country was easy. Getting back in was the hard part. She stopped at the first store she came to to purchase a map and sat in the hot parking lot plotting out her route. Moments later she was on her way, speeding south toward Ensenada.

Once there, however, finding Casa de Cielo proved more difficult. She knew it was south of the town, but that

was helpful only inasmuch as general location. There were
multitudes of properties with private drives leading to the
ocean. The young girl at the dusty cantina outside of
Ensenada had proved far more helpful than the map.

"*Sí*, señorita," she had said in a soft voice. "I know the
place you want. Casa de Cielo. My grandmother and
brother take eggs and vegetables there to the rich woman
when she calls."

Since the young girl had made the trip with her grandmother to the Korchins' villa several times, she was able to
provide Melanie with excellent directions. As it turned out,
the dotted line on the map indicating the road she now
followed ended on the page long before she spotted the
sprawling villa. Now she stood behind a large cactuslike tree
about fifty yards from the estate and considered her options.
To avoid immediate detection, she had left her car about a
quarter mile down the dusty road and walked this far.

Casa de Cielo may have very well been a lavish vacation
home, but to Melanie it had all the appearance of a veritable fortress. The two-level adobe structure was surrounded
by and well sheltered behind a massive perimeter wall at
least 30 feet high. From her vantage point on the slight rise,
she could see bright reflections of light on the top of the wall
and surmised that, either at its construction or sometime
later, the owners had added shards of sharp glass to the
finish layer of sealant. Glass guaranteed to shred the hands
and limbs of anyone foolhardy enough to attempt to climb
up and over.

Melanie bit her lip and studied the wrought-iron gate
guarding the immense circular driveway. Through the dec-
orative bars she could see a long black car parked to one
side. There was no sound of voices coming from within,

just the muted roar of the pounding Pacific surf from far below the cliffs on the other side of the house. For a moment she considered simply walking up to the gate, ringing the call box and demanding to be taken to her sister. There was little doubt such a stratagem would get her inside, but once there, would she be allowed to leave with her sister and niece? It was looking to be the only option when her thoughts were interrupted by the sound of an approaching vehicle. She quickly ducked farther down behind the tree's exposed and weathered root system. Soon, a battered and rusty pickup truck came into view and pulled to a stop in front of the gate. It backfired a few times before settling into a choppy idle and an old woman got out of the passenger side. She reached back in, pulled out a large wicker basket and shuffled over to the gate.

That must be the young girl's grandmother, the one who sells eggs and vegetables here, Melanie thought.

The woman's arrival must have been expected and the noisy truck had certainly announced her presence. Melanie saw a tall, heavily built man dressed entirely in black walk across the courtyard. As he approached the gate, she saw both his face and head were hairless and he moved with a lithe grace—the sign of either a professional dancer or well-trained fighter. Melanie doubted he had ever appeared at the Bolshoi.

Instead of opening the gate, he stepped to one side and Melanie started as an opening appeared in the solid wall, as if by magic. She realized it was a door styled after the town wall portals of medieval times, used for access when opening the gates was too cumbersome. As it was fashioned out of the same material as the wall, it had been well camouflaged. And, no doubt, locked.

The old woman stepped through and the door swung shut behind her.

Acting on a sudden hunch, Melanie quickly stood up and darted across the road to the gate. She glanced nervously over at the young man behind the wheel of the truck, and gave a small wave, trying with all her might to look like she had every reason in the world to be there. He barely acknowledged her presence. With a deep breath, she reached out and pushed on the door. As she had hoped, the man in black had not bothered to lock it for the brief period of time it would take to complete his business with the old woman. Melanie offered up a quick prayer that their business would not be taking place immediately on the other side as she opened the door wider. She stepped through and quietly shut the door behind her.

Trying to look in all directions at once and with the sickening realization she was completely exposed, she was relieved to find herself alone in the courtyard. But the sound of muted voices coming through a side door told her she would not be for long. Throwing caution to the wind, she scurried across the open expanse and through a set of terrace doors. And not a moment too soon. She had just stepped inside when the man in black and old woman reappeared. She moved behind a curtain where she could keep them in view and saw him usher her out the door. Once the old woman was on the other side of the wall, the man shut the door firmly and slid a large bolt into place. Melanie was relieved to see the lock was of the dead-bolt variety. It would make getting out much easier than if it had been a lock requiring a key or combination. The man in black watched the truck drive off and then walked back to the side of the house.

Now that she was inside, she took a moment to allow her breathing to slow and her eyes to adjust to the cool dimness of the interior. It was nothing she had expected. In fact if she had not known better, Melanie would have sworn she had stepped into a museum, and a very good one at that.

The Korchins' home at Blackstone was of a decor reflective of what Melanie termed the neo-antique movement currently sweeping through Southern California. The rooms were an eclectic blend of early American reproduction and authentic pieces with the appearance far outweighing any authenticity. But this was like stepping into the Winter Palace in St. Petersburg. Melanie was standing in a large room with polished tiled floors. In the center a marble pedestal supported a massive bowl carved from green granite and edged with exquisite gold and silver work. Huge paintings done in thick oils of dark, bearded men holding lances on horseback covered one wall. Intricate tapestries were draped on the other walls. A gleaming samovar all but obscured the top of the solid wooden sideboard on which it perched. Wonderfully decorated hand-carved instruments, including traditional *tsimbaly* and a stringed *balalaika* hung from one wall. Glass-covered cases within the room held any number of beautiful objects including a variety of carved wooden icons, *matrëshka* nesting dolls and even a delicate Fabergé egg.

Astounded, Melanie walked around the entire room and stopped in front of a case with numerous leather-bound books. Even to Melanie's untrained eye, they looked like first editions and, she would be willing to bet, probably signed ones at that. On a stand next to the case a large gilt-edged book lay open revealing intricate and bright illuminations on the pages.

Melanie shook her head at the sheer volume of precious and valuable objects. But she forced herself to move on. Under different circumstances, it would have been marvelous to linger and study the items. But she was here on a mission, and one in which time was of the essence. Quietly, she tiptoed from the room to an outer hallway. Looking to the right and to the left, she saw that it extended about fifty feet in either direction before making right-angled turns. Across the hallway was a wall of glass overlooking an inner courtyard. She surmised the hall ran in a complete square around the courtyard with the house's rooms constructed off the outer side. It was massive and she hesitated a moment, daunted by the challenge of finding her sister.

She had not yet seen another soul in the house, but could now hear the faint sounds of a piano coming from a room several doors down. Knowing her sister hadn't a musical bone in her body, she swiftly walked in the opposite direction and found herself at a wide stairway leading to the second story. Gambling that Anatanyia would want to keep her reluctant guest on an upper level, and thus more easily constrained, she rushed up the stairway, stopped on the upper landing and peered around. At least half a dozen closed doors faced this side of the square and she suspected the other three hallways held as many rooms. Where to start? Once again, she lucked out and before she could move, a door just to the right opened a crack. She could just make out the shape of a body on the other side before it was thrown wide open and she was looking directly into the face of her sister.

"Melanie!" Ariel cried. "Is it really you? How did you get here? Quick, come inside!"

Before she could speak, Melanie allowed herself to be

pulled into the room by a now-crying Ariel. Once the door was shut behind her, her sister threw her arms around her and, sobbing, buried her head on her shoulder.

"I'm so glad you're here," Ariel gasped between sobs. "I'm so afraid."

Melanie held Ariel close. "Shh, it's all right. I'm here now. Everything's going to be fine," she said with a great deal more confidence than she felt. Looking over her sister's shoulder, Melanie spied an ornate bassinet standing next to an equally elegant cradle. Disengaging herself from Ariel's grip, she walked over and saw for the first time her niece— Mitch's baby. She was completely unprepared for the wave of unconditional love that surged through her, making her almost dizzy. "Hello, Kathleen," she said softly. "I'm your aunt Melanie. It's nice to meet you." In that moment she knew she would die before letting any harm come to this small bundle that was, at least in part, of her flesh and blood.

Oblivious to the significance of the moment, Kathleen opened and closed her small mouth, made a cooing sound and promptly fell back to sleep. Unnoticed by Melanie, Ariel had come to stand by her, still sniffling.

"Tell me what's going on here," Melanie said. "But do it quickly, we have to get out of here before Anatanyia or that thug downstairs knows I'm here."

Ariel pulled herself together and looked with huge eyes at Melanie. "Anatanyia doesn't know you're here? How did you get in?"

"It's a long story, and one that will have to wait. We have to leave now. I mean *right* now. My car's about a quarter mile up the road. If you can't walk there with the baby there's a great tree to hide behind and I can come and get you…. Ariel? What on earth?"

Tears had once again sprung to Ariel's eyes and she had sat down hard on the bed.

"You don't understand. There's no way out of here. Don't you think Kathleen and I have tried to leave? This place is in the middle of nowhere, and that creepy Mikhail is everywhere!" Ariel buried her face in her hands, weeping again.

With a sigh, Melanie sat down next to her sister on the bed and put an arm around her. "Tell me everything," she said. "But do it fast."

Ariel nodded and gave one last huge sniff.

"At the dinner party I named Anatanyia as Kathleen's godmother. She'd been so helpful, setting the nursery up at the guest house, and so good with the baby. It seemed to really bring us closer together. I think that's why she invited me here."

Melanie nodded, doing her best to cover the surprising waves of hurt and resentment at the news that Anatanyia, not she, had been made Kathleen's godmother.

"I told Victor I wanted him to be the godfather. He loved the idea. Oh, Mel, you should have seen his face, and the way he held little Kathleen in his arms and rocked her back and forth."

"Did Victor know about Anatanyia's invitation to you to visit this place?"

Ariel shook her head. "I'm not sure. We were alone when she invited me to come here. Anatanyia said she would fly down here a day or so before us, to make sure the villa was open and our room suitable for the baby. That was fine with me, because, like I told you earlier, I wanted to spend a night with some old friends out on the town while Steph babysat Kathleen…" Ariel sniffed and wiped her eyes. "She took Kathleen and checked into the suite while I met with friends at a favorite restaurant. I thought it would be easier to rent the suite for Steph and Kathleen because it was so close to the restaurant, in case Kathleen got fussy, or whatever. You know. But when Steph called me, I was at the nightclub then, and she sounded terrible. She asked me to come to the hotel right away. So I did, and well, you know the rest."

Melanie nodded.

"When I got here, Anatanyia told me she had called the hospital and everything was fine with Stephanie, it was just a bad case of food poisoning. She fixed me a nice meal and took care of Kathleen and let me rest. At first, it was wonderful," Ariel said. "So much had happened, Mitch dying in the awful accident and then the baby being born…" She looked directly at Melanie. "And worst of all, losing you. For the first two days all I did was sleep by the pool and eat little meals. I was so exhausted after everything that had happened. But then, things started getting strange. The second night we were here, Anatanyia wouldn't let me take Kathleen back up to my room after supper. She said the baby preferred being with her, and that she thought it was best if Kathleen's crib was moved into her room. That way I could get better quality sleep and recover from the birth more quickly. At least that's what she said, but Melanie, she had Mikhail take me to my room and when I tried to get out, the door was locked!"

"Mikhail is the bodyguard?"

Ariel nodded. "The man in black. He never speaks. He's creepy. Ever since that night, Anatanyia only lets me hold Kathleen when I have to nurse her, and then that's only for an hour at the most.

"Last night, Anatanyia started screaming at me during supper, accusing me of all sorts of dreadful things having to do with Victor. Then she said that she was a better mother than I would ever be and that no one but her would ever raise Victor's child. Mel, I really think she's insane."

Melanie was inclined to agree. And that made her more determined to get the three of them safely out of there as soon as possible. But she was halted by a sudden thought. "Ari," she said, "why didn't you call me before today?"

"When I arrived here Anatanyia took my cell phone away. She said I mustn't have any distractions—rest and peace was what I needed. Actually, it didn't bother me then. There was nobody I wanted to talk to. I just wanted to sleep. But when she started acting strange, I looked for a phone. I couldn't find her landline in the house, and I looked everywhere, believe me. Then, this afternoon, I found my cell phone in a kitchen drawer while looking for a clean dish towel. That's when I called you."

"But you were caught?"

"She came onto the balcony while I was talking to you. I tried to hide it from her, and then I sneaked it back into the drawer. She never said anything. She was singing a lullaby to Kathleen. I wasn't even sure she saw me, but if you're here, she obviously did. She must have called you and told you how to get here."

"No. She called me and warned me not to come. Tell me about the bodyguard."

"His full name is Mikhail Stanislavovich Komeninski. I don't know anything about him other than he is never far from her side. I can't believe you got past him without being seen."

"All the more reason to hightail it out of here. We're running out of time. Get Kathleen, Ari. We have to hurry!"

Ariel picked Kathleen up and whispered soft words into her daughter's ear, and Melanie grabbed a few of what she thought to be the most essential things needed for a baby, extra clothes, diapers and a blanket, and started for the door.

"Wait!" Ariel said.

"Now what?" Melanie said with more than a little impatience. She was growing more certain discovery was only moments away.

"The little bear, please."

Melanie looked in the direction Ariel was pointing and saw a nondescript stuffed brown bear.

Ariel sniffed and said, "Mitch bought that for the baby a few weeks before he died. It's...it's the only present Kathleen will ever have from her daddy."

Melanie felt the familiar stab of betrayal in her stomach, but grabbed the bear and pushed Ariel through the bedroom door, where her sister froze and let out a cry of despair.

"Ariel, we have to be quiet and——" Melanie looked past her sister and her whole body went rigid as she saw the stately woman standing there.

"Melanie. What a nice surprise. How good it is to see you," Anatanyia Korchin said. "You must think me a rude hostess not to have greeted you upon your arrival."

CHAPTER FIFTEEN

KENT WAS CURSING himself for what must have been the one hundredth time for his ambushing Korchin with the old news clippings, when he spied a young surgeon coming from the O.R. and looking around the waiting room. Seeing Kent, the doctor walked over to him.

"How is he?" asked Kent.

"It was touch and go, still is in my opinion," the doctor said in that detached, impersonal medical tone Kent had come to loathe. "We've inserted a temporary shunt to keep him alive, but no guarantees."

"Can I talk to him?" Kent said.

"The patient is far from being out of the woods at this point. He coded three times on the table but we brought him back. We're still waiting on some tests and for the chief cardiologist to take a look at the results, but my guess is we are looking at a triple, maybe even quadruple bypass. Installing the shunt was a temporary procedure just to keep him alive."

Kent took a deep breath. "Is he conscious?"

"Barely. He couldn't withstand general anesthesia in his current condition so we performed the emergency surgery using a spinal block. The procedure went well, and his blood oxygen levels are rising, but like I said, he isn't out of the woods by a long shot."

"Can he respond to questions?"

The doctor looked disgusted and shook his head. "I'm not even sure he knows his own name. Look, you don't seem to understand the gravity of his condition."

Kent was about to explain that the information in Victor Korchin's head not only held the clue to the murder of two women, but also the location of at least two others who were in very real danger, but before he could, a condescending voice said, "No, he doesn't, doctor, but I do. If you don't mind, I'd like Mr. Korchin placed in a private room with no outside visitors allowed at all."

Kent whirled around and came face-to-face with Daniel Marquette.

"Who the hell are you?" said the doctor.

"I am Mr. Korchin's attorney. It is my considered opinion that this man here—" Marquette gestured toward Kent "—is largely responsible for my client's current condition. It was during the antagonistic questioning at the hands of the LAPD, and under direct supervision of this man, that Mr. Korchin suffered his heart attack. There is no medical or legal reason to allow him access to my client."

Pompous ass, Kent thought to himself. "Look, Marquette, you know as well as I do you can't keep me from questioning Mr. Korchin." Turning to the doctor he said, "Victor Korchin is the only man who can help us. Legally and ethically you have to let me talk to him."

"You will do no such thing!" Marquette said. "And while I can't keep you from asking questions, I promise you I will advise my client not to answer them!"

"Hold it, both of you," the doctor said. "I'll decide what is medically and ethically best for Mr. Korchin. He may be your client—" he looked at Marquette "—and he may be your suspect—" he looked at Kent "—but for the time being, he's my patient and this is my O.R. The two of you can shut up and sit down until we have Mr. Korchin fully stabilized and moved to an intensive care bed."

With that he turned and went back through the O.R. doors.

Kent and Marquette glared at each other for a moment and, to Kent's immense satisfaction, it was Marquette who looked away first. Muttering dire threats about "slander" and "police brutality," the attorney retreated to the bank of pay phones in the corner of the waiting room, and began making calls, casting furious glances in Kent's direction.

Two can play at this game, Kent thought, walking to a row of phones at the opposite wall, pulling out some change and punching Murphy's number.

His boss sounded tired when she picked up on the third ring. "How's our boy?" she asked.

"Not so good." Kent filled her in on the doctor's dire prognosis and finished with Marquette's untimely and intrusive appearance.

"Okay, Kent, hang tight. The only one who can keep us from talking to Korchin is Korchin."

"Unless Marquette gets to him first and advises him to keep quiet," Kent said.

"Well then, it's up to you to make certain Korchin sees the wisdom of coming clean," Murphy said. "You also might want to remind Marquette that, as unfortunate as Korchin's heart attack was, it occurred while in police custody, meaning we are legally responsible to keep an officer with him at all times."

Marquette had been, predictably, red-faced with rage

when he realized Kent had every intention of conducting a bedside interrogation. But after fifteen minutes of bluster, he was forced to concede—with none too good grace— there was nothing he could do about it. Kent would be lying to himself if he tried to deny the pangs of guilt he felt at the prospect of questioning a man who was, quite literally, on his deathbed. But he ignored them and told himself there was no other way.

Flanked by a flock of outraged doctors and trailing the still muttering Marquette in their wake, Kent had been ushered in to Korchin's room. What he saw made him instantly regret what he knew he had to do. The man in the bed bore little resemblance to the one he had questioned only hours earlier. Korchin's skin still held an unnaturally pale pallor and hung in loose folds from his face. There were dark smudges under his eyes and his breath was shallow, his chest rising and falling ever so faintly in time with the monitors clustered at his bedside.

"Thank you, Doctor," Kent said. "If you will please leave us?"

Lips pressed into a thin line, the head surgeon ushered the staff out of the room.

He knew getting rid of Marquette would not be as easy. "I don't suppose there's any point in my asking you to leave?" he said.

Marquette did not even answer. He just grunted and sat down in the folding chair nearest the door. Kent shrugged, turned away and pulled the only other chair in the room as close to Victor as the machines around him allowed.

"Mr. Korchin... Victor..." he said softly. "This is Lt. Kent Mattson, it's important we speak, sir."

No immediate response.

"Mr. Korchin, please, lives may depend on what you know...."

"For the love of God, man, this is inhumane." It was Marquette.

Kent spoke without looking around or raising his voice. "Mr. Marquette, at least three lives depend on what Victor Korchin can tell me. I'm asking you as one professional to another, let me do my job."

More grumbling from Marquette's direction, but he did remain blessedly silent.

Kent tried again. "Mr. Korchin, I'm sorry to have to tell you this now, but we are afraid Melanie, Ariel and your wife are all in trouble. We need you to help us find them."

At this, Victor's eyelids flickered open and his lips moved.

"What's that, what did he say?" said Marquette.

"Listen, I'm asking you for the last time, shut up or get the hell out of here!" hissed Kent. "Mr. Korchin? What was that?"

It was not loud enough to be termed even a whisper, but by putting his ear almost to Korchin's mouth, Kent could make out the words.

"Don't hurt my beautiful Anatanyia..."

"We won't hurt her, we want to help her," said Kent.

"She is so beautiful. She has so much talent. Life was so cruel to you, my little Tanyia. Don't worry, I will protect you. No one will harm you anymore or make you do those things again. But you have to trust me."

What followed was lost to Kent as Victor lapsed into Russian and appeared to slip into unconsciousness. He leaned over the bed, his heart squeezed in a tight fist of desperation.

"Victor, your wife could be in danger. Do you know where she is? Ariel could be with her, and Melanie. They could all be in danger."

Victor roused. His eyes flickered open, but it was obvious he was no longer in the hospital room. Instead, he had retreated to a place and time thirty years prior, a place and a time which just happened to coincide with the missing portions of Rachel's biography. Was it the shock of seeing those old Russian news clippings that sent Victor there? Kent could not begin to guess. He was startled when Victor suddenly called out, "Tanyia! Tanyia! No, no, please, leave her alone. She is only a child!"

"Who's hurting Tanyia, Victor? What are they doing to her?"

Kent was taken aback when he saw a tear slide from beneath Korchin's eyelid.

"Only a child, a child…" Victor mumbled before again reverting to his native Russian.

"C'mon, Victor, stay with me," Kent said. "Tell me where Anatanyia is. I can help her if you tell me."

But Victor was firmly entrenched in reliving the past, and try as he might Kent couldn't steer him back to the present. Finally, hoping that he could fast-forward the story, Kent stopped trying to direct the conversation and instead encouraged Victor to keep talking. It felt like forever, but eventually the story of Victor and Anatanyia came to light. On numerous occasions Kent had to guide Victor back into the English language, and he was not completely certain of the time line, but he was confident enough he had the facts. And, should they be corroborated, they supplied more than enough motive for murder.

"Victor," Kent asked when the older man had seemed to run out of words. "Victor, can you tell me where Anatanyia has taken Ariel?"

The ghost of a smile appeared on Victor's lips, and his almost inaudible words chilled Kent's heart. "If she took them anywhere, it would be to heaven."

EVEN AS KENT was leaving the I.C.U., doctors and nurses, each casting burning looks at Kent, were coming into the room to fiddle with machines and check Victor's vital signs. "He seems to be stabilizing, no thanks to you," were the doctor's parting words.

Kent had walked in a daze from the room to the elevators and out of the hospital. But with renewed determination, he started his rental car and headed for the police station. A half hour later, it was Murphy's turn to look stunned as she sat, openmouthed, across Kent's desk.

"Well, I have to say, it does explain a few things," she said.

Kent nodded.

The captain sprang to her feet, pacing. "So, let me make sure I understand. According to what Victor told you, when Anatanyia had her accident during the Olympic competition that knocked her out of competitive skating for good, she was beholden to more than the Russian government."

"That's right," Kent said, looking at his own notes. "On paper, she was fully sponsored by the old Communist regime, something that was fairly common in those days, despite prohibitions against professional athletes in Olympic competition. But several of the governmental officials had pretty shady backgrounds. Sounds like they were dangerous characters with close ties to the Russian mafia. Grooming champion athletes was big business with big payoffs. The other side of that, of course, were the equally big and far more common losses."

"Losses that were made up in the various illegal operations the mob ran, including porn film production," Murphy said.

Kent nodded. "Had she refused, according to Victor, her family members would have paid the price. She had no choice but to follow their orders. Victor knew about the threats to her family, and he knew that getting her and her family away from the mob would be a risk bigger than any he would ever take, but against all odds he snatched the entire Komeninski clan out from under the noses of the Russian mob and, with the help of a network of fellow dissidents, he spirited them out of the country."

"But *where?*" Murphy said.

"All I could get out of him was that they holed up in this safe place for over a year before moving to California and during that period of time he and Anatanyia had wed."

Kent would gladly give up a year's pay and then some to know where Melanie was. The only clue he had was Victor's cryptic comment about "taking them to heaven." He was going through his notes from the interrogation for the fourth time, thinking he might have missed something, when Murphy took a call.

"We might have something," she said, hanging up the phone. She opened her office door, disappeared for several moments, then reappeared and plunked a file folder on his desk. "The officers searching Blackstone just sent this over. They found it in Victor's private office. It's copies of deeds to various properties owned by the Korchins. Before sending it up the guys downstairs made an indexed list. It's on the first page."

Kent flipped to it and whistled under this breath.

"That was my reaction, too," Murphy said.

Kent scanned the list. Along with the Blackstone estate, impressive taken alone, the couple owned a bungalow in Hawaii, a deluxe condo in Vail, a Manhattan townhouse, an entire island in the Bahamas and a villa on the French Riviera.

Kent swore under his breath. "There's not one damn place listed that you can drive to easily from here," he muttered.

"Colorado isn't all that far," Murphy pointed out.

He shook his head. "When Melanie spoke to me she said she was going *down* to get her sister…"

"Down?" Murphy was looking at him intently. "You're just remembering this little detail, after I put out a state-wide APB on her vehicle?"

Kent met his boss's sharp gaze and remembered with an equally sharp twinge of guilt that he'd treated Melanie's imperfect recall the same skeptical way. "Victor went into cardiac arrest while I was talking to you on the phone." Kent shrugged an apology. "I thought I told you, I must not have. You can throw the book at me, cashier me, make me stand in the corner. Just help me figure out how to find her before we have more victims to deal with. Melanie said she was going down to get her sister. Down meaning south? South of the border? Mexico, maybe…?"

Kent paced to the window. "But where?" He narrowed his eyes on the busy streets below, his thoughts racing. "When I was reading through Rachel's draft, it briefly referenced the estate where Victor and Anatanyia spent their tenth wedding anniversary. There was no mention of the location, just that it was a private hideaway that they called *Cielo*." Kent spoke slowly, rehashing everything he knew, trying to fit the pieces of the puzzle together even while knowing that every second counted in the race to rescue Melanie from certain danger. Suddenly the pieces clicked and he turned to Murphy with a surge of excitement. "Of course! *Cielo* means 'heaven' in Spanish!"

"You've lost me."

Kent flipped his notebook to the last page. "The last thing Victor told me was Anatanyia had probably taken Ariel and the baby to 'heaven.' I thought he was rambling about something sinister, but what if they own a property in Mexico, someplace within driving distance, a private hideaway they didn't want anyone to know about?"

"A property that might not show up on their portfolio?" Murphy said.

"It could be held in any number of ways, as a corporate entity, in a friend's name... How the hell would we ever track something like that? What about under her maiden name, Komeninski?"

Murphy shook her head. "We've already tried that and all we came up with was the fact that four Komeninskis, all related to Anatanyia, are employed by Korchin Productions. Detectives are questioning all of them, just in case they know anything at all about where Anatanyia is."

Kent paced the office, consumed with a growing sense of helplessness. "Damn it, we need information *now.* We need the pilot who flew Ariel and her baby out of the city to resurface. We need Melanie to turn on her phone. We need a miracle. How do we track someone who's just driven off into the sunset and doesn't want to be found?"

"There may be a way." Murphy stood. "Follow me."

Kent trailed Murphy up a flight of stairs into the LAPD's technical nerve center. It was a domain he rarely entered, being suspicious of computers that required special languages to operate. Murphy slid her ID card into the door scanner and it opened remotely. The entire floor was open and full of cubicles, each with a flat screen computer and a departmental staffer monitoring any number of programs, information streams and surveillance operations.

"Thank you, Homeland Security," Murphy said, walking down one of the aisles. "The feds paid for most of this. Grant money to fight terrorism." She stopped at a cubicle in which a young woman with more visible piercings than Kent had thought possible was downloading files. "Kent, meet Tess," Murphy said.

"Hi," he said, holding out his hand to the woman.

She took it and laughed. "I'm Wendy," she said. "This is Tess." She pointed to the humming computer. "Tactical Electronic Surveillance System. Access to the best and most sophisticated satellite imaging available. Take a look."

Kent leaned over while Wendy punched in a series of numbers on the keyboard. The screen flashed and suddenly an overhead image of the LAPD squad house appeared.

"Impressive," Kent said.

"Ah, that's nothing. Where are you parked?"

"The upper lot," Kent said.

"Watch this." A few clicks of the mouse and the screen again changed to show the upper parking lot. "Which end?"

"South, middle section." More clicks and Kent's rental car could easily be seen, as if someone had taken a photo of it and placed it on the computer.

"Okay, enough show and tell," Murphy said. "We need real-time images from Highway 5 to the border of Mexico and south of that as well." She handed Wendy a sheet of paper. "We're looking for this suspect's vehicle. All the information you need is there. It could be on the road or at an isolated and probably waterfront villa. Can you also reference highway images from the past three hours?"

"Sure," Wendy said. "They're stored in the main brain for at least three days. But it could take some time."

Kent and Murphy looked at the screen where the real-time satellite image was showing grid after grid of highway, cars and trucks frozen in place. Zooming in close enough to identify the vehicles. Trying another grid. Zooming in. Section by section. Kent swore under his breath and turned away, running his fingers through his hair. "That could take forever."

"It's a long shot, but right now it's all we have," Murphy said. "We can keep trying to triangulate her position using her cell phone, but unless she activates, we're out of luck. All we can do is wait and hope Wendy can find her vehicle."

"No, that's not all we can do," Kent said, turning.

"Where are you going?"

"To look for Melanie," he shot over his shoulder, walking fast. "I can fly a hell of a lot faster than Wendy can bring up those satellite images."

"Hold on, Kent," Murphy said, hurrying after him. "I told you before, you're off the active end of this case. What you're going to do is get your butt back to your desk and finish those profiles. I'll get a hold of the border patrol. They can send planes up…."

Kent whirled to face her. "You don't understand. Melanie's in trouble because I screwed up. I should never have let her out of my sight. I promised her I'd keep her safe."

Murphy raised her hand in warning. "You're not doing this, Kent. You care way too much about this young woman and you're not thinking rationally. You can't fly across the border without the proper clearance."

"So get me the proper clearance," he snapped.

They squared off, each angry. "As of this moment, you're officially off the case," Murphy said. *"I mean it."*

Kent was closer to losing it with his boss than he'd ever come before. He drew two steadying breaths and then nodded, reached inside his jacket for his pistol and police ID and laid them both on the nearest desk, startling the technician who watched in wide-eyed silence.

Without another word he took his leave of the police station, perhaps for the last time. He felt numb as he crossed the parking area to the rental car and slid behind the wheel. The interior was scorchingly hot. He started the engine and boosted the air-conditioning to max. The sun was low in the western sky. There wasn't much time for visual flying. Two hours at the most. With a little luck, he'd find her before darkness closed off the search. Okay, with a lot of luck. In fact, if he found her at all it would be miraculous, but the odds would be a whole lot better if he had a spotter on board....

As he pulled out of the parking area he realized the futility of what he was doing, but he couldn't sit and do nothing. A swift flash of movement exiting the side door of the building caught his eye and he hit the brake just before pulling out into traffic. Murphy approached the car at a brisk walk, chin high, dark eyes burning. She opened the passenger door and slid in, laying his pistol and police ID next to him. She gave him the briefest of glances before slamming her door. "No way am I letting you do this on your own," she said. "Besides, facing down a hostage situation in Mexico without proper clearance beats the hell out of my regular meeting with Brannigan."

CHAPTER SIXTEEN

IT HAD BEEN TEN YEARS since Kent had last crossed the border into Mexico. He and Susan had flipped a coin on who'd get to choose where they'd spend their next vacation, and Susan had won. She had paused for a moment, considering all the tempting choices they'd discussed, and then smiled that mysterious smile of hers. "I think this year we'll vacation in El Dorado," she announced.

"Where the hell's that?" Kent asked. "We never even talked about a place called El Dorado."

"It's north of Mazatlán, south of Los Mochis, east of Durango."

"Sounds Mexican to me."

"It's very Mexican, and the exchange rate is excellent. We could retire today, the both of us, and live there for the rest of our lives in relative prosperity on our earnings to date."

"And we can drive there," Kent guessed.

"Oh, yes. Every wonderful inch of the way."

Susan hated to fly as much as Melanie did...maybe even more. On long flights she'd taken tranquilizers that zonked her to the verge of unconsciousness, but only when Kent was along to chaperone. If he'd won that toss, she'd be stocking up on tranquilizers, but instead of hiking from pub to pub across the English countryside or exploring the foothills of Nepal, they drove from Taos to El Dorado and spent two incredible weeks holed up in a beachside shack with metal roofing and siding fashioned from packing crates huddled between two ancient mesquite trees, with a Coleman cook stove and cooler, a box of groceries, bottles of water, jugs of wine and each other. They swam in the Gulf of California, searched for gold coins from legendary shipwrecks along the graceful curve of the private beach and pretended they were the only two people on earth, not hard to do in such an isolated place.

On the fifth day the stray dog showed up. A pup, really, all skin and bones and strange wiry fur. Ugly as sin. Of course, Susan immediately adopted it. "We'll call him Loki," she said. "We need a good watchdog." Kent had looked at the sorry excuse of a dog, thinking that it probably wouldn't live out the week, and shaken his head, but Loki had returned with them to Taos and outlived Susan. Such were the ironies of life. Now he was returning to Mexico, also because of a woman, though this could hardly be considered a vacation trip.

"Penny for your thoughts." Murphy's voice came over his headset. She was scanning the ground below with a pair of binoculars as he flew, which was a tremendous help. Also helpful had been her connections to the border patrol and a few key contacts in Mexico, without which they would undoubtedly have attracted a hostile escort of F-16s from Mirimar Naval Air Station as soon as they crossed the border.

"My thoughts aren't worth that much," Kent responded, blinking the sting of weariness from his eyes. It felt as though they'd been in the air for hours. He checked the fuel levels for the thousandth time. It was unnerving watching them deplete and not knowing where he was going to land, or when. The landscape below was bathed in rose and gold, the final colors of a glorious sunset over the Pacific Ocean. Kent wondered, as the sun began to sink into the vast, sparkling waters, if he would see the green flash that Melanie had spoken of. He tried her cell phone number again. No answer. Not surprising.

The tension that had been building steadily in him since she'd disappeared had reached a level that was almost unendurable. Images of Susan's body kept flashing through his tormented mind. Would Melanie suffer the same fate because of him? Why hadn't he been able to put the clues together quicker? Why couldn't Wendy call them with coordinates to Melanie's location? Why didn't Melanie turn on her damn phone so they could triangulate her position? Was she already dead?

"Kent," Murphy said, lowering the binoculars and focusing on him. "We're going to have to turn back."

He shook his head. "No. She's down there somewhere. We have to find her."

"We're running low on fuel."

"There's an airport in Tijuana. We can refuel there, or in Mexicali."

"We're running out of daylight, too," Murphy pointed out, "and there isn't an airport in the world that can provide us with more of that."

"We have another half hour or so, and our fuel will last that long. She's down there, Murph. She's in trouble and needs our help."

"Kent…" Murphy began, then stopped as the plane's

com was activated. They listened to the call sign and Kent reached to trigger his mike with a fresh surge of hope.

"Go ahead, Wendy," he said. "What've you got? Over."

"Bad news, I'm afraid," came Wendy's voice. "TESS is temporarily down. Some sort of glitch with the server access. It shouldn't last that long, these things never do, but it's holding things up, and once it gets dark we're out of luck. I've scanned all the images in the main brain back to the time you requested. So far we haven't come up with a silver Mercedes sports coupe. Over."

"Damn it, her car has to be somewhere on that highway. Look harder!" Kent snapped.

"Yes, lieutenant. We'll keep looking."

Kent ended the transmission with a silent curse. He could feel the band of tension tightening across his chest as he radioed back to headquarters. "If Melanie Harris tries to contact my office, patch the call through on SelCal."

He slumped back in his seat, filled with a sense of desperation like he'd never felt before. In a matter of minutes, he would have to turn back, find the nearest airfield and refuel. In a matter of minutes she could be forever lost to him. *If you never talk to me again, Melanie Harris, talk to me now. Talk to me one last time. Answer your goddamn phone and tell me where you are!*

But there was no call from Melanie. Nothing came through SelCal. There was nothing but a darkening sky and a fuel gauge that began to speak more loudly than the pounding of his heart. With a silent curse he turned the plane around and headed back for Tijuana. They'd stopped there once already after crossing the border, landing for a customs check. Kent knew he could refuel the plane there.

He also knew they could rent a car. Kent wasn't going to give up. Neither darkness nor distance could keep him from finding Melanie. Nothing was going to keep him from finding her.

He expected protests from Murphy after he'd refueled and parked the plane. He expected her to demand that they return to L.A. and mastermind the search from there, but she never said a word, just accompanied him to the rental counter and stood quietly while he filled out all the information and gave the clerk his credit card. They walked out to the car together, and Kent paused before unlocking the doors. "You can go back if you want. I'd understand," he said. "It was a crapshoot, flying down here like that."

"I know." Murphy reached for the door handle. "But if I'm ever lost or kidnapped, you're the one I'll want looking for me."

WHEN MELANIE'S initial burst of panic faded, she was, as always, struck by Anatanyia's statuesque and classic beauty. Anatanyia Korchin was one of those women for whom each year of maturity brought with it increasing levels of grace and charm. The problem was, in the movie industry those natural attributes meant little when compared to the breathtakingly gorgeous young women who flocked to Hollywood by the thousands. Anatanyia had seen them as competitors for Victor's attentions, affections and leading roles, in spite of his constant assurances to the contrary. It had always struck Melanie as a tragic irony that the only one who did not recognize Anatanyia's worth was Anatanyia. In all the time Melanie had known her, though they'd never been close, she'd regarded her with a mixture of admiration, respect and, at times, envy. But never fear. Not until now.

While Anatanyia outwardly appeared and behaved as elegantly gracious as always, there was something not quite right about her expression. Her eyes were almost too calm, too placid. And there was that ominously large man in black looming behind and to one side, hands clasped behind his back and expression solemn, as if awaiting her next command.

"You will, of course, join us for supper," Anatanyia said. She looked at Ariel, who was awkwardly holding the squirming and fussing Kathleen. "I'll take her from you now," she said. "You look tired, Ariel. You haven't been resting enough. Did you have a nap earlier, like I suggested?"

Ariel said nothing, just tightened her grip on Kathleen, who began to cry, and shook her head.

"Anatanyia," Melanie said. "Ariel told me that she'd named you as Kathleen's godmother. I think that's wonderful, but right now Kathleen needs to be with Ariel. A baby needs her mother."

Anatanyia's calm eyes suddenly blazed. "I know that!" she hissed. "I am not a fool. Mothers should *never* abandon their babies, no matter what they have done or how badly they have failed." She turned back to Ariel, who was unsuccessfully trying to quiet the crying baby and looking as if she were about to start crying, too. "Give her to me, Ariel. She needs for me to sing her favorite lullaby."

With a choked sob, Ariel handed Kathleen to Anatanyia. The baby immediately ceased to wail as Anatanyia sung a few lilting words beneath her breath and gently rocked her back and forth. She looked up and the madness had vanished from her dark eyes. "We will take supper in an hour. Is this acceptable to you?"

Melanie nodded, her mouth dry. "Yes, of course."

"Good. Mikhail? Would you please show our new guest to the bedroom in the east wing? And Ariel, please try to have a nap before supper. An actress about to start filming a movie needs her beauty sleep."

Anatanyia turned and walked down the hall and out of sight, singing softly to the baby she held in her arms. Melanie had no chance to offer any words of comfort or encouragement to her sister before she felt Mikhail's hand on her arm, guiding her firmly from the room. He stopped only long enough to shut the door firmly behind them and turn the lock, but not before Melanie saw her sister standing like a statue next to the empty cradle, tears rolling down her face.

Mikhail escorted her down the hall without speaking, and Melanie had the eerie sensation that he was some kind of android. When she asked if he was related to Anatanyia, he made no response. When she asked if he realized that it was wrong to lock houseguests in their rooms and keep them there against their will, he remained predictably silent. He opened the door to the guest room and gestured her inside, closing it behind her. Melanie waited until she heard his footsteps recede, then tried the door. Locked. She pulled her cell phone from her purse and dialed Kent's number, her hand trembling. It was miraculous the man in black hadn't confiscated her phone.

Or maybe he'd known, as she was discovering now, that cell phones wouldn't work within the walls of this room. For some reason, she was getting no signal at all. She turned the phone off to conserve the battery and returned it to her jacket pocket with a moan of frustration. She paced the room, berating herself for the hundredth time for not being more forthcoming to Kent about her plans. If only she had confided in him before mounting this failed one-woman rescue attempt. If she had, help would undoubtedly be on the way. As it was, no one outside of the villa had any idea where they were. Worse yet, her sudden disappearance from the hospital probably only cemented her guilt in Kent's eyes. For all she knew, he and Captain Murphy were right this minute swearing out a warrant for her arrest. There was fine irony. Melanie recalled her fears of earlier that day when she had sat in the cold, stark interrogation room, so sure she was moments away from incarceration. Now, here she was, held in a very different type of jail, but a jail nonetheless.

A quick inspection of the room showed the door was the only way out. There was a window, but it was still light enough outside to reveal a suicidal one-hundred-foot drop to the ocean below. The private bathroom connected to the room also had a window, but it, too, overlooked the cliffs. The house was totally silent inside and out. The only thing Melanie had heard was the sound of a car arriving not long after she had been locked in. More guests for supper?

The room grew dark and Melanie turned on the bedside lamp. According to her watch, she had been in the room for just over an hour when she heard a tap on the door and the key turning in the lock. She stopped her pacing and tried to prepare herself for whatever was coming next. The door swung inward to reveal Mikhail.

"The mistress awaits the pleasure of your company in the dining room," he said in a heavy Russian accent, bowing slightly from the waist. "She requests that you dress for dinner."

It was the last thing Melanie had expected to hear. She looked down at her rumpled clothing that was somewhat the worse for wear. No doubt she'd be an affront to Ana-tanyia's deranged sensibilities at the dinner table. "I'd be happy to," she said. "But since I wasn't really planning on staying, I don't have a thing to wear. In fact, I don't want to stay for dinner. I'd really rather take my sister and her baby and leave, if you don't mind."

Mikhail gave her a blank look and entered the room, crossing to the closet where he opened both doors wide. Without another word, he retreated from the room, leaving the door ajar. Melanie peeked out, and wasn't too surprised to see Mikhail waiting just down the corridor, wearing that same solemn expression, hands clasped behind his back.

"You do realize that by keeping my sister and me pris-oners here that makes you an accomplice to kidnapping and murder?"

Mikhail crossed his arms in front of his massive chest and said, "When madam is ready, I am to escort you to dinner."

"Madam will be ready in her own sweet time!" Melanie slammed the door shut, an act which gave her a brief, if short-lived, feeling of satisfaction. With no solutions to her predicament presenting themselves to her, she decided the best thing to do was to play along, stalling for time. She walked over to the closet and examined the clothes within. "Nothing off the rack here," she murmured, looking at the gowns by Dior, Chanel, Versace and de la Renta. She knew Anatanyia loved formal dining. Melanie figured the gowns were kept on hand as window dressing for the older woman's elaborate parties. Melanie selected the soft blue Dior, then chose a matching pair of shoes from the collec-tion lining the closet floor. Drawers built into the side of the closet were well stocked with nylons, undergarments and various toiletries, all still in their packaging.

When she was appropriately dressed, Melanie carefully searched all the cupboards and drawers in the bathroom and bedroom, looking for scissors or a nail file, anything she could secret away in her handbag to use as a weapon, but found nothing. She wondered if she dared carry the cell phone in the handbag, then nixed the idea. Sooner or later Anatanyia would think to search her. Instead, she slid the phone between the mattresses on the bed and smoothed the coverlet down carefully. She drew a deep breath and examined herself in the bathroom's full-length mirror. "Good luck," she told the pale-looking reflection, and walked out of the room to the waiting Mikhail.

PREDICTABLY, the dining room was furnished and decorated in traditional old Russian style. A massive cut-glass chandelier hung from the ceiling, bathing the heavy oak table below it in golden light. Silver candelabra arranged on the table held flickering candles. Three place settings of delicate china, shining silver and glittering crystal were arranged at one end of the long table. Ariel was already seated, but she sprang to her feet when she saw Melanie.

"Melanie!"

Ariel flung her arms around her and Melanie was able to murmur, without Mikhail overhearing, "Try to be calm. I'm going to work on a way to get us out of here."

Any further conversation was halted by the entrance of Anatanyia. Looking every inch the grand *tsarina* of the estate, and holding the baby in the cradle of one arm, she glided toward them. "Good evening. If you will please take your seats?"

Melanie took Ariel firmly by the arm and they went to sit at the table. Anatanyia sat at the head of the table and gently placed Kathleen in the ornate bassinet next to her seat. She then picked up a small bell and rang it twice. Mikhail, who had left the room after delivering Melanie to it, reappeared, bearing a large and ancient-looking porcelain soup tureen, which he placed in front of his mistress.

Anatanyia lifted the cover from the tureen and ladled generous portions of Russian borscht into three bowls. After everything she had learned that day about Anatanyia's Mexicali shrimp dip, and what a homicidal hit it had been at her last dinner party, Melanie watched her hostess very closely and waited until she'd taken several spoonfuls of the soup before trying any herself.

"Do you like it?" Anatanyia asked.

"It's very good," Melanie said. "Who's your chef?"

Anatanyia reached to give a pacifier to Kathleen. "I am so very busy, it is not often I get to cook, and I do enjoy the time in the kitchen. Everything you eat tonight, I prepared just for you."

Then you can bet I'm not eating a thing until you have first. Images of Stephanie on the floor of the Beverly and poor, dead Shakespeare ran through Melanie's mind.

The soup course was followed by a lamb stew with yogurt, fragrant with cinnamon, cardamom, ginger, garlic, cloves and saffron and served with buttered noodles and a platter of traditional *tvorozhniki*—small flat cakes made of cottage cheese and accompanied by dollops of sour cream.

Anatanyia divided her attention between the meal and Kathleen, who was dozing peacefully in the bassinet beside her, while Ariel picked at her food and cast frightened glances in Melanie's direction every chance she got.

Melanie hoped Ariel would refrain from saying something that might dangerously anger Anatanyia.

"I couldn't help but notice the impressive collection of art and antiques you have here," Melanie said.

"Yes, they are impressive," Anatanyia said. "But not because of their monetary value, which is quite large, but because of what they represent."

"Oh?"

"Sacrifice. Hope. Promise. Freedom," Anatanyia said. "Things I doubt you would know anything about. Everything you see here, every painting, every book, every statue, they were gifts. Gifts from the grateful refugees who have passed safely through Cielo's doors."

Melanie was at a loss how to respond to that, but Anatanyia herself kept the conversation going, after shifting the topics to her favorite Russian poets, musicians and painters. It was as if she were presiding over just another typical dinner party at Blackstone, not holding two women and a baby prisoner on the Mexican coast.

Over coffee and apple dumplings, Anatanyia asked Melanie if she had seen Victor during the past two days.

"No," Melanie said, not sure why she lied, but suspecting it might be helpful to withhold the information about Victor's police questioning and hospitalization until such time as it was useful to divulge it. Besides, for all she knew, Victor was dead.

"This troubles me," Anatanyia said, stirring her coffee with a tiny silver spoon. "He usually calls each evening. I hope nothing is wrong."

"He's probably busy getting ready to start shooting *Celtic Runes*," Melanie said. "There's so much to do before they start filming."

Anatanyia seemed satisfied with that answer and nodded. "Yes, that sounds like Victor. Always working." She set the spoon at the edge of her cup. "It is getting late and you must be tired after your long drive. Mikhail will show you back to your room. Ariel, the baby needs to be fed. Kathleen has been colicky lately, don't forget to burp her afterward. Can you manage? Good. I'll be up in an hour or so."

Ariel went immediately to the bassinet to retrieve her baby and Melanie turned to Anatanyia. "Thank you so much for that wonderful dinner. Would it be all right if I spent some time with my sister? It's been so long since we've talked."

Melanie realized her mistake when Anatanyia surged to her feet, her eyes flashing. "*Now* you wish to talk to her? You would not come to my party. You did not wish to see her then. That was only days ago. But now, you drive all the way to Mexico to see her? To talk to her? Do not mock me. Go to your room. Your conversations with your sister have waited for six months. They can wait a little longer. In the morning you can go. You and your sister. I will be glad when you are gone. There will be peace here then!"

Melanie had no further chance to talk to her sister, as badly as she would have liked to. Ariel had looked on the verge of a complete breakdown as she was escorted from the room by Mikhail, who returned immediately for Melanie. His hand closed firmly on her arm as he led her down the corridor to her room. The sound of the key turning in the lock drove home to Melanie the seriousness of her situation. She was alone in a foreign country with absolutely no idea how to get out, and no one outside of this estate knew she was here. Sitting on the bed, she felt the first stirrings of real despair.

"What have I done?" she whispered. She now knew she had let her wounded pride and misdirected anger toward Kent rule her actions. It had been foolhardy beyond belief and now, in all likelihood, she, her sister and her niece would pay the price.

BY 1:00 A.M. they'd already burned up two tanks of gas. Kent was on his eighth cup of coffee and Murphy was dozing in the passenger seat when he came out of yet another all-night cantina with yet another cup of coffee and slid back into the driver's seat to study the map. They were just outside the tiny town of El Rosario. Between Tijuana and El Rosario there were scores of bars, restaurants, gas stations, grocery stores and gambling houses, and Kent had stopped at every single one to show Melanie's picture, to ask about Anatanyia Korchin and a place called Cielo. So far he'd had no luck at all. Nobody knew nothin' about nothin' and even if they did Kent knew the odds of them saying anything to a gringo, even one who spoke fluent Spanish, were long. Not even the money he'd flashed had gotten him anywhere.

Kent switched on the map light and took a swallow of coffee. The tamales they'd eaten hours ago were still sitting in his stomach, causing him no end of heartburn. He stared down at the map of the Baja and blinked the burn of exhaustion from his eyes. He had a hunch they were a long way from where they needed to be, but that was all it was. A hunch. And his hunches were becoming punchy with fatigue. His window was down and he could hear the sound of the waves against the shore. There was no traffic. He tried Melanie's cell phone again and her answering service picked up. He left another message. Sooner or later she'd listen to them…if she could.

He switched off the map light. Leaving Murphy in the car he walked down the graveled shoulder and into the desert that skirted the shore. The ocean was a vast, dark entity breathing in the night, the waves rushing in and out, brushing up against sand and gravel and the toes of his boots. He sat down near the water's edge, pricked his hand on something thorny, and stared out at the horizon. Took another swallow of coffee. Studied the stars. Listened to the ocean and breathed its warm, salty breath. Listened to his heart beat and thought about Susan. Thought about Melanie.

Then he stood and slatted the remnants of the bitter coffee onto the sands. She was north of here. He'd drive down every damn side road between here and Tijuana, looking for her car. He'd bang on every door if he had to, looking for her. He'd never give up until he found her.

Murphy roused when he slid back into the driver's seat. She glanced at the luminous dial of her watch and brushed the hair back from her forehead. "Where are we?" she murmured, sitting up.

"We're too far south." Kent started the engine, pulled the car around to reverse direction and began driving north.

CHAPTER SEVENTEEN

MELANIE SPENT the better part of the night tossing and turning, trying to figure a way out of the danger in which she now found herself. By 2:00 a.m. she'd come up with an escape plan, of sorts. If she could just get outside and far enough from the villa's walls, there was a slight chance she could place a mayday call to Kent. It wasn't much of a plan, she realized, but it was all she could think to do. With that slim hope firmly in mind, she finally fell into a fitful sleep.

Several hours later she dressed hastily in her clothes from the day before and, with no real expectation of success, tried the door. To her great surprise, she found it unlocked. Apparently, some time during the night Anatanyia and the silent Mikhail had reached the conclusion there wasn't any danger of Melanie running off, surrounded as she was by desert and ocean and with her car safely locked away. She quickly retrieved her cell phone from between the mattresses and, tucking it into the pocket of her blazer, stepped into the hallway. As it had been the day before, the house was eerily silent. Before she did anything, she wanted to check on Ariel. She walked swiftly down the hall and knocked on her door. She heard the scrape of a chair from the other side and a moment later the door opened and Ariel's pale face peeked out.

"Melanie, thank God! I thought you were that horrid Mikhail," she said, opening the door wider.

Melanie quickly slipped in to the room and put a finger to her lips. Whispering, she said, "Ariel, listen to me. I think I might have a way out of this. For whatever reason, neither Anatanyia nor Mikhail searched my purse or my room, and I still have my cell phone. Where were you when you called me on your cell phone?"

"I was on the upper terrace. At least, that's what she calls it. It's more like a balcony, and it's practically on the roof."

"That's what I thought. There's some sort of block on cell phone reception within the building but I'm going to sneak outside just as soon as I can and get word to the authorities. When that happens, can you keep Anatanyia occupied for a while?"

Ariel looked uncertain. "I can try."

"You have to do more than try, Ari, for all our sakes, especially Kathleen's!"

"But she's crazy. You've seen it, haven't you? At first I really liked the idea of her taking care of Kathleen. I mean, nothing I do seems to stop the baby from crying. It's like she doesn't want anything to do with me except when she's hungry, but Anatanyia? She picks Kathleen up and sings one of those Russian lullabies and she stops crying. Melanie, she's taking over completely. All I am is a wet nurse! And last night when she took Kathleen away she was ranting at me. A lot of it was in Russian, but the gist of it was about you. You had ruined everything by coming here and she was going to have to do something to fix that. Melanie, I'm telling you, she's crazy. *Crazy!*"

"I know that. She's already killed two people, Stephanie and Rachel."

Ariel's face paled in shock. "Rachel, too? How?"

"Anatanyia put poison in the Mexicali dip she served at the dinner party."

"Oh, my God! I might have eaten that!"

"Ariel, calm down." Melanie gripped her sister's shoulders and gave her a firm shake. "Listen to me. If you help me, we can be far away from here and safe from Anatanyia by the end of the day. But you have to keep Anatanyia and Mikhail occupied while I get outside the walls of this building long enough to place a phone call. Can you do that?"

Gradually the blank hysteria left Ariel's eyes and she nodded. "I think I can."

"Of course you can," Melanie said, hoping it was true. "If you can land the lead in a blockbuster movie, you can dream up something to keep those two occupied. And I promise, we're going to get out of here."

That vow binding them, the sisters left the room only to find themselves face-to-face with Mikhail, who was waiting in the corridor to escort them to breakfast. Melanie gave Ariel's hand a reassuring squeeze as they followed him down the hallway to the villa's east sun room, where Anatanyia was reading a Russian-language newspaper with Kathleen nestled in the bassinet next to her, sleeping the dreamless sleep of a newborn infant.

"Good morning," Anatanyia said when she saw them. She folded the paper and stood. "It's such a beautiful morning I thought we could take our breakfast outside. Mikhail, would you show our guests to the upper terrace?"

"Certainly, madam," he bowed. "This way, please."

With a furtive glance at each other, Melanie and Ariel made to follow him out of the solarium and up the stairs.

Suddenly Ariel stopped and turned around. She dropped
to her knees and uttered the most ungodly keening noise
Melanie had ever heard while she stretched her arms
toward Anatanyia and wrung her hands together. "Please!"
she said. "Please, I beg you. I beg you with all of my heart.
If you've ever felt anything at all for a mother's love, let
me take my baby. Let me hold her. Give her to me, Anatanyia. I beg you!"

Anatanyia had risen to her feet and was bending over
the bassinet, preparing to carry the baby to the upper
terrace. She appeared shocked by Ariel's over-the-top
hysteria and straightened. "What in heaven's name is the
matter with you?" she said.

"I'll admit I'm a terrible mother, just awful!" Ariel
wailed. "But I love my little girl, I truly do. I love her, and
I need her. Oh, Anatanyia, plee-ee-ease! I..." In midwail,
Ariel suddenly slumped forward, falling onto the floor.

Melanie felt Mikhail brush past her as both he and Anatanyia rushed to Ariel's side, and in the ensuing chaos, she
turned and raced up the few remaining steps to the terrace.
She heard the ongoing commotion behind her but ignored
it as she whipped the cell phone out of her jacket pocket
and rapidly dialed Kent's number. She heard his phone
begin to ring even as she heard the scuff approaching footsteps up the stone steps. She looked around wildly for
some place to hide the phone and spied the flower arrangement in the middle of the breakfast table. Leaving the
phone activated, ringing for all she knew or with Kent
already talking away on the other end, she tucked it into
the midst of the blossoms and greens, then dropped into a
chair just in the nick of time.

Anatanyia walked out onto the terrace with the baby in

her arms. Right behind her came Mikhail, his hand on Ariel's arm. Ariel looked somewhat disheveled and very miserable, but she sneaked Melanie a questioning glance before sinking into one of the breakfast chairs and bursting into tears. "I want my baby," she sobbed into the curve of her arms as she prostrated herself on the table. "I want my baby!"

Anatanyia looked askance at Ariel. "If you do not stop this childish behavior, you will ruin our breakfast!"

"Anatanyia, please," Melanie said. "Give the baby to Ariel. If you don't, I'm afraid we'll have to leave here. We'll have to leave this beautiful red-roofed place just south of Ensenada, this place you call heaven, Cielo. Give the baby to Ariel, Anatanyia. Please." Melanie could only hope that the call she'd initiated had connected. In the meantime, all she could do was continue to stall for time, talk loudly and hope that Anatanyia didn't go completely berserk.

By 7:00 A.M. Kent and Murphy had retraced their steps to Tijuana, where they exchanged the rental car for Kent's airplane. Once again they were airborne, this time with a list, admittedly incomplete, of all private airstrips on the Baja. The list had been provided by one of Murphy's contacts on the border patrol. For an hour they flew a search pattern that left no ocean-front villa unexplored, but all they really had to home on was Melanie's vehicle, and that could be tucked away inside a garage. TESS was back online but Wendy had been unable to come up with anything but one satellite photo of Melanie's car, which placed it on Highway One just north of Santo Tomás at 5:00 p.m. the day before. Murphy was manning the binoculars, looking as ragged as he felt after their long and sleepless night.

"Come on, Melanie," Kent muttered as he made a low-level pass on the south leg of his grid. "Talk to me. Tell me where you are."

And then suddenly, as if somehow heeding his desperate plea, he heard something through SelCal. He increased the volume and static crackled in his headset...but not all of the transmission was static. In the background he heard voices. Distant voices. He maxed the amplitude, forgetting to breathe, while Murphy lowered the binoculars and leaned forward in the copilot's seat, her expression equally intense as both struggled to make sense of the noises they heard.

Noises that made Kent's blood run cold.

Screams. Sobbing voices. No, one voice, a woman's voice, faintly crying? Too distant to make out any words. But then another voice in the background, even more distant but with a Russian accent, unintelligible. Kent's heart thumped a rapid cadence in his chest. He reached to trigger the mike and try to reach Melanie but Murphy stayed his hand. She shook her head vehemently, and even as she did Kent heard Melanie speak. Her voice was much closer and clearer than that of the other two, though still muffled, as if she held the cell phone at a distance. She was apparently in no position to speak directly to him.

"Anatanyia, please. Give the baby to Ariel," he heard her say. "If you don't, I'm afraid we'll have to leave here. We'll have to leave this beautiful red-roofed place just south of Ensenada, this place you call heaven, Cielo. Give the baby to Ariel, Anatanyia. Please."

Ensenada!

Kent snatched the air chart close and studied it even as he concentrated on the voices in his headset. He pushed up the throttle and banked the plane sharply around. They were too far south. Ensenada was north by about twenty-five miles, and Melanie was just south of it, in a villa with a red roof. They were close. So close!

"No, that's not true," he heard Melanie say in a strong, clear voice. "We like it here very much. Please, Anatanyia, don't be upset with us. I know you're angry about so many things, but it's such a beautiful morning. To look out at this view, to see that little island with all the white birds, what did you call it? Isla Bellita? It's so close you must be able to swim out to it. How wonderful this place is. Of course we'll stay, won't we, Ari? Just give Ariel the baby, Anatanyia. Please, she…" The static level rose, obliterating the voices.

Kent traced his finger on the air chart, following the coastline south of Ensenada as he listened to Melanie plead with Anatanyia. There! A tiny island off the Baja. Isla Bellita. Melanie had been looking right at it even as she spoke those words. Good girl, he thought with a rush of gratitude. She'd managed to tell him right where she was.

"Okay," he said to Murphy as he guided the plane up the coastline. "Keep your eyes peeled for a little island covered with white birds."

"Got it," Murphy said, staring through the binoculars. "Dead ahead, two, maybe three miles." She pivoted in her seat, scanning the coastline. "And there's a red-roofed villa on the cliffs directly across from it. It looks like there's a small airstrip behind it, maybe a hundred yards from the main building."

"That has to be it," Kent said. The static level dropped in his headphones and the voices continued coming over the SelCal now in what sounded like an argument. Kent could make out the words "coffee" and "not hungry."

Neither voice sounded like Melanie's, and as he scanned
the landscape below, a burst of static suddenly blocked
out the conversation, followed by several minutes of dead
air. But as he prepared to set up his approach to the
private landing strip, the line cleared. What came next
made him clench the plane's controls until his knuckles
turned white.

"...so you poisoned them both at the dinner party?" he
heard Melanie say.

"They left me no choice. It was an easy thing," the
Russian-accented voice responded.

Static crackled again, and this time the line went completely dead.

Kent glanced at his boss. "You hear that?"

Murphy nodded. "Your girl's in the clear. Let's get this
bird down."

"How the hell do we land there without being seen or
heard by Anatanyia?" Kent muttered as he veered inland,
losing altitude quickly and scanning for the airstrip
behind the villa.

"We don't," Murphy said, who had resumed scanning
the estate with the binoculars.

"So much for the element of surprise. I'm looking at the
shortest airstrip I've ever seen," Kent said. "Tighten your
seat belt, Grandma. Looks like we're a good two hundred
feet shy of roll-out requirements for this bird, and the landing's going to be rough."

MIKHAIL SERVED the continental breakfast on the upper
terrace. Coffee, juice and fresh pastries. Anatanyia poured
tiny cups of the strong coffee, and while she did Melanie
chanced a glance at the cell phone secreted inside the flower

arrangement and saw the red activation light weakly blinking, indicating the batteries were running dangerously low.

Ariel was sitting next to her, sniffing loudly. When Anatanyia placed the cup of coffee in front of her she pushed it away abruptly, spilling the black liquid. "I don't drink coffee," she said. "The caffeine would get into my breast milk and make the baby sick. *You* told me that, Anatanyia, and yet now you offer it to me? Why?" She stood. "I'm not hungry, and I wouldn't eat with you even if I were. Or drink your coffee, either, for that matter. What's in it? Arsenic?"

Anatanyia's dark eyes flashed. "Very well. Take Kathleen and feed her in the solarium. She, at least, needs to eat, if you don't."

Left alone, Melanie and Anatanyia regarded each other with mutual hostility. It was Melanie who broke the silence. "Anatanyia, I don't think Victor would approve of what you're doing here. Does he even know?"

Anatanyia stirred sugar into her coffee, and added a tiny bit of cream. She lifted the cup and saucer and took a small sip, regarding Melanie over the rim. "I no longer care what my husband thinks."

"Victor loves you. He'd do anything for you, but he wouldn't want you to hurt anyone, you must know that," Melanie said.

Anatanyia set the cup and saucer down with enough force to shatter both and spill more coffee on the tabletop. "What do you know of love? Real love?" she raged as she rose to her feet. "The kind that burns in your soul and fills your spirit so completely all else is blocked out? You say Victor loves me, but you don't even know what love is. The kind of love you know is one built on physical needs that take but never give. Oh, yes, I know that kind of love all too well!"

Melanie remained carefully silent. In the distance, Melanie could hear the drone of a small plane. It was getting closer. Anatanyia paced to the railing and gazed out at the ocean, but she was obviously not admiring the scenery. She was in another place, in another time and did not seem to hear the approaching aircraft.

"When I skated, the people loved me," she said. "They would call my name over and over and throw roses onto the ice at my feet. They had love for me because I could give them pride in our motherland with my medals, in spite of the poverty and corruption." Her fingers tightened on the iron railing. "I was good, but my skills came at a price. I practiced so hard every day that my bones and muscles ached and I could not sleep at night. But then during the Olympics I fell, and that love from the Russian people stopped, the same way my mother's love stopped when the government first took me from my family to teach me to skate. She sent me away to live in the big city and then, when I could skate no more, she told me I could not come home. My family was poor. So poor. There wasn't enough food. There wasn't enough money. I was sixteen years old. What was I to do?"

Melanie remained silent, waiting for Anatanyia to continue.

"I had no home to go to. These people who trained me to skate told me they had paid a lot of money for my training. They told me I must repay my debt to the Soviet people." Anatanyia turned to Melanie. "I had no money. I had no job. I told them this, and they said they would feed me and give me a place to live and let me work off my debt.

How kind of them, I thought. After I failed them, they are giving me a second chance to prove myself. I thought maybe if I repaid my debts, maybe my mother would let me come back home." Anatanyia's laugh was bitter. "The job was an easy one, they said. All I had to do was let them take pictures of me. They said I was pretty, and that pictures of me would pay big. I thought, why not? So I went with them to this place."

She turned and looked back out at the ocean. "The pictures they took were filthy ones. Degrading. Pornographic. I told them I would not do that, I would never do those things, and they asked me if I had ever heard of the work camps in Siberia. They said they would send my father and brothers there to pay off my debt if I could not do it myself. I loved my father and my brothers and I knew how terrible those work camps were. So I let them take their pictures. Movie pictures. I let them do things to me that were terrible, because I loved my father and my brothers."

"My God, Anatanyia," Melanie said, genuinely shocked.

"I learned these people were part of the Russian mafia. It was they who threatened me and my family. I cried and begged, but they would not listen. No one would listen. Such cruel men, all of them. All but one. One man cared, and one man was brave enough to rescue me and my family from all that."

"Victor," Melanie said.

"Yes. He was there in that horrible place when I arrived. Such talent he had as a filmmaker, even then. He told me he had borrowed money to get his father out of the country, a great deal of money, and when he couldn't pay it back fast enough, they forced him to run their cameras. He hated it, but like me, he was trapped. Victor was so kind, so gentle. He saw what was happening to me and was determined to stop it. He had been saving some money up, little by little, and this money allowed him to purchase tickets on a freighter bound for Mexico. Tickets not just for me, but for my parents, brothers and small sister. Together, thanks to Victor, we all escaped.

"It was a terrible voyage and our rooms were in the deepest part of the ship where it was always cold and dark. We had to leave Russia so quickly, we could only bring a few treasured things—some books and a small icon. My mother became very ill and died before she saw land. I was hoping she would tell me that she was sorry that she had sent me to the government school and sorry she had told me I could not come home again, but she did not. She just died."

Melanie could see Anatanyia was crying now.

"The voyage seemed to last forever. When it finally ended, Victor's father was waiting for us and he brought us here, to Cielo. When I turned twenty-one, Victor and I were married. He went to Hollywood, and as soon as he could he sent for me. We worked hard together, and life got better. Soon, we were able to contact other relatives and friends in Russia and help them get out of the country. We saved many people over the years."

"Whatever became of Petra?" Melanie asked. "Your best friend?"

Anatanyia shook her head. "I kept in touch with her over the years, but she would not leave. She loved her parents too much, and they would not think of abandoning the motherland. She married a good man and had five children.

Five." She turned to face Melanie again. "All I wanted was one. Victor gave me everything. My life, my pride and my hope. There is nothing I would not have given him, but there was one thing I could not. I could not bear him a child. Such a thing was not possible for me, though it was what he wanted more than anything."

"Why didn't you adopt?"

"Adopt!" Anatanyia fairly spat the word. "No, Victor deserved a child of his own blood. And now, finally, he has one."

"What do you mean?" Melanie said, an uneasy feeling beginning to take hold. Listening to Anatanyia was like trying to put together a jigsaw puzzle with half the pieces missing.

"He has Kathleen."

Melanie shook her head. "I don't understand. Mitch Carson was Kathleen's father. Everyone knows that."

"The baby is Victor's," Anatanyia said. "She will grow up proud of her father. She will never find out about his past, or her godmother's. I have made sure of that. Mitch Carson could not be trusted. So few people can. Even my dearest friend Petra betrayed me when she told Rachel Fisher about my past."

"Rachel contacted Petra, didn't she?" Melanie said. "She found out all about what you were forced to do. You were afraid she'd put it in the biography."

"No, I knew she would not," Anatanyia said. "But the foolish woman could not keep silent. She told her lover about it. She told Mitch Carson. Mitch came to me afterward, demanding I speak to Victor and convince him to give him a big role in *Celtic Runes*. When I refused, he told me what he had discovered and he threatened to make our past in Russia public knowledge. Victor did not think Mitch was a threat, but I knew he had to be dealt with."

"So you killed him? How?"

"Mikhail took care of it. He is very loyal to me."

"What about Rachel and Stephanie?" Melanie asked, dreading to hear the answer.

"I could no longer trust Rachel. She was not loyal. She might talk to someone else."

"But why Stephanie? What did she have to do with all this?"

Anatanyia's eyes narrowed. "She and Rachel were good friends. Always talking together. They shared everything. Besides, Rachel had told me how helpful Stephanie had been in gathering information from old Russian newspapers."

Melanie's head was spinning. *Oh, Stephanie!* Melanie remembered the feeling of relief several years ago when her best friend had told her she was accepting a position with a leading entertainment publication and leaving the world of investigative reporting behind. Relief because Stephanie's pursuit of increasingly dangerous and high-profile stories was placing her in dangerous situations. But now it appeared the entertainment beat had not been as benign as she had believed.

"So you poisoned them both at the dinner party," Melanie said.

"They left me no choice. It was an easy thing," Anatanyia said. "My mother had been trained in the ways of herbal medicines and she taught me. There are as many ways to bring about death as there are to bring about healing."

Melanie's heart was pounding and there was a dull roaring in her ears. Another furtive glance at the cell phone and she saw the activation light had winked completely out. So much for the battery, she thought. She could only hope it had been enough. The low-flying plane was now directly overhead. Anatanyia looked up. "Ah, perhaps that is Victor, coming to visit his daughter," she said in a pleased voice, as if she hadn't just been discussing the murder of several innocent people. "He has been away from us too long."

Melanie shivered. She did not know what was more disturbing—Anatanyia's rantings or these odd moments of apparent lucidity. Taken together, the mood shifts were, at the very least, the indicator of a deeply troubled mind. But Melanie feared it went far beyond that. She was growing certain the wife of her dear friend Victor was completely insane.

"That day at the restaurant, when you fell against me," Melanie said. "That was no accident, was it? You wanted me to fall over the cliff. And the poisoned dip you sent to my apartment, you were hoping I'd eat it. Why did you want to kill me, Anatanyia?"

"For the same reasons. You were all friends who talked amongst yourselves. Besides, you would want the baby. Eventually, when Ariel grew tired of motherhood, you would claim her, and the baby belongs to Victor." She glanced skyward again. "I do hope that was Victor in that plane. It sounded like it was landing at the airstrip."

Melanie stood with a surge of anger and frustration. "That's not Victor, Anatanyia. The day after you abandoned him to his fate the police started blaming him for the murders. He's not going to be coming to see you or Kathleen or anyone else for a very long time. The police think that *he* killed Rachel and Stephanie. Is that what you wanted them to think? Did you plan it that way? Did you plant the poison in his garden shed?"

Anatanyia looked confused for a moment, then her eyes became dangerously vacant. "I loved Victor very much, but in the end he, too, betrayed me. He took from Ariel the one thing I could not give him. I knew once Mitch was dead that he would choose to be with Ariel and he would no longer want me." She looked directly at Melanie, who felt an involuntary shiver run up her spine at the blankness in Anatanyia's eyes. "I knew that would happen, but I had to kill Mitch Carson. He would have destroyed the both of us. He was a nasty, evil man and he deserved to die."

Anything Melanie might have said in response was forestalled by a loud scream and the sound of breaking glass behind her. She whirled around. Unnoticed by either Melanie or Anatanyia, Ariel had returned from the solarium with Kathleen in her arms, just in time to hear the end of Anatanyia's statement. In obvious shock, Ariel had screamed her reaction and backed into a side table holding a huge crystal vase, knocking it to the marble tiled floor where it smashed into tiny fragments that to Melanie symbolized all of their shattered lives.

CHAPTER EIGHTEEN

MURPHY RADIOED back to headquarters their approximate position and requested backup from local authorities seconds before the wheels touched down. Kent was correct about the landing. Their roll-out ended roughly, a good one hundred and fifty feet beyond the end of the landing strip. The plane's wheels dug deep ruts across a sandy patch of cactus-studded desert and the left wingtip clipped several tall ocotillos before Kent was able to stop the plane. He pivoted the aircraft and taxied back onto the airstrip. There was a small cinder-block building at the end of the airstrip closest to the villa, and Kent cut the plane's engine right beside it. Both he and Murphy checked their weapons before tucking them back out of sight.

"I don't have to remind you that we won't have any backup for at least a good half hour, assuming headquarters alerted the proper Mexican authorities," Murphy cautioned.

"Then I guess we'd better keep out of trouble, hadn't we?"

"And I also don't have to remind you that we're out of our jurisdiction here."

"I promise to play by your rules, captain," he said, opening the door of the plane. "Whatever you say goes." He glanced over his shoulder. "And by the way, thanks for coming along for the ride."

"I'll always back you up, lieutenant. You should know that by now."

They disembarked on full alert and stood behind the sheltering fuselage of the plane for a few moments, studying the villa which loomed above them at least one hundred yards away, across a disturbingly open expanse of Sonoran desert scrub brush. They could discern no alarm at their presence. There were no barking dogs, no armed guards, no one calling out a challenge or watching with suspicion. In fact the place seemed strangely quiet, just the faint, lonesome hiss of a warm ocean wind through the mesquite and creosote and the even fainter backwash of surf crashing against rocks…until the peace of the moment was shattered by the far-off sound of breaking glass and a thin scream that shivered up and down a plaintive scale and galvanized both of them into instant action.

"Party time," Murphy said, and they sprinted across the open terrain together. They were both out of breath when they reached the villa's perimeter wall. A quick scan of the building's exterior after they'd shot open the locked iron gate barring the circular driveway had shown no easy way in. The ground floor had small barred windows set into the thick adobe walls. Large glass terrace doors were also protected by a closed metal grate, and the only door was an arched, massive expanse of thickly hewn timber at least ten feet tall and half as wide, strapped with huge wrought-iron hinges.

"Great. Now what?" Murphy said as she studied the massive portal, after finding it locked from within.

"You'd think there'd be a servants' entrance, a delivery dock. Something," Kent said.

"Maybe not. One entrance to guard beats two or three,

and this door looks like it would take a mortar round without flinching."

"What the hell. Let's try getting in the old-fashioned way." There was a massive iron door knocker and Kent used it to good effect. The noise was loud in the stillness following that terrible scream. He waited a few moments, then repeated the clamor, slamming the knocker against the metal plate. "*¡Tengo una carta para* Anatanyia Korchin!" he bellowed. "*¡Es muy importante! ¡Muy importante!*"

The long silence that followed made it seem as if the place was abandoned, but then Murphy touched his arm. "Someone's coming," she said.

Kent heard the approach of heavy footsteps on the other side of the huge door. "*¿Quién es?*" a man's gruff, threatening voice said.

"*Soy un amigo de* Victor Korchin, *y tengo una carta para* Anatanyia. *Es muy importante.*"

There was a brief pause, then they heard the sound of a bolt being drawn back with a heavy, rasping sound. Murphy took a step back into the shadows at the base of the villa as Kent drew his pistol. One side of the massive door began to swing outward, and as it did Kent heard an ominous sound from where Murphy had moved; a sound he'd heard before, and one that instantly diverted his attention from the danger lurking within the villa. He turned his head. Murphy was pressed against the adobe wall, but instead of watching the door open, her gaze was fixed at her feet, where a Western rattlesnake of considerable size had curled itself into a tight coil, rattles buzzing and head held high, ready to strike. Murphy must have startled it when she unwittingly walked into its territory.

"Don't move," Kent said, shifting ever so smoothly to

do two things: keep the door from opening any farther and give himself a better shot at the snake. He took the shot instantly, there being no time to do anything else. Western rattlesnakes were known for their aggressive behavior and when they acted like they were about to strike, they usually did. The moment he squeezed the trigger he felt the door explode outward, hitting him in the shoulder and throwing him off balance. He spun, trying to bring his pistol back up, but he was too late. Kent never even saw what hit him, he just felt the hard, numbing blow that drove him to the ground, then another stabbing pain as a booted toe buried itself in his gut. As he rolled away from the attacker he heard a cry from Murphy, one of her bloodcurdling karate shrieks, and could only imagine what kind of surprise she was giving the bastard.

Go, Grandma, he thought as he struggled to rise.

Murphy had the situation under control by the time Kent was on his feet. A bald, burly man in black lay on his back, not too far from the writhing body of the headless snake, while Murphy trained her pistol on him. His nose was bleeding, his lower lip was split and his eyes were wide open and very startled. No doubt it was the first time he'd ever been decked by a fashionably dressed, gun-toting grandmother.

"You all right?" Murphy said, glancing briefly in his direction.

Kent nodded. "Cuff the bastard before he gets any ideas, and shoot him if he does," he said. "I'm going in."

MELANIE HEARD the shouts, followed by the sudden gunshot, and damned Ariel's untimely entrance onto the terrace. Had she not been present, Melanie might have tried to overpower Anatanyia in those initial moments of confused distraction, but now it was too late. At the sound of the gunshot Anatanyia swiftly crossed the terrace and wrested the baby from Ariel's submissive arms. Ariel was weeping, and for the first time Melanie had the distinct impression that those were real tears streaming down her cheeks.

"You killed Mitch," she sobbed, shaking her head. "You killed my Mitch! How could you do such a thing?"

Melanie watched with bated breath as Anatanyia walked around the corner of the balcony, baby in her arms, to look down into the courtyard.

"Mikhail?" she called down. "Mikhail, who is there? Who comes?"

But there was no reassuring reply from the man in black. Anatanyia retreated from the balcony railing and returned to the room. She was clearly nervous, her dark eyes darting like a caged animal. "Someone is here," she said. "Inside the house."

Please, please let it be Kent, Melanie thought, clenching her hands into tight fists.

"I knew he was murdered," Ariel was sobbing. "I knew it all along, but nobody believed me. Why did you kill him, Anatanyia? Why?"

Anatanyia ignored Ariel, turning and crossing the terrace. She stepped inside the French doors and went to a small desk set against the wall. Shifting the baby into the curve of one arm, she opened the top drawer and pulled out a small black case, resting it on the desk to work the clasp open and lift the top up. She reached inside and drew forth a very small pistol. Melanie caught her breath as Anatanyia stepped back over the threshold and faced them, holding the weapon in her trembling hand.

"Please understand that there is no turning back for me now," she said. "I can run no further from my past."

TOO EASY, Kent thought. Way too easy. And only one guard? Highly unlikely. In a place this big, owned by the wealthy Korchins, there would no doubt be a host of servants as well. He listened for movement within. Nothing. He leveled his pistol in both hands and went through the doors at a crouching run, ducking immediately behind an ornate fainting sofa upholstered in dark gold velvet. He stumbled against a heavy floor lamp beside the couch, nearly dropping his pistol onto the gleaming tiled floor and knocking the heavy red velvet shade, complete with gold tassels, from the lamp. It clattered to the floor beside him.

Good going, Kent. His lungs burned from the exertion of the past few moments. He needed to rest and catch his breath. He hoped no one had heard his clumsy entry, but if they had, they weren't investigating. He peered cautiously from behind the sofa.

The walls of the Korchins' Mexican fortress may have been made of adobe, but there, its likeness to Chimeya ended. This was no place Kent would ever want to live. He scanned the room with a sense of having left Mexico behind in the hot courtyard and stepped into a Russian museum. The room was cold and forbidding, the sort of place where a child would be held tightly by the hand and warned not to touch anything because every object or piece of furniture was some sort of priceless antiquity or collectible. In the room itself there were at least ten armed guards, all of them hanging on the walls and immortalized in dark oils, their fierce eyes watching every move Kent made. The furniture was heavy, dark and oppressive. Just being in this room made him feel as if he were suffocating.

Kent stood, and a wave of dizziness brought sweat to his forehead. He gripped his pistol and tried to catch his breath. The bastard must have broken some ribs with that kick. He hoped Murphy had gotten in some killer kicks of her own. He moved out of the museum and into a hallway that wrapped around the inner courtyard and connected all the rooms. There was no cover in the wide, gleaming corridor, and he moved swiftly, on silent tread until he found a wide set of stairs leading to the second level. He could hear voices coming from upstairs. Faint, but audible. Women's voices.

He climbed the stairs as quickly as he could but halfway up he had to stop once again to catch his breath. He leaned his shoulder against the wall, sweat stinging his eyes. He could hear Melanie's voice. Melanie was okay. In fact, she sounded remarkably calm and composed. Relief made his knees weak and he slid down to sit for a moment on the marble step.

"We all have ghosts in our pasts, Anatanyia," he heard Melanie say. "We all have things we'd rather run from than face. You're not responsible for what happened to you in Russia. You were victimized. None of that was your fault."

Good girl, Kent thought. Keep talking to her....

"I can't believe you murdered my Mitch!" another voice choked out, a high, histrionic voice that grated on Kent's nerves. "You killed my baby's father!"

The Russian-accented voice continued, ignoring the emotional outburst and addressing Melanie's statement. "Victor told me the same thing, but nobody would believe

I wasn't at fault. If that information got out, my life would be ruined. I had no choice but to kill those women and Mitch Carson. I knew that Victor would want to divorce me. But there was nothing else I could do. "

"Oh, Anatanyia, that's not true. You didn't have to kill anyone. Victor would never divorce you. He loves you."

"He loves Ariel, and he is the father of her baby. I know this is true."

"How can you know this? What proof do you have?"

"Ariel never wanted to have the baby," Anatanyia replied. "She wanted to get an abortion, is this not true, Ariel? You did not want to get fat. You were afraid a baby would ruin your acting career. I overheard that conversation between you and Victor, Ariel. I heard how he tried to convince you not to end the pregnancy. He pleaded with you. He begged! He put his arms around you. I saw this! I looked into the room and I heard everything and I saw it all. That is how I know that Victor is the father of your baby."

"Wait a minute," Kent heard Melanie say. "You mean Victor knew about the baby? And he was going to give me away to Mitch on my wedding day?"

"He knew about the pregnancy, but he didn't know the baby was Mitch's," Ariel sobbed.

"It wasn't Mitch's baby," Anatanyia said. "It was Victor's!"

"That's a lie!" Ariel delivered this in a raging scream that made Kent want to plug his ears. "*Mitch* was Kathleen's father. I never slept with Victor and I never wanted to! He's an old man, old enough to be my grandfather!"

"Victor may be old, but he is more of a man that you'll ever know," Anatanyia shot back, curiously defensive of a

husband she believed had fathered another woman's child.
"He is a fine and honorable man!"

"Yes, he is," Melanie's voice broke in. "Which is why
you should know that he would never have an affair with
Ariel. He loves *you,* Anatanyia. He pleaded with Ariel to
keep the baby because Victor holds all life sacred. You
above all people should know that. Victor nurtured all of
us. That's what he does. It's how he brings out the best in
all things, everything from prize roses and garden vegetables to Academy Award-winning performances from the
actors who work under his direction. That's what makes
him great, and that's why we all love him."

Melanie was obviously stalling for time, and sooner or
later time would run out. He couldn't sit here on this step
forever. Kent pushed to his feet. The burn in his lungs
doubled him over and made him reach for the stair railing.
Damn that man in black for breaking all his ribs. He had
to get up there. Had to tell Anatanyia that the gig was up.
Had to get home, because the boys would be worried, and
Stannie would never stop nagging him about being late,
always being late, and she'd wonder where the mustard
was, the Colman's mustard, and scold him for forgetting
it, and would Susan have died if he hadn't been so
goddamn focused on his career? Would Melanie ever
forgive him for not trusting her? Would she ever return to
Chimeya and light the place up again with her life and her
love? He had to see Melanie, tell her how he felt about her.
Stannie had been right. Life was too short to keep a beautiful woman waiting…. And what the hell was he thinking!
He could not seem to keep his mind from wandering.
Focus!

"Victor does not love me anymore," Anatanyia said,

but her strong voice was faltering now, as if unsure of the uncharted waters ahead.

"How can you say such a thing?" Melanie again, her voice compelling, filled with emotion. "He worships you. He always has, and he always will."

Two steps. Three. Pause for breath. The cramping burn in his chest was becoming unbearable. Kent bent over, stifling a cough against his forearm, and was dully surprised to see a spatter of blood on his shirt sleeve. Coughing up blood was a very bad sign. On a sudden hunch he put his free hand to where the bald man had struck him, and felt a warm, sticky wetness. He stared at his bloody hand in disbelief. Knife. The bald bastard had knifed him. He swallowed back a wave of queasiness. Being knifed was so much worse than being shot.

"I could not give him what he wanted. I could not give him a child of his own," Anatanyia was saying, but her voice was definitely becoming shakier. She was heading for the reef in the crashing surf, a ship adrift and doomed in a storm of her own making.

"Victor doesn't care about that," came Melanie's firm voice. "He only wants you. He only ever wanted you."

"But he asked Ariel to move into the cottage when the baby was due. He wanted her close to him because he was in love with her." She was defending her beliefs now, trying to hold on to the reason why she'd poisoned two women, committed murder...

"No. He knew you wanted to be close to the baby. You did, didn't you? Didn't you volunteer to take care of it when Ariel went back to acting? Didn't you decorate the study and turn it into a nursery for her? Didn't you *want* Ariel living at the cottage so you could take care of her baby?"

"Yes." The response was barely whispered. Anatanyia's impenetrable walls were quickly crumbling.

Kent had reached the top of the stairs. His pistol was still in his hand, but as he took those final steps he remembered Victor's plea from his hospital bed.

Please don't hurt my Anatanyia.

He holstered the weapon and moved into the doorway. The first thing he saw was Anatanyia, baby in the curve of one arm, pistol in her free hand. She was pointing that pistol at Melanie, but when she spotted Kent she took a step back and the pistol swung to cover him.

"Stay away," she said, her voice as unsteady as her hand. "I am warning you, come no closer!"

WHEN KENT stepped out onto the terrace, it was all Melanie could do to retain her composure. She wanted to run to him, run to the safety of his arms, but she knew she had to remain perfectly still. Just a look passed between them, the briefest of glances, yet he spoke volumes to her in that moment. She could only hope hers had said as much.

"I have a message for you, Anatanyia," Kent said. "From Victor. He sent me here to deliver it in person."

Anatanyia blinked rapidly. The baby stirred in her arms, waving tiny arms and clenched fists. "What is this message?"

"Come home."

Those two simple words had a profound effect. Anatanyia's regal composure dissolved. Her face became a mask of intense pain and her dark eyes brightened with tears. She shook her head. "I can never go back."

"Victor needs you," Kent continued. "He's had a massive heart attack. The doctors put an emergency shunt in, but he has to undergo a quadruple bypass operation just as soon as he's strong enough to survive it. He needs you more than he's ever needed you. He needs you to come home."

"Heart attack…?" The hand holding the pistol drooped as Kent's words sank in. "Oh, Victor…" Her voice broke and she half turned toward the balcony, gazing sightlessly out at the ocean. "What have I done?"

"You've killed three innocent people for no reason at all, that's what you've done!" Ariel shrieked. "Give me my baby, you murdering bitch, before you hurt her, too!"

Melanie moved to her sister's side and took her arms in a fierce grip. *"Shut up,"* she hissed under her breath.

Kent moved forward into the room at the same moment as Melanie went to her sister, and Anatanyia turned back to face them, the wariness returning to her tear-filled eyes and the pistol coming back up. She shook her head at Kent. "Please, do not make me shoot you."

"I don't think you want to shoot me, Anatanyia," Kent said.

She shook her head. "No. I did not want to hurt anyone. But there are dark angels…"

"I know all about dark angels. I have a few of my own. You don't have to listen to them, Anatanyia. Look at that baby you're holding. Do you see any of your dark angels there?"

Anatanyia looked down at the infant and shook her head again, tears flowing down her cheeks. She never even looked up as Kent deliberately crossed the room to where she stood. Melanie watched, scarcely breathing, as he reached for the pistol and took it from her yielding hand. "Everything's going to be all right, Anatanyia," he said. "Victor will be all right." Kent was reaching for the baby as he spoke, and Anatanyia handed little Kathleen into his arms with the most heart-wrenching expression Melanie had ever seen.

Kent had the baby. He had the little pistol. He glanced over his shoulder at Melanie, who moved swiftly to take Kathleen from him and hand her into Ariel's protective embrace.

They heard footsteps swiftly ascending the marble staircase and Captain Murphy edged onto the terrace, pistol held at the ready. She took the situation in at a glance and then holstered her gun. "Sorry it took me so long. I checked out the rest of the villa. There's no one else here. I see you have everything under control."

As Melanie moved toward Ariel and the baby she heard Kent suddenly shout, "Anatanyia! No!"

Melanie spun around to see that Anatanyia, in that moment's diversion over Captain Murphy's arrival, had rushed across the balcony. She stopped at the railing and whirled to face Kent. "I can never go back home. Victor will be all right, but only if I never go back."

"That's not true," Kent said, moving slowly closer. "He loves you and he needs you."

She shook her head, her hands gripping the top of the railing. "I have hurt him, and if I return I will only hurt him more. He is a good man and I loved him the best that I could, but the dark angels…I could not fight them. Tell Victor I tried, but they have won."

As she spoke the last words, she turned to throw herself over the railing. Melanie cried out even as Kent lunged forward, his hands reaching the place where Anatanyia had been but catching only handfuls of air as the tormented woman vanished from sight. There was no scream, no sound at all but the shocked silence of those left behind and the distant crash of the surf against the rocks below.

KENT'S DESPERATE LUNGE had driven him hard against the iron railing and he hung over it, staring in disbelief at the shattered form of the woman sprawled on the rocks far below. He felt another wave of nausea and weakness, and wondered if he was going to be sick. He should have seen that coming. He should have read her better than that. Should have moved faster. Should have saved her.

But for what? Life in prison, or some institution for the criminally insane where she would be tormented incessantly by her dark angels?

"There was nothing you could have done," Murphy said, moving up beside him and looking over the rail. "She'd gone over the edge, literally and figuratively, and—" Murphy's hand touched his upper arm. "Kent, for God's sake, you're bleeding!"

Kent straightened from the railing and turned. He saw Melanie moving toward him like a bright angel of light and beauty. She was safe. Melanie was all right. At least one good thing had come of this awful day….

"Oh, Kent," she said, wrapping her arms around his waist. She looked up at him, her eyes filling with tears, and in that moment just before the darkness came, while sunlight still dappled through the twining bougainvilleas that shaded the balcony and his own arms held her close, in that moment he saw the green flash in her eyes and he knew that she had just banished forever the dark angels from his own past.

CHAPTER NINETEEN

MELANIE DROVE her car through the familiar streets of Beverly Hills with the delicious feeling of playing hooky from school. The day stretched ahead of her, gloriously empty of commitments. There would be no babysitting a cranky infant this afternoon, no listening to Ariel complain about still being two pounds overweight while she read and reread her *Celtic Runes* lines aloud, scuffling back and forth across the living room in those awful pink slippers. Oh, it was impossible to escape them completely. Baby toys were strewn across the seat and passenger-side floor and strapped in the back was the state-of-the-art child's restraining seat, empty at the moment. On the seat beside her was a bag of baby supplies: mostly diapers, some baby formula and bottle liners, and a new little stuffed animal. A cat, this time. One that looked a little like Shakespeare.

On a day such as this, it was almost possible to forget the horror of those final moments in Mexico—almost. Melanie knew she would never completely be free of the images of Anatanyia making her desperate plunge over the balcony railing, or of Kent lying unconscious in his own blood after risking his life to save them. As she had cradled his still form in her arms, the room seemed to suddenly fill with uniformed Mexican police officers responding to

Captain Murphy's call for backup. Soon after, a unit of American agents arrived to help process the scene. A kindly female U.S. border agent took charge of Melanie, Ariel and Kathleen, shepherding them into a waiting van, thus sparing them the sight of Anatanyia's broken body being lifted from the rocks below and brought into her beloved Cielo for the final time.

Driving along now, Melanie offered up a quick prayer that the troubled woman had finally found her heaven and was at peace.

From her seat in the van, Melanie had watched as Kent was rolled out of the villa on a stretcher, oxygen mask on his face and Captain Murphy trotting along beside him to a waiting ambulance. She watched it drive down the dusty road, lights flashing, until it was out of sight. She had closed her eyes and then opened them almost immediately at the slight tug on her hand.

"Mel…" Ariel had said.

"Yes?"

"How, how can I, we, Kathleen and I, ever thank you? You saved our lives. I always knew you were the brave one. But for you to come here, after all I have done…" Ariel's voice trailed off and Melanie put an arm around her sister's shoulder.

"Ariel, I love you. There was no way I was going to lose you—again."

Ariel looked up, tears brimming in her eyes. "Does that mean you can forgive me?"

"I already have," Melanie said. "But can you forgive me?"

"What do you mean?"

"I never should have abandoned you the way I did. If I

had been there, you never would have fallen victim to Anatanyia like this and maybe our friends would still be alive and…"

Ariel held up her hand. "Stop it, Mel. There's no use playing the what-if game. Believe me, I know. I'm just glad we have each other now. And that Kathleen will grow up knowing her brave and fearless aunt!"

Melanie had known the wounds between them were deep, but sitting in that van outside the elegant villa, the healing process was well underway. And she realized that though the road ahead might be rocky at times, as the older sibling she would always be her sister's keeper.

Close to a month later, Ariel was trying to wean Kathleen, now that filming was about to begin, and Kathleen wasn't being very cooperative. She preferred the breast to the bottle and was fussing endlessly, and Ariel seemed incapable of dealing with the multiple and unending stresses of motherhood. The cottage at Blackstone, where Melanie and Ariel had taken up residence at Victor's insistence, had been a comfortable enough place to recover from the terrible episode in Mexico, and initially she had appreciated her time spent with Ariel and the baby. But three weeks of playing aunt and nurturing older sister was enough.

Never had she been so relieved as when Ariel announced that she was amenable to Melanie's suggestion of hiring a full-time nanny, and she even let Melanie pick the right woman, a proper British grandmotherly sort who had no problem making Ariel toe the line. It was time for Melanie to get on with her own life, and to that end she had spent the morning at the studio catching up on paperwork.

She hadn't seen Kent since that one visit in the hospital. She'd felt so awkward, sitting in his private room on that plastic chair, hands folded in her lap while nurses came and went and fellow police officers hovered outside the door like a flock of protective, sharp-eyed eagles. It had been impossible to do much more than make small talk, something she had always failed at miserably. She had stayed barely ten minutes, and she'd said none of the things that were in her heart.

He'd been out of the hospital for a week now, but he hadn't called. She told herself she was being foolish to think that he would, but a part of her still clung to the hope that what she felt for Kent was at least in some part reciprocated. It was on a whim that she decided to take the afternoon off and visit him at his private office. At least there they would have no constant interruptions and she could give him the little gift she'd bought, with no prying eyes watching. She parked her Mercedes in the office building's parking garage and headed for the elevator. Was it only three weeks ago that she'd last been here? It felt like a lifetime.

Amazingly, the receptionist remembered her. "Ms. Harris," she said, rising from her desk as Melanie entered the waiting area. She glanced in confusion at the appointment book. "I'm sorry, I don't seem to see your name...."

"This isn't an official visit," Melanie said. "I know I should have called, but I was hoping I could speak with Dr. Mattson. It won't take long, but if he has another appointment..."

The receptionist shook her head. "He has no more appointments, Ms. Harris. Please wait and I'll tell him you're here." She returned almost immediately, leaving the door ajar behind her, and smiled. "He says to come right on in, and forgive the mess."

Melanie nodded her thanks. Clasping the package in her hands, she walked through the open door. Kent was standing behind his desk, dressed pretty much the same way he had been the first time she was here, in blue jeans and a chambray shirt. The only thing different was the sling on his arm. He grinned with what appeared to be genuine pleasure when he saw her, causing her heart to skip several beats.

"When I was here last, you told me if I should ever have a change of heart to stop by your office again," she said, the words sounding stilted and rehearsed, which they were.

"Your change of heart came just in the nick of time. Ten minutes later and my shingle would've been off the door."

Melanie glanced around the room. Cardboard boxes were stacked haphazardly. All of his books and pictures had already been packed away and the walls and shelves were bare. "So, you're really giving this up? Abandoning the big bucks, the Hollywood scene?"

"Don't worry, Ms. Harris. I'll always find time for you." He gestured to the chair. "Please, have a seat. Would you prefer hypnosis or electric shock treatments? Same price for both."

Melanie laughed and sat, but once she was seated the awkwardness returned in full force. She felt her cheeks flush under his scrutiny. "How are you feeling?" she asked.

"Good as new. How're things going with you?"

"Oh, pretty well. I'm working things out with Ariel and falling in love with my niece, which wasn't as difficult as I thought it would be. In fact, she makes it pretty easy." She placed the package on his desk. "I brought you a little something I thought you could use."

Kent unwrapped the package with one hand and opened

the small box. He withdrew the mud-colored toadlike ceramic casting from within and placed it on his desk, where he regarded it with a thoughtful expression. "Thanks. I've always wanted one...I think. What the hell is it?"

"The gypsy woman who sold it to me told me this object has great protective powers."

"Is that so. Then why was she selling it?"

Melanie smiled. "I asked her the same thing. She said she didn't needed protecting."

He raised his eyebrows. "And you think I do?"

"Well, it couldn't hurt."

Kent pushed the squat, ugly object around in a circle with his forefinger for a few moments, then glanced up. "The only reason that big bald dude in black got his knife into me was because I was preoccupied with a bad-tempered Western rattlesnake."

"Exactly my point," Melanie said. "Better keep that thing on your desk at work, or better yet, carry it with you at all times."

"Yes, ma'am." Kent dropped into his chair and kicked back, eyes narrowing on her. "So tell me, Ms. Harris, how are you *really* doing with everything that's happened?"

"Better, little by little. I started work again today, which helps. There's a lot to do, getting ready for a new production." Melanie laced her fingers together in her lap. "I can't stop thinking about how Anatanyia's jealousy and insecurity caused three innocent people's deaths. How she wanted to kill me, too...and how none of it was necessary." Melanie leaned forward. "Kent, I have to ask you this because it's been bothering me. I know you're a trained psychologist, but how did you know Anatanyia wouldn't try to shoot you when you took the baby and the gun from her?"

"I didn't."

Melanie stared. She had expected him to give her a logical recitation about body language and eye movements and how they all related to a suspect's capacity for violence. "Then why did you do it?"

"She was ready to snap and you were in danger," he said with a casual shrug. "She could have shot you at any moment."

Melanie pushed out of her chair and paced restlessly to the window. She wanted to tell him so many things but didn't know where to begin. "Victor came home from the hospital last week, the day after you were released. He's doing all right, but he never mentions Anatanyia."

"It'll take him a while to come to terms with everything that's happened."

Me, too, Melanie thought. She turned to face him and drew a painful breath. "Well, I won't take up any more of your time. I just wanted to stop by and see how you were."

"I'm glad you did." He stood, looking as awkward as she felt. "It was great to see you. I almost called you a couple of times, but..."

Melanie felt a faint glimmer of hope. "Why didn't you?"

"I didn't dare. I figured you were probably still mad at me."

"Why would I be mad?"

"Because of how it all went down. You know," he explained with another shrug. "The disastrous dinner we had, then that awful lunch, followed by Victor's massive heart attack..."

"Oh, Kent. I'm not mad. I realize you were just doing

your job." With a painful wrench, Melanie realized she could stand here all afternoon fumbling for something profound to say, but Kent wasn't going to sweep her into his arms. She'd been a fool to believe there was anything more between them than a murder investigation. She started for the door, then paused. "How are the boys?"

"Good, good!" Kent moved around the desk as he spoke. "They ask about you. Every day, in fact, sometimes more than once. Stannie does, too. I think if Loki could talk, he'd be asking. They all want to know when you're coming back." He crossed the room to the door, glanced out into the reception area and then closed it firmly. "Look, I know you're going to be pretty busy getting this new film of Victor's up and running," he said, "but would you like to have dinner some time?"

Melanie felt that lonely space inside her fill with a slow, tingling warmth. "I'd like that very much. It would be nice to get away from a fussing baby and a demanding sister."

"How far away?" he said, his words painting a significant picture.

"There's this ranch I know of high in the foothills of the Sierras that has a certain peaceful appeal."

Kent's gaze intensified. "When do you think can you go?"

"Whenever you want me." Butterflies danced and her heart kept apace.

He reached his hand out as if he feared she was a mirage that might vanish at any moment. "Woman, I've wanted you since the day we first met," he said, his voice rough with emotion as his fingertips traced the side of her face. "How does *now* sound?"

"I think that's the sweetest-sounding word I've ever heard." She'd had three whole weeks to discover that life without Kent was as unthinkable as life without fresh air, sunshine and warm summer rain, and if he was inviting her back to Chimeya for another try at a romantic dinner, she was more than willing to accept. She was well aware of the risks that accompanied falling in love, but with Kent, she was more than ready to take them. In fact, she already had.

"Think you're ready for your next flying lesson?"

Melanie nodded, not trusting herself to speak around the lump in her throat.

"Good. I could use your help. Flying can be tough with just one arm." His hand brushed the hair back from her temple, then curved to fit the nape of her neck in a warm caress. "But before we go, there's something else I've been wanting from you since the day we first met."

His kiss took her by surprise. There was no time to worry about things like keeping her eyes open or closed, or about trying not to mess things up or come across as being too awkward and shy. One kiss from Kent and she forgot all about silly things like that. Just one kiss, and she knew she'd been given a second chance for happiness.

She wasn't about to let this one get away.

OPEN SECRET

by *Janice Kay Johnson*

HSR #1332

Three siblings, separated after their parents'
death, grow up in very different homes,
lacking the sense of belonging that family
brings. The oldest, Suzanne, makes up her
mind to search for her brother and sister,
never guessing how dramatically her
decision will change their lives.

Also available:
LOST CAUSE (June 2006)

On sale March 2006

Available wherever Harlequin books are sold!

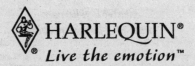

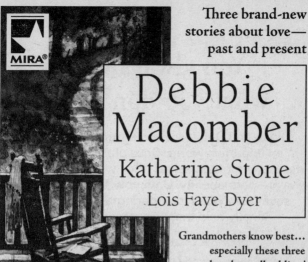

You always want
what you don't have

Dinah and Dottie are two sisters who grew up
in an imperfect world. Once old enough to make
decisions for themselves, they went their separate
ways—permanently. Until now. Will their reunion
seventeen years later during a series of crises
finally help them create a perfect life?

My Perfectly
Imperfect Life

Jennifer Archer

HN34

Available March 2006
TheNextNovel.com

Detective Maggie Skerritt is on the case again!

Maggie Skerritt is investigating a string of murders while trying to establish her new business with fiancé Bill Malcolm. Can she manage to solve the case while moving on with her life?

Spring*Break*

by *USA TODAY* bestselling author

CHARLOTTE DOUGLAS

HARLEQUIN®
Ne**xt**™

Available March 2006
TheNextNovel.com

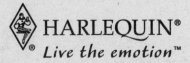